HAMILTON ROMANCE

A HAMILTON-TORONTO NEXUS

by

DAVID BEASLEY

DAVUS PUBLISHING
Davus sum, non Oedipus

FOR J.E.A.B.

copyright 1996 David R. Beasley

Beasley, David, 1931-
  Hamilton romance: a Hamilton-Toronto nexus

Sesquiecentennial ed.
ISBN 0-915317-05-2

  I. Title.

PS8553.E14H34 1996   C 813'.54   C96-900036-7
PR9199.3.B3762H34 1996

DAVUS PUBLISHING
DAVUS SUM, NON OEDIPUS

150 Norfolk St. S., P O Box 1101,
Simcoe, Ont. N3Y 2W2. Buffalo, N.Y. 14213-
Canada 7101, U.S.A.

When living in a short street with a long name, Schultzstrassnitzkygasse, in Vienna, Austria in 1957, I wrote this novel about the place in which I was born and raised and which I had left a few years before to seek knowledge of the world. Some problems the novel depicts and their attendant hypocricies remain today. The narrator's youthful criticisms and biases will always be valid from his viewpoint and have shaped his character forever, regardless how the passing years may have invalidated them. They and the conflict among the other protagonists imply underlying changes brought by World War Two, the battlefields of which were geographically distant but emotionally close. As Hamilton, Ontario celebrates its sesquicentennial in 1996, it may be interesting, possibly enjoyable, to return for a few hours to this particular past. Moreover, I feel I am doing justice to the characters of the novel by releasing them from a long imprisonment in manuscript.   D. R. Beasley.

CHAPTER 1

Everybody ran down to the centre of the city it seemed. People were all over the place, a huge sweating mob that pushed against things with a joyous common delirium. Little Gore Park, wedged into the centre of King Street, couldn't be seen for the shoulders, heads and intoxicated faces. There were ribbons all around the trees that framed the park so that one knew where it was; and that sedate iron statue of old Queen Victoria was standing up above everyone and looking grimly at the drug store across the street. The pigeons, too, were up above everyone because they couldn't find a safe landing place on the ground.

As I pushed through the crowd in search of the excitement, I saw that the windows of the corner jewelry store had been covered with great paintings of our biggest war heroes. The paintings were of that slick, commercial variety that we get too much of, and which was over-doing our real national pride as if some phony were trying to propagandize our peace as he had done our war with that fathers-of-the-nation business. I won't say I was happy when a big army type in his undershirt and khaki trousers put his fist through Mackenzie King's jaw and then began to rip away the cardboard, but I felt that a new time had come because the day before he couldn't have done that without being pounced upon as a traitor. As it was, those who saw him either laughed or pretended not to notice, and the mood in the air was all for him.

Soon there were spaces between clusters of people so that one could, if one wanted to go faster, brush in and out of the crawling multitude. A band had started up quite close, and it was when I was hurrying away that I ran into Skip. He had seen me a split second before I hit him, and he tried to wheel back on his bad foot, but he was knocked for two little steps to the side and sat down on the pavement. Thank God he had a sense of humour. He laughed when I tried to lift him up under the arms, but he was no help at all in getting himself standing. He waved aside any apology I tried to shout above the noise of the band, and, throwing one arm over my shoulders, he motioned for a drink with the other. It was obvious the way he tossed back his head that he meant liquor, but the only bar in the centre of town was in the hotel, and, in that crowd, it seemed miles away. I saw a Honey Dew sign and we plunged toward it.

The atmosphere inside the restaurant was cool and sober, making us gasp at the abrupt ceasing of noise as the double doors swung shut behind us. A plain girl in white was the only person in the room, and she was watching the celebrations through the wide street-window.

"Well, we can't get drunk here," Skip said.

I didn't know what he had expected so I agreed with him. "Do you want to get drunk?"

"No. I'm merely protesting that America's run by gray-haired mothers." I was just twenty and not wised-up the way I should have been at that age. I thought he was griping about his mother so I didn't say anything.

We sat down in one of the booths, and the girl brought us two Orange Dews. Even with the air-conditioning, the room was too warm. I watched pills of water run down the outside of our glasses. Skip had already introduced himself as Charlie Burke and said that he had come back from Europe about six months ago with a leg wound. He was very excited about V.E. Day as weren't we all. He never stopped smiling and his big chest heaved as if he'd come in from a long run.

"Whereabouts do you live in Hamilton?" I asked him.

"Just arrived here last week, and I'm looking for a decent place. I've got a job with an insurance company."

He saw me glance at the door and he laughed.

"I won't hit you just yet."

"You'd better not because I haven't got any money. I'm a student."

"Where?"

"Osgoode."

"A lawyer, huh! I wanted to do that too, but when I finished high school I joined up."

I felt guilty because I was born at a better time than he was.

"Where did you come from?"

"The east," he said. "Used to play hockey in Montreal."

"Wait a minute!" His face was fading in and out of my memory. I could feel the pulsation in my brain. "Are you Skip

Burke?" The name was so easy; it just slipped off my tongue and I hadn't said it for years, seven at least.

"That's right." His smile showed all his front teeth.

I saw those square blue cardboards again with the pink powder from the bubble-gum which we kids blew off to reveal photos of our hockey idols. Before the tank and machine-gun sets came into vogue we used to swap them. I remember collecting as many as I could of Skip and sticking them all over my bedroom wall because I used to hear his name a lot in the National League meets over the radio. He was a star in the play-offs one year. He got the name Skip because he'd skip down the ice after the puck. The radio announcer used to make a lot out of that.

"Do you play hockey too?" he asked.

"Oh no. I haven't got enough stuff for that. I never enter into any sports where I can be broken in two."

"Well, you really know your game because no one else remembers I used to play." He looked pleased and sat straighter. "But I'm just as happy. It's better to leave the past where it belongs."

I thought of his bad leg, which wasn't really so bad, just 'tender' he said, and I guessed he was unhappy he couldn't play again. "A little publicity ought to help you sell more insurance," I suggested.

He laughed. "No thanks, no personality cult for me."

We finished our drinks at a gulp and turned to look through the part of the window where the girl wasn't standing. The band had begun to move, and looked as if it intended to parade about the park, but it kept being pushed back, so that the best it could do was to march around in a little circle with its tubas appearing like brass dolphins above the waves of people, and, its leader, a tall man, looking like a confused and frightened Captain about to lose his ship.

"That mob looks pretty happy, doesn't it?" Skip said. "The victors, and none of them have ever been anywhere near the war."

"They're really celebrating the end of their worries," I said.

"You're right. I forgot people could have parents that might worry about them. God! Victors! A stupid remark. You know," he smiled, "sometimes it's a good thing that America is run by gray-haired mothers. That old home-spun rationality."

I realized he must be lonely in a strange city, especially when everyone was with friends. I wondered if he'd accept if I asked him back to dinner. I didn't want to be embarrassed by a refusal. "My mother's visiting in the country, but my sister Nancy cooks okay. If you want to come, we'd like to have you."

"That's swell!" Skip looked appreciatively at me. "How old's your sister?"

"Two years more than me. Not bad either, I guess."

"I'll come then. That's swell!"

As it was the middle of the afternoon, I gave him the address and he said he'd come about seven. We pushed through the doors into the crowds, and he walked a block with me before he cut down north towards the bay. I guessed he was living in one of those cheap hotels in the north end. There was the odd tavern down that way so he could get a drink when he wanted it, but he'd have to associate with all the roughnecks. I had hardly ever been down in the north end.

In front of the Court House, I stood watching the Loyalists' monument. It comprised the young family with arms entwined, standing in the centre of the great lawn, so still and apart from all the jubilation in the streets. The determination carved on its faces expressed concern for the freedom it fought for and had to hack out of the woods north of Niagara. It was strange to think how the Loyalists had influenced the shaping of the country; yet their influence was so unobtrusive that no one ever realized how profoundly it formed the basis of the nation's thought.

After a while, I found a phone booth behind the Court House and called Nancy. At first she didn't like the idea of cooking extra in a hot kitchen for a friend of mine until I told her that Skip was in his late twenties. That changed her tone all right. Good old Nance, she was always ready for a little adventure.

CHAPTER 2

Skip arrived wearing a cool blue suit. I could tell he was good-looking by the way Nancy was interested in almost every word he said so that I was soon beginning to feel like a third party.

We ate in the back sun-room at a table with candles to light when it got dark. When Nancy brought in the main course the sun was blinking red at us through a space between the trees in the garden. We had an upper duplex, and, in the summer, we could sit at the back surrounded by our thirteen windows and watch the sun go down.

"Its very nice here," Skip said.

"Wonderful in the evenings," Nancy agreed. Her adjectives changed depending on whom she was talking to. With a girl friend she'd say 'terrific'; with me, 'not bad'. "But in the middle of the day it's like the Sahara."

I could just see old Nance on the Sahara with her blonde hair swept up like Cleopatra's crown, those small breasts she was fond of encouraging caught in a strip of white sailcloth leaving her midriff bare to below the belly button, and the camel she was riding looking not unlike those dopes who took her dancing.

Skip seemed to like the cooking, and, with every mouthful, he became a little more chummy with my sister. He didn't leave me out of the conversation though; he kept referring statements to me for verification until I was ready to object just to start a direct argumentative interchange between him and myself.

I noticed, however, that his easiness was forced; he seemed to be trying to cover up a timidity, as if he were afraid he was being watched for his manners. Then I saw that he was holding his knife from underneath the handle instead of from on top, and, when he had finished, he let his knife and fork lay apart instead of putting them together. I thought that would have finished him with Nancy, but, for once, she didn't seem to care. All she said was, "Would you like some more?" in a good-hearted Aunt Jemima tone ending on a note that hinted if he didn't he should signal so. Skip glanced quickly at our plates, put his knife and fork together and began to redden. I think Nancy was embarrassed too because she whisked the dishes away to the kitchen, which was contrary to her usual slow 'posy' movements when clearing the table.

"How do you find the people in Hamilton?" I plunged after the first generalization I could think of.

"Hard to get to know," he said, "but it's like every other city."

"Everyone's got his clique, I know. It's tough on newcomers. I'm finding the same thing in Toronto a bit, even after a year and with friends of the family there. Next fall I'll have to start the same process of getting to know people all over again. And at that my territory won't go much outside Osgoode and the University. You never feel a part of the city; you're lucky if you feel a part of your own little district, like Rex Hill or Rysdale's Hollow or wherever you are. Not that I'd ever want to feel a part, you understand."

He saw me shiver, and he laughed. "That's the trouble. No one wants to feel a part of the land. What are they so afraid of? They all hide in their superficial class circles and throw up barriers to conceal the eating, the drinking, and the whoring inside."

I couldn't help showing surprise at the force of his language, and he saw it and immediately apologized.

"You know, I've been in the army where if one gets a chance to think it comes out sort of strong like that."

We heard the telephone ring and Nancy answering it.

In the sky, streaks of clouds were painted scarlet and blue and purple with a few yellow wisps around where the sun had disappeared. The outside world lay rock still except for a tender breeze reaching through the open window to touch cool finger-tips to our faces. Below in the garden, the deepening shadows of the trees made them seem as if kneeling on the ground in subservience to the approaching night god. The poplar by the back fence turned over several of its leaves as if in protest at the inevitable coming of dark.

Just after the street lights clicked on, Nancy came. She brought us ice-cream in mother's best dishes, which were kept in the tall glass-doored cabinet that had belonged to my great-grandmother. We opened the cabinet on special occasions.

ROMANCE

"Tom, that was Cathy. She wants us to go to a party in Westdale, so I said we would."

"She asked Skip too, didn't she?"

"I'm asking Skip," she said, playfully seductive.

Skip must have been as surprised at her change of tone as I was, but he merely looked up and made eyes right back at her. "Sure," he said. And he forgot about all that knife-and-fork business.

"Is Cathy alone?" I didn't want to appear interested so I said it as casually as possible.

"She always is, isn't she?"

Cathy was not the kind of woman you could corner easily. At a party, if anyone were talking alone with her, those passionate blue fires, called her eyes, would be circling around looking for something better. She was difficult to take out in a group because she didn't stay long enough at the side of any one man for that fellow to claim her as his date. There were guys who took her out and guys who brought her back and you were lucky if you belonged to both groups on the same night. Of course, there were always other girls with these other fellows, but they didn't have any control over their partners when Cathy was present. She acted as if only the men existed and I think that's why she was so unpopular with females; she was one hundred percent woman.

"Tommy dear, take out the dishes when you're finished while I dash upstairs. She'll be by in a minute."

"Do you know who this Cathy is?" I asked Skip. "She's dynamic!"

"Uh huh." He was still in the after-effects of Nancy.

"Her father's John Rymal, one of the brewery family, but he doesn't have to work."

"Oh, I know, Trans-Canada stuff. Yea!"

"There's a chance to sell some insurance."

He laughed and slapped his knee. "I'll wait a week or so," he joked. But I could tell he was pleased.

Nancy had lit a few candles. To anyone passing in the street, the room must have looked like a tower with two ghouls tea-spooning ice-cream. But there was no one out in the night, and we could hear no noise through the open windows. Our residential district was quiet. It was on the fringe of the big houses of Hamilton's socially successful at the foot of the mountain. If one went three or four streets higher, one could start feeling rich just looking at the houses and one would begin climbing too because the mountain slope was steeper there. It became too steep for houses and the land remained wild until one came to the ridge of the escarpment where new housing estates were being set up.

Yet the foot of the mountain had not always been "the" place in which to live. The older families of the city used to hold sway in large houses in the east end. But since the Crash and the thirties, those families found that the securities they had been holding were worth little of their original value, and, with their social monopoly gone, they forsook their houses to developers who replaced them with apartments and super self-serve groceries. The big industrialists who lived at the foot of the mountain in the south were as far distant as possible from their blazing ovens along the bay shore in the north. They were the leaders who carried on the tradition of adding to their fortunes and doing nothing toward the improvement of anything outside their front gardens.

There was a slight hope for improvement though. Far in the west end of the city, there sprung up small, modernly designed houses and tree-lined roads close by the woods, as if the area wished to cling to the semblance of country. It was agreed by the south-enders that the wealthier people from the west were "nouveau-riche," but I think the objection was that they were "nouveau." The new district was called Westdale, and a university had its campus in the heart of it, so that periodically opinions on cultural and landscaping improvements emerged from the Art faculties. There were moments when it seemed these ideas would not only take hold in Westdale but threatened to spread to other parts of the city. Lately, because of the national demand for researchers in physics, some wealthy donors abetted the cluttering of the campus grounds with monstrous concrete installations, which completely emasculated the humanities and further removed the dream of a Hall where ballet, opera, and symphonies might visit.

We heard a horn play a tune in the night air and I went to the front of the house. A Buick waited in the street below, and I could see the tiny points of lit cigarettes inside it. I called Nancy to hurry and went to the porch for Skip.

ROMANCE

Nancy came wearing a blue polka-dotted calico which matched Skip's suit better than the dress she had worn before. She had sprinkled on some perfume too, and her movements, haloed by the fresh scent, seemed like pretty bobs. Obviously, she was going to play the role of the fairy-footed maiden, defenceless, all alone in that forest of men.

A blast from the horn greeted us when we reached the street, and the car filled with laughter. Cathy was behind the wheel and there were two girls sitting beside her. We filed into the back seat where we squeezed the poor fellow who was there against the window because Nancy refused to sit on anyone's lap for fear she'd spoil her dress.

When Cathy drove, the back seat was the worst place to sit. She hurtled through blind crossings and, without slowing, honked in case someone were coming along the other streets. One prayed that there was no other Cathy driving in the neighborhood. But her tendency to speed added to the sparkle of her charm, and, once she was on the main road, having passed through the valleys of death on the side streets, she became Diana, goddess of the hunt, carrying our hearts on the back of her flying arrow. The after-effect, when the ride was over, was to think of her as goddess of the moon.

I was glad to see that there was only the one fellow in the car with her, and it seemed he was only there because he was a brother to one of the other girls. Since Skip was taken up with Nancy, I felt pretty certain of getting a good share of Cathy for the evening. I began to imagine that light touch on the arm, the firm figure at my side, floating there as if I could lift it high merely by cupping my hand on the small of her back. And if we'd be dancing then I'd feel the touch of her raven hair against my cheek.

The car passed by an electric plant that was the last outpost of the city proper before the streets merged into Westdale avenues. We turned several sharp corners and stopped in front of a stuccoed house where the porch, shaped like an entry to a Norman castle, was lighted gaily and where Satchmo Armstrong's voice sang from the open window.

Skip and Nancy had been doing most of the talking and laughing. I spoke a little with Cathy, but it was discouraging craning my neck over the front seat and being interrupted by the chattering women who were there. I was first out of the car and helped Cathy step out. Skip left Nancy for a second to speak to me. He was looking uncertainly at the house.

"You're sure it's all right for me to come?" he asked. "I'm older than the rest of you, and I might be a stick-in-the-mud."

"We'll risk it," I smiled.

It was amusing to think that anyone could feel uncomfortable because he was older than the rest of us. I suppose there is a real age difference between those who have been to war and those who haven't. Anyway, Cathy was worth bothering more about at the moment than Skip. Yet I understood why he spoke to me rather than to Nancy. My sister, like most of her set, was not of the confiding sort. To her, confessions from a man were a sign of weakness. Besides, I don't think any man could believe that what he said to her in confidence would escape repetition in several different versions on as many different occasions.

When we entered the house, however, Skip's fears were groundless. There were all ages from twenty to forty and even some other veterans who were drinking beer and wandering among the younger people with an air of experience. The party was large. From one room to the next and up to the second floor groups conversed, forming and breaking up and re-forming. The large comfortable-looking rooms with their all-blue or all-red-brown colorings offered plenty of easy chairs and thick carpets to sit upon. Along the walls, were landscape and portrait paintings, lit from underneath and adding to the reserved yet welcoming atmosphere. This was further enhanced subtly by the drawn shade, which made it dark enough to cut any glare but light enough to prevent the opposite sexes from getting too close together.

We wandered through the first room, where none of us knew anyone personally, although I recognized a couple of the veterans as belonging to families who had been friendly with mine. But in a second, Cathy suddenly cut loose to waltz in on a group of young people, half-standing, half-sitting so that we followed her and joined in the salutations. Nancy introduced Skip to everyone standing round about but, as he was a stranger, no one took any interest in him. As Cathy had soon disappeared among men somewhere else in the room, and as Nancy was taken up with answering questions from some of her more insistent friends, I chatted with Skip to keep him from feeling shunned. From my year in Toronto I knew what it was like standing alone on the circumferences of groups.

"Let's wander around a bit," I suggested, and I thought of how angry Nancy would be when she discovered that I had taken him away.

In the next room, which was a study, there were some girls I knew talking among themselves. I introduced Skip to them, and we spent an exhausting ten minutes trying to make conversation, but unfortunately, neither Skip nor I was very interested in the latest movies so we drifted away and began looking at shelves of books lining one wall.

"The fellow who lives here has a good selection of classics," I said. Skip leafed through some volumes, and yawned disinterestedly.

"Wonder whose house we're in," I said.

"My uncle's," a girl's voice spoke softly by my elbow.

She was a demure blonde, about eighteen, with big understanding blue eyes. Her figure burned fire in her red dress, but she was the type who tried to lessen its accentuation with cover-up frills and bad posture. She looked shy so that it was surprising to find that she was not.

"And who are you?"

"Melanie."

"I haven't seen you in Hamilton before, not that it's that small, but surely, if you'd been here, I should have seen you."

"I'm from Toronto, on a visit. I don't come often."

There was obviously an attraction and I sensed it in her too, the way her eyes avoided meeting mine, and the fact she was standing alone as if appearing from nowhere to speak to me about nothings.

"Your uncle reads a lot."

"I think he collects more than he reads. He doesn't find much time away from his office."

"Then he collects a lot. It's a good hobby."

She looked across the room at a painting. Her blonde tresses enframed her face in an intelligent seriousness, yet there was no definite expression, merely a vague intimation that she might have been thinking.

"When are you going back to Toronto?" I felt as if I were guiding her thoughts rather than interrupting them.

"Tomorrow."

"You must leave me your address. I'm studying there."

I entered what she told me in my book. I was beginning to tremble slightly and it was difficult to write clearly.

"Isn't anyone dancing?"

"Upstairs," she said, and she was as eager as I.

I looked around for Skip, but he had gone. For a moment I felt guilty at leaving him to find a break in the wall of this party, but then I remembered that Nancy would be with him, and I followed Melanie up the stairs.

Slow, soft music came from a long-player in one corner of the darkened room we entered. I noticed that several other young couples were huddled together in the dark before Melanie came against me. We stuck as if waxed. Her hip bone rubbed below mine. For a long time we were pressed as if by an invisible clamp, and we had to breathe in soft gasps. Both our faces were wet, and drops of sweat ran from my armpits down my side. She was shaking and had to press hard against me. My head spun but I clung to her, breathed her hair, and kept us moving so that the others wouldn't notice.

The music had stopped and I saw the shyly interested faces of other couples looking at us before I could deaden my blissful expression, move away from Melanie awkwardly and pretend that everything was normal. In the doorway, I met Nancy with a partner.

"Where's Skip?" she frowned with surprise.

I shrugged and led Melanie downstairs. Her hand was hot in mine, and when I looked in her eyes it was as if she had fever, they were so strong. And they no longer shifted shyly away. No one was in sight and I kissed her hard and long.

"I'll get down to Toronto soon." It was summer time and college didn't open till the Fall. The hotter the woman, the greater the inconveniences cluttering the way to her.

Some boys came up the stairs, and we pretended to be looking at a small photograph enframed on the wall of the landing. One of them stopped and asked Melanie to dance. He was friendly with her, and I saw her give him the look Eurydice probably gave Orpheus when she was on her way back to hell. I watched her fade away and continued to descend the stairs with a relief that Orpheus must have experienced. I felt momentarily delivered as if fate had

ROMANCE

suddenly eased up on the pressure she had clamped on my soul.

Cathy, laughing in a group, turned in eager anticipation as I stepped in the room as she did automatically at the promise of something new. Her eyes probably hadn't expected or wished to be set on me, but once they were, so were those of the rest of the company, and she had to follow up her cue by crossing over to me. It was hard for anyone to believe that he was not of world importance when Cathy approached him with her special party lustre. Her charm had a sparkle as real and as convincing as the stones set in the bracelet her father had given her. I was alone with her in the centre of the room and feeling fantastically lucky.

"Tommie Davis, where have you been all this time? Here!" Cutely, she held her glass of cocktail out so that I might drink from it. "Oh ho! That's enough now. You'll have to fetch me another glass." She frowned at me then. "Have you seen your friend? He's boozing in the front room. How on earth did you ever come to know him?"

"He was a hockey star long time ago."

"Well, he's a drinking star now. People have been asking me who he was because he came in my car. Honestly, I'm embarrassed."

She led me to the doorway from where I could see Skip sitting with some older men and drinking beer.

"He doesn't look drunk to me," I said.

"He's been arguing as if he were."

"It's just politics. Come Cathy, let's...." I was going to say "dance" but I remembered that Melanie was dancing, and I didn't want to risk driving one bird in the hand to two in the bush; better two in the hand, so that I suggested she step onto the porch for some air.

With raised eyebrows she assented, and the blue sheen from her dress flashed happily at me as she stepped from the lights of the room. Stopping at the railing, she stared across the front lawn, cut like a cake into dark shadows by the street lamps, and she stood waiting while I came from behind her, held her, and kissed her as she turned her face up to me. There was no passion with Cathy. She was more like a pearl that one held for a precious moment before passing it on to the next man for admiration.

"So my girl friend's kid brother has taken to kissing big girls," she smiled, knowing her smile was perhaps the prettiest in the world.

"Only lovely big girls."

"Oh ho!" She turned and snuggled against my chest.

"And experienced too."

"Everything's new with you," I said.

She threw her arms about my neck and laughing, swung at arm's length in front of me, gradually pulling me down to kiss her again. An excitement exuded all over her, giving us both a giddy sense of adventure.

"Let's go for a run in the car!" she cried. She seized my hand and impulsively dragged me across the lawn, completely taking me by surprise.

A loud grumbling of voices came from the house as if the gods of heaven themselves were suddenly jealous. She stopped, and I could see myself slipping from first place as another became her new curiosity.

"That's your friend, isn't it?"

Skip was standing between two of the veterans with his arms outstretched against them holding them off from each other. The other guests hung back with white faces and watched him try to cool the men's anger. He was talking quietly to them about the party being a private one and that they weren't in a barn but in someone's house, when one of the men hit him in the jaw and jumped at his opponent. Skip fell on the arm of a chair but, within an instant, he stood up and, stooping, began rabbit-punching at the fracas on the floor with furious precision. One of the men rolled away, while the other, breathing heavily, charged Skip still stooping, with the intention of knocking him over. But Skip gave him one of the most beautiful body checks I have ever seen. He lifted him up and over, gracefully landing him in an easy chair where the poor fellow tried to win back some of the wind that had been knocked out of him. There was a moment's suspense while the other veteran got to his feet; but he recognized the situation and hanging his head in embarrassment he retreated behind the guests into the next room. Smiling, a gray-haired, deeply-tanned man came to clap Skip across the shoulders. I guessed he was Melanie's uncle, because at this sign of goodwill, the talk started up again and the party carried on as before. Skip joked for a moment with the host and some other people who had come around him and then, feeling Nancy's arm slip over his own, he said something to her.

"What a man!" Cathy said. Her eyes shone and her breasts rose on the crest of a full breath.

"Yeah, I told you he was a good guy," I said, but I felt uneasy.

Skip and Nancy came to us and suggested that we leave.

"Come on, then," Cathy smiled at Skip. "The others can get a ride back with someone else."

When I sat in the front seat with Cathy, we were not as intimate as I hoped I might have been. In spirit, Cathy was in the back seat with Nancy and Skip, and, for the moment, I felt I was baggage to be dropped off at the first opportunity.

"Where are you going, Cathy?" Nancy's voice nervously awoke from a long kiss.

"Taking you and Tommie home," she said, "then I'll drop Skip wherever he wants to go."

"No." I was well enough acquainted with all the intonations of my sister's voice to recognize this as one of ruthless command. "Skip's tired. Drive him home first."

"Okay!" Cathy was almost singing. "Where do you live, Skip? Oh, way down there! You'll have to move up close to us so we can see more of you."

There was silence from the back seat so that Cathy asked him another question. She kept piling question on answer until I knew that if my sister had had a gun, Cathy's life would have been worthless. Finally, we let Skip out in front of a smudgy hotel in a dimly-lit side street. When he said good-bye to me, I saw that he had drunk too much to have noticed the warfare between the girls. We watched him unlock the door to the hotel under a yellow lantern light turning his brown hair to copper, and he waved.

The drive back to our house was very quiet and the atmosphere was tense with silent insinuations. It was my dove-like presence that kept them peaceful.

CHAPTER 3

A month later I saw Skip again. I knew he had taken Nancy out several times, but I was never at home when he called, so that I was pleased when after driving the tennis ball a foot too long over the baseline, and looking at the verandah to see if anyone had seen the fool stroke, I saw Skip smiling at me as he was climbing the stairs with Nancy. He was wearing a sports shirt open at the neck even though it was Sunday afternoon and it was not done to go without a tie in the street. He sat in one of the chairs by the railing while Nancy went into the club house, and he pretended he was settling down to watch me play.

The set was almost over. I slapped the ball into the net twice, returned some fair drives and won on a fluke wood stroke by the net. The guy I was playing with looked disgusted, but I didn't mind. I was willing to take any excuse to get out of the sun and shake the red dust from the courts off my feet. While I was showering, Skip came down and called me. He wanted to know if I would tell him my strategy; not that he ever played, rather so that he could warn others.

Then I heard him talking with someone about insurance. He wasn't trying to sell it; the other fellow sounded like a co-worker. When I was dressed and went up to the verandah, I saw that his friend was bland and serious with glasses. Tim Lake was his name. I sat down with them and saw that we were separated from the rest of the people on the porch by several empty chairs. I guessed that Skip had been shunned by the others and had retreated to the end of the porch. Even with Tim and me for company he looked self-conscious. I could tell that he wanted to sit up with the smart set all in their Sunday-afternoon best and chat with whomever he pleased. But when he glanced at them, it was with the eyes of a man who had been given a cold shoulder.

For my part, I could see nothing frightening about those people. They came only for a few hours on very few Sundays and never played tennis. They belonged to the older social set which had once reigned over the courts between the wars, and they returned to watch occasionally because they wanted to remember the games they had played. But since the club was forced financially to become more plebeian, the patricians found it too uncomfortable to appear at just any time alone. If on a Sunday afternoon the weather was beautiful, and if it was not in mid-summer when most people were holidaying in the north, they arrived, sat in the sun, and added to the prestige of the club by the very infrequency of their visits.

"Where's Nancy?" I asked.

Skip pointed to the end courts, and I saw Nancy in a mixed doubles. "They're booked for the first court when it's free."

A slow lob sent a ball into Tim's lap instead of onto the other side of the court. He juggled it as if it were a snake and threw it back at the players, who were laughing with the man who had made the bad stroke. A player wearing a white peak remarked about his opponent's tennis elbow slipping, and since he was an old member, the verandah patricians laughed politely.

Tim still looked a little frightened, but the good humour around him brought a smile into his broad face. He relaxed by asking Skip what premiums his company was then paying on fire and theft.

I looked along the verandah and saw Cathy coming towards us. Mr. Rymal was behind her, but he stopped to speak with a man who had grabbed his arm. Skip welcomed her with his wide smile, the one that I knew from the bubble gum photo.

"Long time no see," she laughed.

Cathy hardly ever came to the tennis club. I thought it was more than a coincidence that she came then. She could plan almost as well as my sister.

"We're leaving for Muskoka next week," she said. "So I'm glad we've met again before I go."

"Going for long?" Skip asked, politely concerned.

"About a month and a half," she smiled. "We're on a lake and it's fun. Why don't you come and visit us?" She looked at me too so that the invitation wouldn't appear forward. "Bring Skip up with you, Tom, why don't you?"

"I've never been before," I said. "I don't know where it is."

"Oh well then, I'll tell Nancy, and we'll have a weekend party. You do get holidays, don't you, Skip?"

"Maybe they'll give me a week at the end of August. I'm new, you know."

A ball skittled along the railing and careened against Tim's chest, making him jump in his chair and almost lose his glasses. He looked so much as if he thought he were an intentional target that everyone laughed. The player with the white peak apologized and remarked that it was luck the court time was almost up because his opponent's tennis elbow was getting worse.

Mr. Rymal, smiling, took big strides over the floor boards and clapped Tim solidly across the shoulders.

"No place to hide here, mister," he croaked. "They've got all our numbers."

We all laughed with Mr. Rymal because his personage carried the fame of many hundreds of practical jokes. And when he thought something was funny, he used his booming hoarse voice and big frame to elect himself the patriarch of humour in a crowd where his wide smile and twinkling eyes fathered laughter in everyone about him.

"Father," Cathy said just before Rymal was about to say something more, "you know Tom Davis?"

I shook hands with him and introduced him to Skip and Tim.

"You two are new here, aren't you?" Rymal took the chair beside Skip.

Tim confessed that he was born in Hamilton. He looked frightened of Rymal as if he suspected the joker would bite him when he wasn't looking.

"Skip's just started up in insurance here," Cathy said.

"Good, good," Rymal laughed. "I'll give you a list of names to call on. They're all friends of mine--just tell them I sent you."

Skip laughed with him.

"Oh father, be good!" Cathy said.

Skip was feeling at home with Rymal. The tenseness had gone from his face, and he leant back in his chair ready to joke.

"No, it's all right Cathy," Skip said. "I wouldn't mind at all as long as he went with me."

"Well," Rymal chuckled, "I used to play right middle in Varsity football, and you don't look so weak. We wouldn't do so bad, you know. You didn't play football?"

When Skip shook his head, I said he was a hockey star.

"Burke," Rymal repeated. "In Montreal you say." He kept us waiting while his mind went through the sports pages of the last fifteen years. Rymal could tell you what horse won on almost any track in every race that ever took place within his lifetime.

"By golly, I remember. I won a hundred bucks on you. More than that, you gave me a moral victory over an old pal whom I'd been trying to beat for years.

"You were playing Detroit when they had that big scorer they used to call the Slugger. Do you remember? By Gosh! and I bet on your team when you were two goals down in the last period. Detroit also had a beaut of a defenceman named Mulligan. If the Slugger wasn't firing in goals, then Mulligan was taking out anybody who came down his end of the ice. You got two quick goals if I remember right and then the Slugger got a penalty. By Gosh! And my old pal, who told me he'd never lost a bet, went down behind the Detroit box and talked to Mulligan when he was off resting for a minute. I never saw anything like that Mulligan when he was after you. Whenever you went near him he tried to knock you over the boards. Do you remember that? Then in the last minute of play, you came storming down with the puck and Mulligan was so interested in slamming you, he forgot about the other players and after sucking him to the side you passed in front of the net and wham! I won! It was real genius, that play; there's no doubt about it. And I found out my old pal had promised Mulligan a lot of dough for trying to get you out of the game so he had a hell of a big bill that time. He never took a bet with me again." He laughed as he remembered his poor pal, and we laughed as we pictured him too, his pockets empty. "Say, where are all those boys now?"

"Slugger and Mulligan are dead," Skip said. "They were in the RCAF."

"Yeah. Well, they come and go," Rymal said. "They come and go."

"I asked Skip to come and see us at the cottage," Cathy said.

"Good idea, good idea." Rymal slapped his knee. "Sometimes it gets pretty boring talking nothing but golf and tennis and a little fishing. It'd be a pleasant change to reminisce about hockey in the middle of summer. Sure, come on up and pay us a visit. And if you don't come there, come and see us here in the city. The house is always open to a guy who brought me a hundred bucks!" He left an impression of good humour on the patrician crowd listening in to the conversation when he stood up and held his hand out to lead Cathy away. "We've got to run home to eat or your mother'll be angry."

"I'm staying here, father. I can eat at the bar."

Rymal let his hand fall to his side. "All right."

"And father, will you leave me the car?"

"How am I going to get home? You don't expect me to walk with my flat feet?"

Everyone laughed, and the man who had spoken with him earlier stood up smiling. "I'll take you back, John."

Rymal went away grumbling good-naturedly, and I saw the group on the verandah smile with him until he was gone. Then some of the women exchanged mocking looks indicating their disapproval.

"What are you and Nancy doing after she's finished playing?" Cathy asked me.

"She's with Skip," I said.

"Nothing," Skip said.

"Now that I've got the car why don't we all go out to the quarry?" Cathy could make any suggestion sound attractive merely by her warming tones, and although the quarry was twenty miles away, and we had no bathing suits, and it would be getting dark when we arrived, yet we three men wanted to go. "I'll bring some food out for us," she said, and she went into the club room.

Nancy and her partners moved to the first court, which had been vacated by the older club members. Nancy's game was faster and more interesting. She was a fair player, Nancy, and, even though she was a woman handicapped the way her shoulder-bones were formed, she managed to hit a serve similar to a man's. She knew she was good too, and when she didn't have to play hard, she showed off her figure by posing attractively against the red courts, the green trees, and the blue sky.

Skip was, of course, interested. He leaned in his chair with his broad shoulders carrying the force of his frame forward, watching the ball closely and judging the movements of the players as if he were the umpire. And at the pauses between rallies he looked at Nancy admiring this, her latest of achievements, as a complement of all her other assets that went before.

Cathy swung through the screen doors and over to us. She met a suspicious look from Nancy with a disarming smile.

"Do you like ham in your sandwiches, dear?" she called out, "or would you rather have egg."

Nancy, who was about to serve, was caught at the disadvantage of not being able to ask why. It was pointless to hold up the game to ask questions, so she said 'ham' and immediately double-faulted.

Cathy took our preferences and went back inside. I could see Nancy was worried because she didn't know what we were planning, and, as her game was slipping, I answered one of her glances at us by explaining that we were going swimming when she had finished. The knowledge did her good; it made her angry enough to win the game on smashes. From her determined expression though, I expected that she was going to come with us; she would accept any woman's challenge to meet her in bathing suits, even Cathy's.

When the game was over, Tim brought the other girl playing in the mixed doubles with us. With Cathy at the wheel, we whipped around to our different houses, fetching suits, and then sped up over the mountain toward a sun, which was beginning to fall plum-coloured in the sky. Turning off the highway, we threw up dust and stones in our wake, then turned into a lane and bounced over mound and rock until we came to rest at the far side of a large stone quarry where the clear surface of the water sparkled with the welcome of tiny bubbles from springs in the rocky floor.

There were no other swimmers. The water looked like an oasis reflecting the dying rays of a hot sun. The girls changed on one side of the car while we boys changed on the other. When Cathy stepped out from her side, I wished I were alone in that wilderness with her. But she was oblivious to my feelings. After she had tried to tiptoe over the pebbles, she must have seen my expression and returned an irritated look.

"Tommie, you might make yourself useful and carry me over to the grass."

Under such an order, how could I refuse? But Cathy couldn't notice how much I enjoyed holding her. I was merely an animal of burden to be made use of.

Skip was the first to dive in. There were certain places where the rocks didn't shelve out underneath the surface, and they weren't marked. One had to look carefully at where one intended to dive, so that we all followed Skip instead of risking another spot. Cathy dived with beautiful form and called to Skip to race her out to the middle. I watched their arms cut long strokes until they splashed to a stop, their laughter carrying across the water to me where I was treading water with the others.

Nancy hesitated whether to follow them, so I challenged her, and we raced too, even though we both knew I would win easily. It's funny how the press of circumstances can force people to accept second rate joys. Had I been racing Cathy, I really would have enjoyed trying to beat her, but with Nancy, I could only think of the subterfuge we were splashing through.

Nancy screamed, and Skip popped to the surface beside her. While they sprayed one another, I tried to dive at Cathy, but she saw me coming and swam to the side. I tried again and came to the surface to meet an exasperated look.

"Oh Tom Davis! Stop acting the fool and behave yourself!"

There wasn't anything else for me to do but tread water.

Nancy was racing Skip back to shore and Cathy and I crawled along behind them. I thought that Cathy was silly to try to win Skip away from Nancy. She would end up by spoiling the fun for all of us. But she was stubborn, and since she was used to getting what she wanted, she remained an optimist.

The six of us sat on the rocks and talked while the sun went down behind the trees. Cathy brought us sandwiches and orange pop. Against the rocks in the gray of the twilight, we might have been figures from a Matisse, munching under the oriental pattern of hues left behind by the sun in the western end of the sky.

Below us, the pool shivered and grew darker. The far shore began to melt its gray rocks into itself and soon they were totally immersed, existing there only because we knew they did. Over us were dark clouds closing the gaps of white and shifting about relentlessly. The stillness of the quarry was broken by no other sound except when we spoke, when our words echoed eerily as if in violation of the natural isolated surroundings. A sudden breeze came cold to the skin. I saw Tim put his arm about his girl and Skip do the same with Nancy. Cathy began collecting the empty bottles, and I followed her with two more back to the car.

"What are you afraid of? I won't bite," I said.

"Tommie, whatever made you think I liked you in that way?"

"I don't think of your side," I said. "I only think of mine."

"Exactly," she said. "I don't think some men know that women can have their likes and dislikes too. Don't you think we women know what we want?"

"For the moment, perhaps, but then anything may change them in the next."

"Well, then, for the moment, you can consider yourself not wanted."

"What are you so worried about Skip for?" I said. "Why don't you just let him and Nancy be?"

She darted a look at me that would have scared me. Obviously, I had just made our case irrevocably hopeless, for the moment.

"Whatever made you think I had designs on Skip?" She accentuated 'designs' as if I had accused her of treachery which was criminal to any female, because it was almost invariably true.

Before I could answer, she wheeled about and stalked back to the quarry, this time needing no help over the pebbles.

"Time for another dip," she called. "Who's with me?"

"Its too cold," Tim said alone in answer.

Cathy moved along the shore onto some rocks jutting over the water where we could barely see her in the darkness closing upon us.

She laughed, "Oh come on, you sissies! Is everyone afraid?"

I sensed that she was calling at Skip; she used a special tone, rather light and unsure, that I had come to recognize as meant for him.

"You shouldn't go in now, Cathy. It's too dark to see," Skip warned.

I saw her swing her arms ready to dive far out, and in that stance was the defiance of the spoilt girl.

We heard her splash, and the clouds shifted to let some moonlight fall on the water. There were traces of rills. We waited, listening for her to break the surface. It seemed too long for her to be underwater, so I stood up and moved to the edge.

"Cathy!"

If she were playing with us, it was hardly the time for it.

"Cathy!" I called, impatient, but the echo fell on deaf ears, as if it were a spirit mocking its namesake.

Someone rushed by me and I saw Skip's body flash fish-white from the rock we had jumped from earlier.

"Tim! go where she was standing," I commanded while I followed Skip.

When I came up, I saw Skip ahead of me and Tim racing along to stop on a pile of rocks. I felt suddenly scared as I thrashed at the water behind Skip. He went under. I stroked out a bit and duck-dived. It was so dark I couldn't see much. I felt rocks under my hands, panicked for air, and kicked for the surface. On the shore, I saw the two girls holding on to each other. Tim was running to follow us in. Skip wasn't anywhere. I went under and swam in another direction, reaching out at every looming form, scraping the skin from my fingers. I made one last wide arm swing on my way up for breath, and, when I looked at the shore and saw no Cathy, I felt how hopeless were my unsystematic plunges. I then began to measure where she might have landed after her dive and to where her motion might have carried her. I struck rocks with my feet and ducked under, feeling my way down their sides into the cold water of a hole into which I had fallen and from where I could feel a freshness rising against me as I pushed myself deeper clutching at one ledge after another. A movement nearby made a slight impact on me, and I looked up to see a black shape disappearing into the flannel dark gray. I went deeper, seeing nothing and feeling only clammy sharp stone. When I got up to the surface I was desperate. I wanted to yell for Skip. But when I looked at shore the girls were gone, but people were struggling in the water near the bank. At the same time my heart leaped, my arms struck out. I reached them as Tim took Cathy from Skip and lifted her onto the rocks. I clambered up the side and grabbed onto Skip's arm. He was weak from exhaustion. The girls helped Tim carry Cathy to the top where they knelt beside her, rubbing her limbs. When Skip and I stumbled to them, I heard him catch at a second wind.

"Get down!" he ordered me.

Tim and he lay Cathy crosswise over my back, and I felt the weight of arms and shoulders pressing through her onto me and heard Skip heavily breathing the count. I closed my eyes trying to catch up with time and with the events that had taken place so casually that evening. I felt a black fear chasing about inside me. I wanted to spit it out onto the ground like the water coming from Cathy's mouth. I heard a car door slam and feet running towards us stopping, and, holding back, in the tense anxiety that lay heavily around me. Cathy began to choke as if her insides were coming out.

"I've got a rug," Nancy cried shrilly.

They lifted Cathy off me, and I hauled myself to my feet. The night was black on us but by the quarter moon I saw Cathy swathed in a blanket. Nancy and Tim were rubbing her arms, and the other girl was doctoring the cuts on her head, while Skip sat, tired, watching them.

When she became conscious, the nightmare began to lift, and I was free to look at the people working over her as if they were robots from a different world. I looked at Skip, and, although I could only see the cast of his face, I knew that, like me, he felt capable of moving like an individual again. He could think and be conscious that his legs and arms were moving, that he could move them at will, and that he had no more fear. We stood up, and, with Tim, we carried Cathy to the car.

When we were under the light, Cathy spoke weakly. "The cuts? Where are they?"

"All under the hair. Lucky," the other girl said.

Cathy lay back and wanted to sleep so Skip sat with her in his arms while Nancy drove us to town. I couldn't help thinking that it was characteristic of Cathy; she often went to extremes to get what she wanted.

CHAPTER 4

The summer went by pretty quickly. There were a couple of heat spells, the second lasting about two weeks. The city was the place not to be, but that's where I was. More than that, I worked in the heat and smell of a plant where rubber tires were made, all for the sake of money, all for the sake of paying my way through Osgoode the next winter. So when five o'clock came round every day, I was glad to go over to the tennis club for a cold shower and then wander home to read some law with a cool glass of some fruit mixture beside me. Since I didn't have much time to spare, I didn't see much of anyone else. Skip was still going with Nancy, *that* I knew. Also Cathy had written Nancy inviting us all north, but Skip couldn't get any holidays. Nancy was taking hers later and, unfortunately, I wasn't invited to run up alone for a weekend.

Then on a Sunday afternoon in September, after Nancy had left for a two weeks' sketching course in the woods of Quebec, she being another commercial artist with dreams, I was reading an interesting case from Torts on the sun porch when the bell rang.

Mother answered the door, and, just as I became disgusted at the illogicalness of the judge's decision, Skip walked in the room.

"Hi boy!" His smile proclaimed the hero again and I was glad to jump up and turn a chair for him. "How've you been doing?"

"Living. Haven't seen you this summer, Skip."

"Well, I've been working hard trying to get a footing in the company."

"Sure you haven't been getting a footing in people's doors?" I asked.

It was fun to kid him and to see his smile spread wide and his eyes twinkle into yours.

"In one sense, you're just about right," he said. "You know it is hard to meet people in this city. Sure, guys from the company have had me around for dinner with their wives sometimes, but it gets boring when all you can do is talk shop. But if I meet anybody else I never get asked around to their houses or to their parties if they have any. Nancy's

ROMANCE

introduced me to lots of people but when they want anyone to come and see them, it's just Nancy. They leave me in the cold. The only place I was asked back to was at the house where that party was, do you remember?"

"Hell, don't worry," I said. "It's only natural. You come from the east, don't you? Wasn't it the same?"

"Maybe, but I was a hockey star remember. Big time, never had to worry with all that bunk. And when I was six years in Europe, every door was open to me. Maybe it's because I was in uniform. I don't know."

"Yes, I've heard Europe's more friendly to strangers," I said. "For that matter, you can go south of the border here and find all the pals you want."

"It's not that!" He looked cross and then snorting, smiled. "It's this closed-in atmosphere that gets me down. It's as if I didn't belong to the place, you know. Here I am trying to make my home here, and all I am and ever will be is a stranger. If no one'll take me in and say, look fellows, he's one of us, then I'm not accepted, am I? I just don't belong."

"You're right, I guess," I said. "But I don't know what to do."

"It's only since Nancy's been away that I've noticed how much I was depending on her for getting around here," he went on. "But now I'm determined to be recognized on my own."

Skip looked as if he was under his coach's orders to get another goal.

"I don't know how you're going to work it," I said.

"Old man Rymal ran into me in the street the other day. He said they'd just come back from their cottage and I was to come round to see them some afternoon. He's a great guy and I like him, you know. But he's so damn casual that I don't know whether he's serious or not. So I wondered, Tom, getting down to the reason for why I'm here today," he smiled, which to me was worth a ten thousand dollar policy. "Could you," he continued, "possibly find the time to go up there with me this afternoon?" He pointed towards the windows facing the mountain and tree-lined avenues with their big houses set back behind long lawns.

I had a sudden fright as if I were about to step naked into a roomful of people at a cocktail party.

"What good would I do?" I protested. "He doesn't want to see me."

"Don't tell me you won't go," he said.

"Of course, I'll go, but I...."

"Well then, come on. Let's go now before it gets any later. We can stay for an hour and then beat it."

On Sunday afternoon, the streets in that area were especially deserted because everyone was in his back garden where he was recuperating either from the morning sermon or from the morning gardening, depending on his allegiance. Occasionally a car would cruise by, its occupants craning their necks to see everything from its windows, and with reason because every large house had its own peculiar but attractive design which, nevertheless, did neither impair the unity nor the visual beauty of the street. Each house had its own separate character. The fountains, the small statues, and the landscaping of the front lawns reflected the glory of wealth.

We began to ascend a steep street. I knew where we were going because at one time in my youth I used to help the morning paper boy deliver his route along these streets, and I could always remember the Rymal's house because it took such a hell of a long climb to get there and the paper boy always sent me with their paper. Moreover, Cathy threw parties to which I had been invited, *grace a* Nancy, so that I was familiar with the mansion that now faced us from the noble mountain seat. It looked down the street we had climbed up, and over the roofs of the neighboring houses, over the city trees and buildings, and on a clear day for miles right to the origin of its wealth, the brewery, a Bauhaus miniature on the Bay shore. This mansion with its wings blocked wide in gothic fashion, with its rows of tall wide windows staring over the lawn and down the slight slope to the street level, gave an air of aloofness, intensified by the underground tunnel, which connected it with its four-door garage built into the side of the slope opening out on the side street with the grass of the lawn running over its roof, thus preventing it from disrupting the landscape. Seen from the front, the garage was completely concealed at one corner so one expected to see the owner suddenly shoot into the street in a black limousine and mercilessly speed down the side of the hill to disappear into the city streets. Since the great house was familiar to me, and, as I led Skip along its front walk, I thought how much more frightened he should have been than I was.

"You ring the bell," he said.

It was strange how small that bell looked. Electricity was wonderfully powerful, I thought. By pressing with the tip of my finger, I could make this place come alive.

"Tommy!" Cathy stood in front of me. "And Skip! What a surprise! Come in! Come in!"

"I was waiting for the butler," Skip laughed.

"It's the servant's day off," she said, "and today is my day for opening the door. Naturally, father had to have a party and I've been on the go all afternoon."

"Oh, Mr. Rymal has company?" Skip froze. "We can't stay, Cathy."

Cathy broke into heart-warming, delicious laughter and gave a flip to her raven hair. "Come along, sissy. If you don't like the party you can stay and talk to me."

In dread, undecided, we followed her through hallways, and into one of the wings where there was a long room decorated heavily with hunting trophies and heads of moose, bear and deer, while along one side several doors opened onto the garden and allowed the sun to stream in to light up the brilliant hues of the rugs and catch the faces and clothes of the thirty odd people gathered there in variations of shade and light. In the centre of the room was ringed the majority of guests. They were screaming with intense excitement over a small rudely-constructed area where two cocks battled amidst blood and flying feathers. Mr. Rymal was standing on a table nearby where he held a fistful of bills and yelled numbers and threw the bills into different piles. Other guests formed small quiet groups at a distance from the uproar, and some of them were strolling in pairs about the garden. Cathy led us to the far side of the room where three people were chatting in the shaft of sunlight that fell through a window. Mrs. Rymal turned and cordially smiled as I introduced Skip.

She had been beautiful like Cathy, Mrs. Rymal. She had the same pretty features: a tender, rounded face that, deepened with age, had given her a sweet look and dark sparkling eyes that threatened to see the humour in everything. The front part of her hair had become gray, perhaps with the help from the beauty parlor some would say, but she was not that type. She was very natural and very hospitable.

"Tom, you know Mr. and Mrs. Birchwood, don't you?" She brought me into their group while Cathy took Skip away to see her father.

Yes, I knew Mr. and Mrs. Birchwood. Their old, slender, genteel forms had been familiar to me since I was a small boy. Their smiles at me when I met them on the street were friendly because I, like them, was descended from an old family; but their family, unlike mine, had to retain a high social position through a series of financially successful marriages until their family, unlike mine, was left with these two old childless remnants, rich and distinguished, but rather lonely.

"How is your mother?" Mrs. Birchwood asked in a silvery voice.

My answer was drowned out by a loud roar from the cock fight but it didn't make any difference to Mrs. Birchwood. She smiled as if she thought I was the nice boy I had always been.

"You're in law, now, aren't you?" said Mr. Birchwood, his voice creaking as if he were straining to keep up with the times.

"Osgoode, sir."

"In the family line, eh?" he chuckled, his eyes bemused.

"I'm afraid so, sir."

He went on chuckling, overjoyed to see tradition standing in front of him.

"Come on and I'll introduce you in the garden," Mrs. Rymal sweetly smiled.

As I went out, I caught sight of Skip, his face red with laughter while he joked with Mr. Rymal. In the garden were more elderly people, and I wondered why Mrs. Rymal was taking me around to meet them all; perhaps she thought direct contact with me would be like injecting youth into their veins and incite them all to getting around the cock-pit and make her husband happy; or maybe she thought I'd enjoy meeting the elect. A few I knew, however, because they were still polite to mother, but others I knew only from hearing stories about them and they, of course, shook my hand with a brevity that ascertained they were only going to know me for this occasion. And there were always the cousins. Whenever you met them at a party, which was seldom, it was understood that you were to maintain a distance as far as their second or third relationships permitted, and if they knew that you knew they were cousins of yours, then they beamed a friendly glint at you which was more of a reminder than a greeting that their relationship was to be kept secret between you. I recognized three or four among the younger ones in the garden and several inside betting on the cocks. Mrs. Rymal left me with a couple in their thirties who seemed youngsters compared to some of the dinosaurs crawling about the garden stones.

"We know your sister very well," the woman said to get us started off in a sure direction.

"She paints well indeed," the husband said. "Has she exhibited?"

"Not yet," I said. Nancy had finished about two oil paintings in her life and, for sure, no one would look at them.

"Exhibit? Where, dear?" his wife asked in a half-mocking, half-curious tone.

"Why, I suppose there must be an art gallery in town," he mumbled.

The woman turned a long intelligent face toward me. The refined nose, the understanding lurking in the eyes, and the simple design of the earrings hinted she might appreciate art. "He, like all the others, doesn't have the slightest interest in art, and even if Nancy did find the chance to hang her paintings, it isn't likely that many people would go to see them."

"My wife is always trying to make out that Hamilton's another Sinclair Lewis' *Main Street*," he broke in angrily with just enough eagerness to betray his satisfaction at being able to mention a literary work in his conversation.

"We've heard that before," his wife said.

Just then another couple, whom I had not met, spoke to them, and, they, falling into married harmony, turned from me, and eager to make an impression, forgot me. I faded away like a disinterested spectator who discovered the crowd had closed ranks in front of him and made it too difficult to see beyond it. I faded away far back into the garden. There I found myself alone, grateful for the respite from the trivial conversations. There I found, too, an apple tree growing between rocks and the wild grass which had tumbled down to meet the foot of the garden. I plucked one of the red fruits, and, like Adam, as I ate it, I watched the other animals in my Eden to see if they were watching me.

Skip and Rymal stepped from the house together, and Rymal called to an older man, one of the city's industrial leaders, who had made his pile, become a little soft-hearted, and retired. I saw Rymal slap Skip on the back and push him towards his new acquaintance. Rymal had picked an easy man for Skip with which to begin his sales talk. That old fellow would buy life insurance for his cat. By the time I had finished my apple, Skip was huddled over and filling in papers while the old man nodded vigorously by his side.

Yet I didn't think it was a good idea for Skip to pursue his business at a social function even though it was obviously at Rymal's instigation. Poor Skip didn't know how far Rymal could carry a joke; for Rymal, the joke was supreme; he was insensitive to any human feeling or to the dignity of another person. And if anyone did not know that, he could not suspect that behind the good will of Rymal's exterior, he was to be the object of his joke.

Rymal stepped from the house again and beckoned to Skip. He must have been waiting for the transaction to end. Skip, smiling with success, came eagerly to him. It may have been the biggest sale Skip had made. Rymal left him standing on the flagstones while he went into the room and reappeared again with the great bulldog form of 0. W. Jones, President of one of the country's largest chain stores. The only thing in common that this man had with Rymal was the love of gambling; otherwise his humour was forced, his outlook was ruthless, and his generosity was non-existent. I could appreciate why Rymal liked to play practical jokes on him. But I feared for Skip.

Jones was angry at being disturbed from the cock-fight and more piqued when he learned that the cause of the disturbance was merely a young man with a wide smile. Nevertheless, he made an attempt to be cordial, and I don't know what Rymal said but Jones managed to laugh. Rymal then left Skip to stroll with him, while he himself hurriedly entered the house and reappeared at one of the long centre windows, where, hiding his form behind the curtain, he peeked out at the garden like the universal fat boy waiting for the firecracker to go off.

ROMANCE

The two men strolled for a distance, Skip talking and Jones nodding in amusement. I noticed other guests looking at them, and I imagined that Skip had suddenly become interesting. Anyone who was walking alone with Jones became interesting. And when both men looked to be enjoying themselves, the other strollers began to smile. But when they came to a turn in the path, where the statue of a Greek athlete sat in a small fountain, Jones lost his smile, and, stopping, he stared at Skip as if insulted. As they had come near to me, I heard the sharp tone in Jones's gruff voice, and I saw his bulldog face look menacingly up into Skip's flushed features. Skip's motions were painful to watch. He stuttered apologies with hands as well as with voice, and he made the fatal mistake of producing an insurance form as a verification of his good intentions. Abruptly Jones turned from him, and, with an expression of angry disgust such as Rymal would enjoy seeing, he moved his thick-set body rapidly back to the house. Skip stood for a moment undecided before he walked slowly to the side of the garden where he was shyly avoiding disdainful glances from those strollers who had no sympathy for one who had fallen out of favor. When I turned to look again at the fountain, I remarked that the athlete was carved looking down so that the trickling water made him look as if he were crying.

Before I got to Skip though, Cathy appeared beside him from the other direction. Following the rules of Canadian discretion, I stopped and hid from their view by standing behind a bush. To my discomfort, Cathy and Skip began walking in my direction. Afraid of being embarrassed, I hid between two fir trees and hoped they wouldn't notice me in passing. Unfortunately, they found that the short range of trees in that spot served as a shield from the strollers in the front of the garden. And so by inadvertent circumstances, I was made an eavesdropper.

"It doesn't matter at all," Cathy was saying. "Father likes his little joke, and Mr. Jones will realize that in a little while."

"But I thought your father was a great guy," Skip said. "It was sort of a dirty trick to pull on me, wasn't it? I mean, for a great guy."

"I'm sorry, Skip; I know it isn't any fun finding out the way he is. I had to learn myself many times because I was never convinced that... oh, that he was that way. It isn't any fun being repeatedly disillusioned when you're young. You have to get used to him, that's all. Then it doesn't matter," she smiled.

"You're right, Cathy, you know. You're all right too."

"Am I? Come now, aren't you beginning to exaggerate? I seem to remember a little episode at a certain quarry where I wasn't a bit right."

"You were always all right," Skip said seriously.

I saw Cathy toss her head in half laughter and her raven hair flick capriciously over the bronzed skin of her shoulders. What her eyes said to Skip I couldn't see, but I could guess, because in the next moment they were embracing.

I was surprised and embarrassed. When my long drawn supposition that Cathy desired Skip suddenly proved correct, it came as a shock. I knew each of them separately as individuals but never thought they would ever come together like this despite their attraction to one another. Cathy was still as lovely to me as always, but it was then that I knew I had no real desire for her. From the moment she had given herself to someone else, she had stepped from being the temptingly attainable to merely a pretty but otherwise uninteresting picture. My half-hearted pursuit of her appeared like a silly exercise done only to pass the time.

Yet I was disappointed in Skip. The way he was holding her so tenderly against him and whispering in her ear like love-sick Romeo was the opposite of what I expected from him. I could hardly believe that he had fallen sucker to Cathy's wiles. He didn't look as if he were playing with her, as if he were out to enjoy himself and then leave before his heart was trapped. Just the opposite. He was hanging on to her like a merchant in possession of a treasure. Almost sickened, I was convinced he was serious.

"Oh God!" I heard Skip say at last. "Let's get away from here."

"I'll get the car," she said. "But say good-bye to mother and father."

"I can't face that bunch again."

"But darling, you must. Besides, there's no other way out."

Skip glanced up the side of the mountain as if left to himself he would really have had the courage to leave the party without any farewells.

"Okay," he sighed.

She kissed him quickly, then looking at him, tapped fingers to her lips. Skip brought forth his handkerchief and wiped at his mouth before he followed her toward the house.

I watched them go with new interest. Cathy's typical proposal to run away in her car evoked the same sense of adventure in them that it used to evoke in me. I thought of where they might drive: to the mountain brow where they'd sit watching the city and whispering vows, to the lovely road by the marsh where, parked under the low branches, they'd love in the company of wild nature, and, afterwards, they'd hold one another with profound solemnity in the city graveyard which they would see up and over to their right. I was not sure what love was, but I imagined it was like that, where the absurd became the reasonable.

After a minute's pause, which was time enough to allow Skip to make his good-byes, I returned to the sports room where the guests were sitting eating buffet-style and reposing after the cock-fight. Mrs. Rymal was near the door so that I made my good-byes quickly, ran from the house to the sidewalk in time to watch the garage doors slide up as Skip and Cathy drove into the street.

"Take me home, will you?" I asked.

Skip reared back, shocked, his eyes betraying the guilt of his obvious situation.

Cathy threw open a back door. "Hurry then."

She speeded through the streets and screeched to a stop near the front of my house. Obviously she was angry that I had interrupted her romance, and perhaps too, because I had caught her red-handed at the theft of which earlier I had accused her.

I looked at Skip and saw that I was a bother to his conscience. He appeared really sorry. I shook his hand to show it didn't matter to me; after all, Nancy was only my sister.

But when I went into the house and heard the muffle of Cathy's car fade in the distance, I was glad that I was going to Toronto the next week and wouldn't be home when Nancy returned from her holidays.

CHAPTER 5

Within a few days of my return to Toronto, I had arranged my courses and settled in at the fraternity house, with a private room if you please--I had to plead insomnia to get it--and began meeting some of the new boys around the house. About the only guy I liked immediately was Maxwell Harley, a fourth-year medical student. He had a good moniker for his intended profession, but it was misleading when one came to the person himself. Instead of being tall, distinguished, suave in manner, and over-bearing in attitude as one could imagine a Harley-Street specialist, he was quiet, inconspicuous with his horn-rimmed glasses, and democratic in his attitude almost to the point of dullness. On meeting him, I was impressed by his straight-forward way of speaking which, however, never bordered on the impolite because his diplomatic turn of phrase made his opinions ring with obvious truth inoffensively. It gave me the feeling that all those to whom I had been speaking previously were merely superficial sophisticates. There was, too, a self-confidence about him that gave a touch of sureness to everything he did and which made me believe that some day he would make a good surgeon.

"With all these war veterans returning, my classes are brim full," I remarked to him after dinner when we were sitting down with newspapers in the reading room.

"Many of them will soon leave," he said. "They come back idealists from the war because their survival is enough to make them optimistic. I don't suppose there is anything more warping to ideals than six months of hard study."

"Still, I have the feeling the profs will take pity on them and pass them at the expense of some of us others."

"Probably," he said. "A touch of gray at the temples and the rank of captain among his pupils should make any prof think twice before flunking a poor paper." Maxwell discouraged further discourse by hiding behind his newspaper. He had the knack of concentrating on his reading so strongly that he plunged the atmosphere into a seriousness that drove those near him into imitating him.

ROMANCE

But half an hour later, he was the one to suggest that we drop in at the corner drugstore for a milk shake.

The breeze of late September sifted lightly the leaves of the large elm outside the fraternity house. Autos coasted noiselessly along the Toronto street. The street lights blinked through bobbing branches, and the night was a play of light and shadow. The silence was broken only by the clicking of heels now and then. We stood listening on the verandah, and we smelt the soft air of fall when the heat of the day had left it.

"The challenge," Maxwell said. "The challenge of a new year. I can smell the pages of my books."

"Which ones?" I encouraged him.

"The biological ones," he said.

Strange as it may seem, there was a sense of death and life in the air. It was the uncertainty of a new academic year. Maxwell had made it seem as if we could determine which it was going to be. When we stepped forth together, the feeling of life was strong within me, buoying me, livening my footsteps, but the presentiment of death lingered within me wh.ch found an echo in the slow swing of the leaves and the coasting of the autos.

Dan's Drug Store was two blocks away. Dan was mythical. No one ever saw him. He owned about half a dozen drug stores scattered throughout the wide rambling area of Canada's second largest city. And in the evenings, it was a sure bet that the younger sets from every area congregated in their own particular Dan's. Ours served a large residential district, so that the chances of seeing pretty girls were high; that is, that variety of pretty girls who had promised to be home by nine o'clock. Sometimes it was rather amusing to see if we could keep them till ten.

Half of the booths were full and some people were sitting at the long shiny counter. Whenever I, coming from studying in the conservativeness of my room, walked into the nickel-plated glare of the druggery, I was super-charged with optimism; it was as if I was graduated and already set up in practice. There was no better mood in which to meet women.

"Do you see anything interesting?" I asked Maxwell.

"Not yet," Maxwell said.

We sat at the counter. The stools allowed us to swing about to see interesting shapes enter the store. They were better than sitting in booths because we could hop freely from one to the other naturally without invitation.

"Tonight is stalking night," Maxwell said, as he looked around at the other boys in the room, some at the counter, others standing by the juke box. In the pharmacy section were two old women. That side of the store did little business at night, and it was kept in half light as if Dan had conceded first place to the soda parlor. But I always sensed that the pharmacy was there, like a first-aid man at a picnic.

Three girls swung through the door. One was chestier than the others and held our attention until they sat down.

"'As evening quickens faintly in the streets, wakening the appetites of life in some......'" quoted Maxwell. "I remember one of them from last year. Wait till I get the old evil eye going, and we can move in."

I turned so that I could watch the girl's reactions in the mirror, and I began formulating an opening line for the chesty one. Maxwell did it just right, really smooth. At the second before the girl turned her head, he removed his glasses, so that when she looked at him he managed to seem attractively uncertain as if, with his glasses off, he was now able to recognize her in his unobstructed long-sighted vision. By focusing on her and distinguishing her so clearly from her companions, he flattered a bright smile over her cute face. And we began to move.

Just as one instinctively anticipates being stopped by a traffic policeman a few seconds before it really happens, and one thinks rapidly between the whistle and the flagging of the arms of different escape routes, all of them hopeless, so, also, when a figure out of the past stands flesh and blood before one, there is the interval of grace before recognition, when one thinks of a dozen escape routes in hopeless confusion.

Such was my confusion when Melanie touched me on the arm as I started from the counter stool. Her face and then her form crystallized in the library setting of her uncle's home. But her name quite escaped my memory.

"Hello," she smiled.

I suppose I reddened because she said, "Do you remember?"

"Of course! I was planning on phoning you."

We sat at the counter, and I glanced in the mirror to see Maxwell jollying a cosy spot for himself between the women in the booth.

"I hope I didn't stop you from meeting your friends," she said.

"No! Good heavens. They're not friends of mine. Maxwell knows them."

Although Melanie was as attractive as ever, it was disappointing to be cut off in mid-adventure like that. I had difficulty adjusting myself to the prospect of a date with her instead of the chesty girl I could see reflected in the mirror.

"Besides, I'm glad to see you again. What have you been doing all summer?"

While she told of Muskoka, of canoe trips and aquaplaning, I wondered if we would have the same electrical attraction as before. Often, after a pause of several months, the reaction dies and one is left like a radio engineer frantically looking for the plug with the current. But on an impulse, I took her hand and I felt a throbbing which corresponded with the deep beat of my heart. She faltered to a stop and looked wide-eyed at me; we, both, shivering a little.

"Are you listening?" she said.

A fellow behind the counter was staring waiting for our order. In his white apron and white face, he was the spectre of social order that kept the world sober and sane.

"Two vanilla shakes," I said, but I must have whispered because I had to say it twice.

"And what happened then?" I asked.

"What happened when?"

"I mean after what you just told me."

"Nothing," she said. "Nothing happened."

It was obvious that conversation was futile. Any communication outside our reciprocal feelings was superfluous. We drank our shakes in silence and very quickly. The less we talked, the sooner we would be finished and could leave the public glare. I saw that another boy was talking with the chesty girl. A sudden touch of envy made me turn on Melanie.

"How come you're here? Were you going to meet anybody?"

Now that she meant more than an adventure to me, I was going to make her run the test of her true intentions. I wanted to have her fib her way into saying something far more valuable to me than the chesty woman across the room. I wanted her to swear her worth to me, to swear that she hadn't come to find anyone else. If I couldn't have the chesty girl, I was going to have a chastity one.

"I live near here," she said. "And I came to get a brick of ice cream for the house."

"Eating it for breakfast?" I asked sarcastically.

"No!" She looked angry. "What's got into you?"

Suddenly the envy went, and I didn't care anymore.

"I was just kidding," I said.

She laughed with me, and we left the store. We walked from one circle of street light to the next under the slow swaying of boughs and the turning of leaves. Melanie was leading us toward the University grounds, and, when we came to the wider, busier streets, I took my arm from around her. As we walked under the arch, I kissed her and we embraced for a long time until my legs ached from standing. On the lawn under a tree in the dark surrounded by the looming hulks of buildings, we made love.

When the ground began to feel hard I sat up.

"That shouldn't have happened," she said.

"Why not?"

Her complaint was so illogical it irritated me. I felt she was trying to call up some guilt and put the blame for it on me. Maybe she hoped it would make me promise to love her. Maybe she really felt guilty.

"Something might happen."

"Is this a dangerous time?"

"Would you marry me if something happened?"

"Don't be ridiculous," I said. "Is this a dangerous time?"

"No," she said.

When we walked from the grounds I was resentful of Melanie. I knew it wasn't her fault that she hadn't outgrown the marriage ideal, but still I resented her. If she wanted to act dumb and tragic I would have no more time for her. There was nothing worse than a girl who was always ready to smother fun in a wet blanket.

When we came to her house, I stopped at the head of the walk.

"I'll give you a buzz sometime," I said.
"Won't you come to dinner? Tomorrow?"
"Not tomorrow," I said. "I'll phone you."
   The streets were deathly still. It was very late. I walked slowly until I heard her front door click shut. Somehow the picture of Cathy kept reappearing in my thoughts. Her gaiety and freedom contrasted sharply with Melanie's sobriety. With Cathy, life was like dancing in green fields; with Melanie, it was like prison walls. Or so it seemed tonight. I began thinking I wouldn't call Melanie ever again. If I could forget about tonight's sexual compulsion, then I might find another girl who was like Cathy; one who wouldn't take things so seriously. But then Cathy was one in a million. Lucky Skip. I was anxious for the weekend to arrive so that I could get home to see what had happened between them.

CHAPTER 6

   On Friday evening I couldn't leave the fraternity because we were initiating the new boys. It was great fun, and true to our nickname, the "Alcohol Drinkers", we drank from bottles with that insidious name printed somewhere on the labels until far into the night. Only in the compiling of initiation tests can one really discover how powerful is the imaginatively sadistic. Many new suggestions had to be turned down because, if attempted, they would have left the victims an inch this side of death. It is lucky that, in a large group, there is a core of humanitarians to keep the true end of initiations in sight; so many others see them merely as a means of torture. In the end, we followed the traditional tests, which had been stiff enough for us. The one or two amendments we adopted compensated for the time we spent in their consideration; otherwise it would have seemed a waste of time.
   Maxwell went through the initiations in great style. Not once did he show any fear, only surprise. He was so reasonable in the way he approached things that he won everyone's admiration. At times he got witty in the most serious places. Finally his cool-bloodedness began to embarrass us; he began to make the tests look like tricks a

small child would pull. We let him off the last few and proclaimed him a true brother, worthy of our house and our name.

I caught a late train the next morning and arrived home in time for lunch. In October, there's a nostalgia in the atmosphere that gives an added pleasure to coming home. The countryside from the train window looks more precious under the stress of new winds, the trees seem to stand independently alone rather than in a cluster, and the meadows look darker and threatening. The wind brushing the long streaks of blown grass seem to accent the need for speed to the impatient traveller rushing homeward. The slipping of the express train into the station, the people appearing in their fall coats, the flints of sunshine lighting the street as if dawn had begun at midday, the wind pushing around corners, still warm but getting rather bold, the warm lunch, perhaps cheese on toast, all mother-prepared, and the sitting with a novel, the pleasant prospects of crumbs on the dark polished wood of the table before one, and the sun sifting through the dining-room window above, were happy home-coming to me. I was even happy to be in the same room with the mirrored, glass-carrying cabinet that had belonged to our great-grandmother.

Nancy was affectedly gay at lunch. I guessed she was feeling humbled at Skip's abrupt change of affections, and she didn't want to show me that she'd been hurt. As soon as she was finished, she went out to visit a girl friend.

About three o'clock or so I got tired of reading and went for a walk. Chestnuts were falling in big, spiky pods that split milkily when I stamped on them. Fresh brown nuts jumped onto the pavement with their white faces up, and it was difficult to restrain from throwing them at something near by. Maple keys were spinning into the air, and I caught a few as they fluttered by me. Leaves had begun to fall but not many yet. There were no piles in the gutter or overflowing onto the sidewalk that I could kick through. But the air lit energy in me, and I thought of watching a football game. There was probably one being played at the stadium, but, as usual, it was now too late to go. I had started to weave in a slow run, dodging tacklers, straight-arming my way along the sidewalk, when a horn blasted beside me, and I turned to see the only car in sight come to a stop beside me.

I must have looked surprised because Skip and Tim were laughing at me and Skip called, "Look out! You dropped the ball."

It was Tim's car, a small practical model, two-toned and shiny such as any insurance salesman would be proud of owning. They let me into the back seat and drove on.

"I'm giving Tim a resume of the speech I'm going to deliver to the Junior Chamber of Commerce next week," Skip explained. "They asked me for an hour's talk on 'The Importance of City Traffic Insurance.'"

While he continued listing the points he would make, I sensed that he was elated at the opportunity of appearing in the public eye, as if by being applauded by a lot of Jaycees he was nearer to being accepted as a native son.

"And, gentlemen, if you stop and think that the percentage of road accidents in the main streets have risen at an amazing rate within the last ten years...."

"I'd say, 'if you consider,'" Tim said.

"Gentlemen, if you consider that the percentage of road accidents etcetera, you will have no difficulty in imagining the importance of city indemnity in the case of faulty traffic lights, street repairs, and insufficient warning signals."

"That's a good point," Tim said. "A good point."

"Except that the population has increased just as quickly as the number of accidents," I suggested.

Skip laughed. "You wouldn't have a chance of thinking of that in the course of the speech. You're supposed to be all caught up in the flow of the words and the ideas like everybody else. So you wouldn't be able to isolate anything to criticize it like that."

"You aren't thinking of running for political office, are you, Skip?"

"Maybe, Tommie, maybe. It all depends on what I can handle. You know, I wouldn't mind being an alderman if I didn't have to spend much time at it and if it helped me sell insurance, which I think it would."

"You can do it," Tim said. "But do you think you'll have time?"

"That's it," Skip sighed, slapping his knee. "Did I tell you, Tommie, that I've been nominated for president of the junior boy's hockey in the city. But I won't have to do much work; it's just a bit of prestige."

I would have hated to have to tell him that instead of furthering his position with the foot-of-the-mountain set, such an honor would drive him in the opposite direction. I don't suppose any company director had ever seen skates since he was a boy, and if he had, they were assuredly only worn by National Hockey League professionals. Skip could have found a way into Westdale society through the door of athletics, perhaps, but never into the houses he had begun to value so much. It was necessary to get rid of that atmosphere of body-sweat and good fellowship, to cover up the shirt sleeves, and to put on a respectable front before he could receive gilt-edged invitations.

"I asked Mr. Rymal about the Yacht Club too," he went on. "He said it was too late to introduce me there this year, but he will next. I think it means a lot to get in with a good introduction."

"That's the place to meet people," Tim said.

"Uh huh... I went as Cathy's guest a coupla times. The sailing was terrific."

Tim drove carefully, slowing down almost to a stop at cross streets, and, on the through streets, he eyed corners fearfully as if he expected a locomotive to charge around on top of us. It was remarkable how his car-driving was so similar to his tennis-playing: in both he pooped along. He pulled to a stop in a small side-street at a gray desolate building which I recognized as the Squash Club.

"Tim says there's a tournament here today," Skip explained.

"It won't be very good because it's the first of the season," Tim added, to rid himself of all blame if it were bad.

We walked past the secretary's office where Tim filled our names in the guest column of a wide black book and signed his own with surprising flourish in the member's column opposite.

"Hi Timmie, Hi Tim, Hello Tim."

We were on his ground. He led us down hallways and through a dressing room where towels were waved in welcome. Skip knew several of the men, and Tim introduced him to others. I wasn't interested in his selling insurance so I studied the collection of trophies encased on the wall. A puff of steam rolled from the open door of a hot shower across to me, and I smelt the dampness and all the other smells connected with it, the rubber of running shoes, the white linen of clothes and towels, and the guts of rackets.

"Come on, Tom!"

We climbed up to the balcony of one of the courts in time to watch a match begin. The player representing Toronto was in his mid-twenties and something of a flash in a show-off way. When he hit a backhand and had plenty of room, he threw out his arms like a ballet dancer and patted the ball to a soft bounce in one corner just above the tin. If he were the one to be caught back, he'd lope in swift strides in time to catch the ball on the edge of his racquet and kill it with a cut spin by rebounding it off the side wall. His serve had to be returned with a drive so that he, waiting plonk in centre court for the ball, looked like a master who could do whatever he wished to win the point. In the rally, he was good too, and, racing all over at a disadvantage, he was likely to win on a lucky shot, after which, he'd walk down the centre and smile and swing his arms at the gallery, or if he lost, he'd lean his head on one arm against the wall and breathe out loud complaints at the plaster, and then, recovering his wind, he'd brush his hand through his blond locks and slump across to take up an unwary stance while waiting for the service. Then, too, he had a spectacular way of smashing a low shot. He'd drop on one knee so that he'd catch the ball at shoulder height and kill it along one side. On the question of energy, he could have given plenty to his opponent, the Hamilton man, who, after the second set, appeared to be dragging his legs in short pants.

"Our man hasn't played since last year," Tim said as an excuse. "At the height of the season I think he'd take this young fellow."

"Yeah, I don't like the Toronto guy much," Skip said. "He's an exhibitionist. What's his name?"

"Pete Miller," Tim whispered because there was a pause in play. "He's been here before."

Miller heard his name mentioned, looked up, and smiled. We, uncomfortable, smiled back. The ball smacked the wall, and we relaxed in the noise of the pounding and scuffing of a long rally. Miller won it on a slow lob shot which split the back corner crease, and a handful of girls, Torontonians, who had been diplomatically applauding him all along, broke into a cheer.

Although he certainly was a grandstand performer and at bottom not a steady player, I enjoyed watching him. His personality seemed to bounce off the four walls and land, slap-happy, on top of us in the balcony.

He was the kind who made sport popular for the non-sportsman. A short, lively man, who introduced himself as Mr. President-elect, pumped Skip's hand when the match was finished. He informed Skip that the club was as happy to have non-playing members as well as any other kind before dashing off to answer a phone call, or to enter a figure in an account book, or to shake somebody's hand, and fulfill the million secret little duties peculiar to club presidents.

Tim suggested we go upstairs. "We can talk there," he said.

The room with the pool-tables was empty, but a lot of people were in by the bar. Some Toronto girls were sitting at a table while they waited for the matches to finish. I led us to the table beside them. After every tournament, there is a party and one never knows what contacts one might strike up. While Skip and Tim discussed Skip's speech once more, I tried to catch the eyes of one of the girls, but I didn't have any luck. They all looked as if they had just become engaged and were waiting for the fiancé who would be by at any moment.

"That's really some speech," Tim exclaimed. "After this, you'll be swamped with offers to talk all over town."

"Well, I hope so," Skip said modestly.

"Who're these girls?" I asked.

"Oh, they're waiting for the party tonight," Tim said.

"Why don't we try and meet them, then? We can get dates for tonight if we want to go." There was nothing I could do alone with these two ducks talking insurance all the time.

"Well, I don't know," Tim looked dubiously at Skip.

"No thanks, I've got my date," Skip said.

"Yes sir, he and Cathy are pretty thick now," Tim winked.

"Forget about her for tonight," I urged. "And we'll have some fun with these."

Skip laughed. "Nope, I've stopped looking at other women."

"Is it that bad?" I said. "Do you mean you're getting serious?"

Skip laughed again and said nothing.

The door swung and Pete Miller grinning, swaggered into the room up to the girls' table where he acknowledged their applause with a little bow and then called at the bar for a round of beers. He recognized us as spectators of his match, and, with a half sentence, he provided the bridge between the two tables, which I had been trying to do like an ogling contortionist for the last fifteen minutes.

"Like it?"

"Fine," Tim said.

"Very much," I said.

"How about you?" Pete's blue eyes smiled at Skip.

"Not very." Skip looked bored.

Pete was not the kind of fellow to be put off or to be outdone in public. He threw back his handsome head, his blond locks flipping briskly as he shook with laughter.

"You Hamilton guys. You're all poor losers."

Surprised to be called a Hamiltonian, Skip rallied to the defence of his adopted city with more anger than was to be expected of him.

"If you'd learnt your squash here, you'd have better court manners."

Pete laughed louder. "What do you know about manners in this stick city?"

Since their retorts were heading them toward a quarrel, Tim put up his hands and cried for peace.

"The match is over," he reasoned.

"Yes, Pete, sit down here with us," a girl said.

Pete took a chair from the girls' table and set it at ours. When he sat down, he sneered a smile at Skip. "What's ta' matter, sourgrapes? Or was that your brother I beat?"

"Not at all," Skip said grimly. "I'm just not as enthusiastic over your game as you are."

Pete looked slowly round at the rest of us with his mouth and eyes wide open.

"I like your game. anyway," I said. "Where'd you learn?"

"The University Courts."

"Oh! You going to U. of T.?" Tim asked softly.

"I'm finishing my B.A.," Pete sighed. "And, man, will I be happy when I do."

"Weren't you in the services?" Skip asked.

"For awhile, but I got out of it."

"You weren't overseas, eh?" Skip looked askance at him.

"Nope, I had flat feet," Pete glanced at the floor.

"Your feet seem to stand up okay pounding the squash boards."

"They're better now," Pete said. He squirmed to the side of his chair and glanced back at the girls as if he wanted to switch the attention to them.

Skip's lips formed 'Zombie' but he didn't say it. He couldn't be sure, and, although he did seem to be making Pete curiously uneasy, he looked as if he thought it was too much bother pushing the issue any further. After all, the match was over.

"Pull your chairs up girlies and meet the nice gentlemans," Pete mimicked.

"We were getting ready to go," Skip said.

The beers came on a large tray. The waiter placed the glasses and bottles about the table.

"Help us drink this first," Pete said. "You can join us in celebrating my win."

I shrugged my shoulders. Torn between meeting the girls and still seeming as if I was ready to go with Skip, I looked indecisively at the two of them and waited for something to happen. Finally Tim, who wouldn't offend anyone, said, "Fine."

Skip looked as if he were accepting poison, but he allowed his glass to be filled.

"Are you staying for the party?" I asked, looking at the girls.

They hesitated before speaking, waiting for Pete to answer, but he said nothing, and I heard a couple of weak yesses.

"Well, I thought I would, but I think I'll buzz off home," Pete said then.

"Good. You can take me with you," said one of the girls who had been wise enough not to speak earlier.

"Me too," said another.

For a moment I thought it was roll call

"Can't take so many!" Pete wailed. "I only got a small car!"

Just then, the president-elect, short and energetic, rushed over to us. He was grinning widely at Pete. He wanted to 'give Mr. Miller the old handshake,' because he'd seen Mr. Miller 'whack out a wallop of a game.' He hoped Mr. Miller

ROMANCE

was 'all strung up' for the party because they had got some 'whacking good records' which Mr. Miller could 'loosen up his bones with' after that 'dog-run around the court.'

"Maybe I will," Pete said. "Maybe I will."

The president smiled at us to show us that although he was busy with his duties as a host, he hadn't forgotten the home-club boys, especially Skip, because he was a prospective member, and he hurried away into the kitchen.

"What a clown!" Pete said. "But ya need a clown to run a club. He's the only guy stupid enough to want to do it."

"Have you ever tried?" Skip said.

"Never been elected, thanks."

"Small wonder," Skip said.

Some of the girls tittered, and Pete flushed.

"Are you looking for something, man?"

"What have you got to offer?"

"Plenty, man, plenty," Pete said and subsided in his chair unwilling to push the argument further.

"We've got to shove off," Tim said.

By that time I'd got the Toronto phone number of one of the girls so that I didn't mind leaving. Before I left, I told Pete I hoped to see him in Toronto.

"Great," he said. "But I hope that monkey isn't with you."

When we were outside, Tim remonstrated with Skip for being so unfriendly.

"You know the Millers are big people in Toronto. They've got loads of dough."

"I could have guessed that," Skip said sharply. "He looked the kind who'd had what he wanted all through life and still thinks he deserves it. The pretty rich boy who gets an army deferment so that he can play around with his cars, racquets and women. All because he was born to a rich father."

"You may be right," Tim said. "Who knows? But it doesn't really matter, does it?"

"Yes, it matters," Skip said. "It matters a hell of a lot."

Skip's face had fallen into the hard lines of unreasonable resentment, as if he were an angry man looking for a prejudice.

CHAPTER 7

The next morning Mother's voice woke me at about the same time that the ripe sun had worked itself around to hit me through the window about the ten o'clock level. I say 'a ripe sun' because it was warm and golden, like a fat juicy peach, and coming in October as it occasionally did, it gave a warmth and glory to the day, which, as it happened justifiably, was Sunday. All glorious mornings happened on Sunday because that was the only day people rose late enough to be able to tell what kind of morning it was. And then with church bells ringing, I suppose 'glorious' was atmospherically suggestive.

Mother was rousing us to go to church. When I was home for weekends, I managed to plead loss of sleep when studying during the week, and I could escape for about three Sundays. But today was the fourth and I really couldn't miss four in a row. I never knew why. It was like an unwritten law, so that I had an hour to prepare myself for church

"Tommie! You have twenty minutes!"

All thoughts of a slow, lazy breakfast under that glorious sun were driven out by the rush for clothes, a swig of coffee, a munch of partly burnt toast, and the dash for church, where I arrived five minutes late just as the minister was parading in behind the choir.

There's nothing at all embarrassing about arriving late for church, though, if you are in the habit of arriving late. The people in the pews behind get used to seeing you rush by, and they like to make a pleasant joke out of it. And if you are in the habit of not coming often, then they are agreeably surprised to see you, as if you had fought off the devilish atheistic influences and were once more back in the fold helping them to support their belief.

As we stood for the fourth hymn, I caught sight of Skip with Cathy in the Rymal's pew up front and on the other side. Naturally Rymal wasn't there; he was a twice-a-year man. But Skip was standing bolt upright and singing with gusto. He was filling Rymal's place in the social ranks without the slightest sign of timidity. I knew I would feel

ROMANCE

dizzy if I suddenly found myself at that height, but Skip was older and more experienced. He was enjoying himself. Cathy looked small beside him. She was more humble in church than outside. She didn't look about but stared in front of her or at her book in a quiet, subdued manner as if she really were holy. During the singing of the hymn, she stood so close to Skip that, even from the back where I was standing, I sensed strong communion between them, which seemed to evoke a declaration of dependency on Cathy's part, something that I felt was particularly dangerous for Skip, especially when it was displayed in front of so many people.

When we were sitting again, it appeared strange to see Skip's head and shoulders mingled with the fancy hats, the expensive dresses, and the white and bald heads of Hamilton's elite.

During the sermon, I tried to pay attention, but I kept dreaming of Melanie and the night I met her in the drug store. If the minister had been talking about original sin, he probably would have kept my interest, but he went on and on about the floods in Greece and about the necessity for fortitude in the soul. With Melanie, I needed fortitude all right, but she hadn't much to do with my soul. Although I hadn't phoned her, I had been tempted to. After all there was no denying her attractions, and my judgement of her had been definitely one-sided. She probably wouldn't have been so melancholy in different circumstances. The sermon ended happily for me because I decided then to see her again.

After the services, I filed out the side door and waited on the sidewalk for Skip and Cathy, who were coming down the centre aisle. I knew it would have been politic of me to go out the centre door so that I could shake hands with the minister and let him know I was still coming to his church, but it was such a bother waiting one's turn. Knots of talkers formed about me, and the pavement at the front of the church grew gay with colours and pleasant talk. Presently Skip appeared talking seriously with an old gentleman whom I recognized as the one usually propped against his wife's shoulder during sermons. Cathy followed chatting with a lady and daughter. I felt uneasy waiting, but I didn't want to break in on them. Finally the old man was called away by his wife, which left Skip alone, looking deserted.

"I didn't know you were Presbyterian," I said.

"Oh, hello Tom. I'm trying it out," he said.

If Cathy could entice him, an experienced man, to accompany her to church, her influence over him was greater than I had imagined.

"You aren't getting any silly ideas are you?" I advised him.

He gave me a straight look, then laughing, he patted my shoulder.

Cathy broke away from another group and came smiling towards us. She was wearing sky-blue and looking fresher and more beautiful than I had ever seen her. The pink in her cheeks rose delicately through the clearness of the skin. Wisps of raven hair curled naturally beside her chin enhancing the light tan of her face. Blue eyes danced with amusement as she saw me with her Skip. And her form, full at the top and long and slender below the waist, was more real than the poster advertisement of American girl youth.

"Tommie, dear!" She held out her hand with an exaggerated stretch of the arm. "How's the old Hog Town treating you?"

"Not bad. It's just as big and dusty as ever."

"Skippie and I want to see you today. Can you come to the Tammy for tea this aft'? Bring Nancy too, we'd love to have her."

Skip retreated a half-step, but he allowed only a trace of the fright he felt to appear in his features.

"I'll ask her," I smiled, "but I don't think she'll come."

Nance, however, did want to come when I told her. She had made a date to go for an afternoon drive with a very nice fellow, but no man for her. She had complete autonomous control over him. If he suggested anything unfavorable, she'd twist his ears off. My sister was as political as most women; if a man gave her a little power, she took short time to set up a dictatorship.

"We can drive out in his car," she said, placing her pencil pensively between her teeth and setting the newspaper's crossword puzzle away from her.

By a streak of luck, she had recently been to the hairdressers so that her blond locks had been pushed smartly on high and curled in a thrilling new style. She selected a tight fitting green dress that reflected its colour in her eyes, and that, I thought, was appropriate for the occasion. With a small black bag to which she had given a green border, she sat on the arm of a living room chair looking out the window for the arrival of the nice fellow whom she had notified of the change in plans.

He came driving his father's Ford, and I saw Nancy blessing her stars that the car wasn't an old one.

"Now, do you know where the club is?" Nancy demanded of him.

"I think so," he said.

"Then you don't," she said.

"Well, I think I do," he said.

"First, turn here," she ordered, "and I'll direct you when it's necessary."

We climbed the Mountain Drive, the high trees arching above us with their leaves beginning to turn into the brilliant colours of the autumn. Here and there a bush had turned red over night, and on the paths winding up through the trees along the ridges, there were leaves blown down before their time, and the tiny weeds growing from the bits of earth caked high on the sheer rock surface along the bends were now yellow. From the mountain brow road, we saw that the small falls was dead. The ravine of sprawling rocks ran down to disappear in the woods. And far over the lip of white rock lay the city stretching long and rolling to the lakeside and complacent in the bright sun of a Sunday afternoon, where people might be arguing whether it was the beginning of an Indian summer or much too early.

Then we turned through the "San" grounds with its far flung buildings where the tubercular occupants sensed they were part of the city below only when they read occasionally in the newspapers that building additions were planned for the sanitarium, or that the ladies' guild had collected several hundred dollars for the patients, or that an Esquimau, in a fit of homesickness, had escaped and been found frozen to death on the mountain side. We fled the sullen stillness and chased along a back highway falling and rising in dips until Nancy signalled a turn, and we coasted round the bends of a driveway which ended at a sprawling house hugging a hill and reigning over a nation of trees.

"A few cars here," Nancy said. "We're not the first."

Cathy's party was on the terrace. About a dozen people were there already. Cathy, the perfect hostess, came forward with arms outstretched and allowed Nancy, her bosom pal, to kiss her on the cheek. She allowed me to shake her hand, and she smiled graciously at the nice fellow. One felt she was the boss; a guy likes to see that at a tea party.

Skip was standing in one corner by the railing where by sipping tea and chatting with someone he managed to have himself the last to be introduced. I watched Nancy's face pretty closely to see what would happen, but, acting superbly, she looked joyfully surprised to see him, and she approached him with a smile that seemed to have forgotten that a month had gone by and he hadn't phoned.

"Hello Nancy," Skip almost flipped his tea on the floor. He was trying to spin his cup like a hockey stick.

"Skip! My heavens, I didn't expect to see you here."

He glanced at me to see if Nancy really didn't know; but I had learned to hold a stone face whenever my sister was talking; I found it paid in the long run, so that he gleaned nothing but a greeting from me.

"Well, Cathy invited me," he said.

All things considered, that was a good answer.

"How nice," Nancy said, her mouth nicely shaping the tones. "Did you know that I got home over two weeks ago?"

"Yes," Skip abruptly took the aggressive. "How were your holidays? Have lots of fun?"

Seeing that Skip could take care of himself, I sidestepped over to another group. I found that I was the youngest amongst the men and that most of the couples were married. It's a strange feeling one has when standing amongst married people. The conversation is flat and not very daring to say the least. Man and wife have usually yapped themselves dry during their honeymoon so that at parties they stick together, talk platitudes, and look about for someone else to give them a reason for living, and all the time they are on the alert to guard their mate against any new influence that might eventually usurp their sexual contract. Perhaps this quietness is natural; I don't suppose the Siamese twins held long conversations after they had learned to talk, except when they were angry.

Cathy was standing nearby, so I began to speak to her, and soon I had her alone.

"You're prettier than ever today," I said.

"Thanks, Tommie dear. I feel it too."

"Is Skip doing this to you?" I couldn't prevent a twist of sarcasm from shaping my smile.

"Yes, he is," she laughed at me. "Aren't you jealous?"

"Very."

A wind kicked up the big leaves of a bush by the railing, and it roared about inside. Cathy's raven hair crested the background of trees and floated in the blue of the sky.

"Poor Tommie," she pouted, amused.

Laughter broke in on us, and we turned to see Skip and Nancy leaning over the railing in the strained attitudes of unsuppressable humour, both of them engrossed in their common feeling divorced from the rest of the party. Cathy looked startled and then blushed slightly when she saw them continue talking as if oblivious to all about them.

"Poor Cathy," I wanted to say, but I was afraid to.

"Nancy's in good form," she said. "Excuse me, I must see if there are still sandwiches left."

Alone, I watched Nancy and Skip. They were in a small world of their own, rather romantic in a make-believe way. She was the coquette, and he was the travelling knight. She Columbine and he Peroquett. They were flirting in game, bantering teasing remarks, and shunning the place and the hour. A maid approached them with sandwiches, probably at Cathy's instigation and by that intrusion the spell was broken. Cathy had waved her wand and now stood contemplating Skip and Nancy, self-conscious in their vacuum. She smiled a 'come here' to Skip from the tea table and he, happily approaching her, reminded me of a spaniel we used to have.

They held hands tightly while she whispered in his ear. Then he stepped to the French windows leading inside just as Rymal appeared there. The two men spoke for a moment before Rymal, his arm about Skip's shoulders, led the way inside.

Cathy and Nancy were glaring at each other. For a moment it was a question of who was going to move first, but since Cathy needed only to wait, Nancy came to her.

No one else was noticing them and so I stepped closer to be near in case of any misbehaviour.

"You had to wait until I was away, didn't you?" Nancy said. "Oh yes you did."

"Skip loves me and I love him," Cathy answered. "It's very simple."

"And what is he doing now?"

"He's telling father that last night we became engaged."

Nancy took a little gasp, her eyes blazing, as they did once when she was a small girl and I had knocked down her sand castle. She threw her tea, cup, and saucer, smack at Cathy. She dashed down the terrace steps and sobbed as she disappeared around the corner.

The front of Cathy's dress was tea-stained and drops of brown water trickled down her stunned features. With my handkerchief, I dabbed at the stains. The others, excited, began to come toward us. I put my arm around her and took her inside. No one followed.

Mr. Rymal was leaning with one arm along the mantel of the fire-place and his big voice was booming at Skip. Mrs. Rymal was sitting in a chair, her hands folded anxiously.

"We hardly know you. What's your background? Where have you come from? I've never heard of that place! Must be in the sticks. No, my boy, we can't allow anything like that. It's nothing against you now, you know. But there it is. You're a nice fellow. But we hardly know you! And besides you and Cathy couldn't know each other yet."

We were, as yet, unnoticed, but Cathy, shaking off her paralysis, ran forward shrieking at her father and then at her mother, telling them that Skip was the equal of any man she had ever met. Her words pelted the room like rain, and, losing herself in a torrent of anger, she threw herself on Skip and clung to his shoulders like a spoilt girl who had just been betrayed by heaven and earth.

The screams could be heard outside. Faces gawked at me.

"Good-bye," I said. "The party's over."

I ran down the steps and around to the back where the cars were, but Nancy was not there. The driveway was the likely place towards which she would run, but I followed it to the highway without finding a trace of her. The shooting range was over the way. I ran along the square of its platform of old boards and looked in the shooting cabins at each end and then down below in the stall from where the clay pigeons were sprung out. The hill ran down like pasture land, and, as I jogged along a path, I smelt the pines in the cool air brushing against my face. First bushes and then the tall trees spreading huge limbs and the rocks clinging in the clay of the hillside and the stream at the bottom hushing the intruder to stop and listen in the new world he had entered. I looked about at my darkened surroundings and I remembered them as the secret place where I came as a boy-scout on Good Friday. The boys in our gang had called it secret because we were sure no one else knew about it. Then a few years later I took a girl there and when I was about to kiss her the heads of dozens of boy scouts popped out from behind trees and bushes on the hillsides around us.

"Nancy," I called.

Three distinct echoes replied.

I ran up in the direction I thought she might have gone because it was toward the city. A crow cawed and beat its big wings between the trees and sailed out into the meadows. I got to the top of the ridge, when I saw a girl in a green dress sitting on a log overlooking the little falls where the stream fell down and sang its hush. Coming quietly from behind her I sat on the log and waited. Presently, she leaned back and laid her head on my shoulder, and I put my arms around her, and we rocked a bit back and forth. After a while, we talked about the animals of the woods, and we made up a story of how a tiny lizard would come from under his rock every morning and wash his face and hands in the stream before he'd lie down to bask in the sun all day.

"Oh Tom!" She suddenly clung fast to me, pressing her head on my shoulder in shame. "I'm sorry, oh, I'm sorry!"

"Look at all the mud on your pretty shoes and on your dress, too," I said.

"Where?"

She looked at her shoes, but she didn't try to clean the mud away. Tears welled up slowly in her eyes again and began to trickle down to her chin. I pulled her close to me, and I kissed one of those big tears just as it was rolling halfway down her cheek.

"Hi Googles, it'll be dark soon. We've got to head home now."

As we were climbing the other side, Nancy stopped me.

"Do you think Skip wants to marry Cathy?"

"Maybe," I said, "but I know she had her hook out for him."

The nice fellow was alone waiting by his father's car when we got to the parking place. He looked surprised at the mud we had collected.

"Gosh! Where were you?"

"Fishing," I said.

"And I've been crying," Nancy said, "cause mine got away." And she strained a smile at me.

CHAPTER 8

When I got back to Toronto late that night, in my mail there was a note from Melanie asking me to dinner on Wednesday, and so it was merely by an affirmation that I found myself staring across the dinner table at three strange faces on the night in question. Melanie's parents were friendly; her younger sister was inquisitive. I think it was an arrangement between them. The younger sister asked me the questions, and the parents listened to the answers. It's surprising how much a guy can be grilled that way.

"How many more years of school d'ya have?" "Where d'ya wanta live afterwards?" "Can ya make lots of money, there?"

Then the little imp turned round eyes on the scoreboards of her parents' faces to see how she was making out.

"Now darling, you leave Mr. Davis alone. Let him have a chance to eat," the mother said.

She was a big woman with a motherly face that seemed to say you were her favorite among all Melanie's beaus, but there was a sharpness in the line of her jaw and certain meaningful inflections of the voice which made you doubt the truth of those pleasant intimations.

"Melanie, perhaps Mr. Davis would like some bread; oh, that is awkward! May I call you Tom? It's so much easier."

"Well, Tom," the father addressed me later in the living room, "so you're going into law."

He was a businessman, but he liked the idea of the legal profession; he had once planned on going into it himself. He would have made a good solicitor; he had that knack of gradually slipping away in a day-dream when someone was speaking to him and then jolting back with a judicial remark on the man's last sentence. His relationship with the family was that of 'good old Daddie.' By daily routine, he kept them in the comfortable bourgeois well being of good clothes, good meals, a summer cottage, and a new car every two or three years.

"Daddie, will you give us the car tonight?" Melanie asked.

Her father put down his coffee cup, took the car keys out of his pocket, and handed them to me in a solemn passing of the powers.

"Where are you going, Melanie?" her mother asked.

There was a hint of suspicion in her voice which stemmed from her disappointment at being deserted by one of her treasures and from her general fear of boy meets girl.

"To a movie, or dancing or something," she said.

We drove away from the quiet residential drive into the city traffic where other cars, like ours, coasted along looking for something to do, somewhere to go.

"I know," I said and sped us into a district I hadn't seen for many months.

The night club was small and packed. A South American band was knocking out Latin numbers on wood and accompanying the beats with more sophisticated instruments, the clarinet, the bass viol, and a flute. There was enough room to sit, but hardly enough to dance. Since most of the numbers demanded plenty of rhythm, the dancers wriggled against one another, trying not to betray that they found any pleasure in it. The main attraction along this line was a pretty blonde who owned a big behind which she jerked and wriggled with fascinating dexterity so temptingly that it became a game to see which male dancer could stay backed up against her for the longest time. But just as I got into position, the music stopped. My luck!

"I'm glad," Melanie said. "It's too embarrassing."

"Why? She didn't know."

"But her partner did. And he was angry."

Like everyone else, I had forgotten her partner. One could barely see him behind her.

Now that the floor was cleared, the waiters were skittling about with trays of drinks. The guests were huddled over their tables indifferent to what was going on about them. Each table was its own party. For that reason, it was more fun to go night clubbing in a group. I did not have much to say to Melanie. There were no questions I could think of asking. If she'd been literary or artistic, we might have found some issue to discuss, but she was just another university freshette, who, when she opened a book did it only to memorize for an exam.

"What's going on at your college now?"

"Nothing much," she said.

"But something must be happening there."

"Oh yes, there's a dance next week. Do you want to go?"

"Aren't there any plays or discussions?"

"Maybe," she said. "I don't know."

We watched the empty dance floor for a while. It was shaped like a figure eight, which explained why there was always a bottle-neck in dancing traffic.

"Do you want to go to the dance?" Melanie asked again.

"Not really, no."

"I'll get the tickets," she assured me.

"Okay."

The atmosphere was stifling. So many people, the cigarette smoke... I couldn't feel any contact with her. If we'd been alone or in a quiet place, those old sex rays would have started impulsively and I would have had a reason for being with her. But with all those babbling baboons around us, with the lights cutting into my vision, the elbow of the guy beside me lodged in my kidney, and Melanie way across the other side of our table, there was no reason. That's the god awful truth. Only other people can give you reasons for living. Alone, you might as well have never existed. And, brother, in that room with Melanie cut off from me, I was feeling very alone. But I knew I'd stick it out till the band came back, and then I could hold her in my arms and sway with her until that mob around us faded into insignificance.

A whack on the shoulder made me start up and look around into a laughing face supported by a red bow tie.

"Where's your pal Skip tonight?"

Pete had a girl with him.

"This is a sardine tin," he said. "Come on out to my place."

Melanie agreed, and I found myself racing behind Pete's car towards the outskirts of the city.

"Who is he?" Melanie asked.

"A squash player," I said.

"Squash? What's that?" she said.

Pete drove a sports M.G. so that frequently he had to stop to allow us to catch up to him before driving on. After half an hour, though, we arrived at a big white house fronted with Corinthian columns and flambeau lamps. Pete led us in a side driveway, and, while he drove into a four-car garage, I parked in the circle outside.

"This way," Pete called.

A white door opened at the side of the garage, and the light from inside showed us a carpeted stairway going up. At the top in a hallway there were three doors. Pete opened the middle one, and we entered a long games-room where beyond the range of billiard tables was a lounge, then a small dance floor and a bar. All along the opposite side were windows through which we could see the city lights far away.

"Wonderful!" Melanie said.

"It's okay now," Pete said. "But it's tough to heat in winter."

Pete introduced his girl as Mag. Her real name was Shirley but he couldn't stand that name; he said it made him think of a doll.

We sat down in the lounge, and Pete went to get us some beer in the bar. Mag told me she had been affianced to Pete for three years. She was a cute, insignificant little girl, who spoke personal problems in a shy voice. She was ever ready to be helpful too; when I took out my cigarettes, she jumped to her feet in search of an ashtray. I don't see how Pete could possibly have given her the name Mag. I think he had got her mixed up with one of his other girls.

He turned on a record player behind the bar, and we slouched in easy chairs in low lighting and listened to Dixieland while we drank our beer.

"That's the damned trouble with this city," Pete said. "Here it's Saturday night and there's no bloody place to go. We were all over downtown before we bumped into you. And now I'm back here again."

"It's nice here," Melanie said.

"Glad you like it," Pete smiled.

I took a long swallow of my beer. If she were going to follow his camp, I didn't give a damn.

"You must have a big family to use all this room," I said.

"Naw, I only got a kid brother. But Pop has lots of visitors. Sometimes we're almost crowded out of the house."

"Are there any staying here now?"

"Naw. Pop's away in New York. No one'll bother us."

A door opened behind us, and a tall, thin, bald-headed man wearing a gray suit and white shoes came into the room. He stopped indecisively when he saw us.

"Come on in, Perkie. It doesn't matter," Pete called. "This guy's Pop's librarian who writes his letters for him and buys his plane tickets. He's a sport, aren't you Perk? Even if he has got a Ph.D."

"I won't be but a minute," the tall man whispered. "I'm looking for a snack to take to bed with me."

"We got two right here," Pete laughed. "You can take your pick."

The tall man's head went red. He smiled uneasily and disappeared behind the bar. When he left, his head faded to a dull pink.

"He's a hard worker. It takes two heads to make all the money Pop has and that guy's his second head, so Pop says."

The records ran out so Pete went over and put on some Glen Miller and we started to dance. After a while we changed partners.

"When are you and Pete getting married?" I asked Mag.

"Soon," she said. "He wants to graduate first and stand on his own two feet, he says. So we've got to wait."

The way she said the 'we' made me think that she really thought Pete was finding it hard to wait.

"He'll be in business soon, then?"

"We hope so," she said.

Pete was doing a double dip with Melanie. He was telling her that the couple was supposed to kiss on the second dip.

"Is he going into his father's business?"

"Not at first," she said. "His Pop says he needs experience."

Pete and Melanie were clasping each other in a long kiss. I kept Mag's back to them so that she wouldn't see them. The record spun out but I held her until the next came on. It was *Under Blue Canadian Skies*.

"Oh Pete," she called. "Do you remember?"

ROMANCE

He and Melanie were dancing again. He, in his white shirt, had his arms folded over her shoulders, pressing her into him, moving forward in roll and shuffle, a bear dance.
"Yeah," he said.
"Our favorite," she told me.
"Perhaps you want to dance it with him," I suggested.
"I wouldn't mind," she smiled.
And we traded partners.
"Did you get his phone number?" I asked Melanie.
She gave me that amused look girls use when they try and tell a fellow without words that they know he's jealous.

But jealousy is such an indefinable feeling; it has so many variations that it's difficult for anyone to tell what kind of jealousy a guy has. I wasn't jealous about her playing around; I just didn't want her doing it in front of me. In my mind, I hadn't bolstered her up with ideals so I didn't care what she did. I wasn't going to have her trample over my pride, so you couldn't say that I was jealous; you might say my egoism had been piqued. I suppose that's one of the danger points which some women, unfortunately, fail to recognize in men. They flatter themselves that a guy fancies them so much that he's "jealous" when really he's only resentful his ego is being hurt.

Jealousy, though, comes when you do build ideals around your girl and you become obsessed with her. Idealism is fatal because a fellow who has it projects it on his object of choice and gets so knotted up with it that his whole being becomes dependent on it. When the object fails to meet the test of his ideals, it fails the man too, for he feels he has failed himself by his own choice, and only violent anger can appease him. Yet why is it that, today, half of us have to be idealistic about a woman before we can take her to bed?

Melanie then began to try the at-arms-length dance with me on the excuse that I was supposedly jealous, but, on glancing at Pete, she saw that he was wound up in his favorite, and, slightly disillusioned, she danced close against me again. But I didn't mind. I was willing to grant that Pete had lots of charms, lots of money, and lots of possibilities, and I wasn't going to hold it against Melanie for realizing it too; so long as she didn't realize it in front of me again.

The warmth of her body began to engulf me. Her hair was like a pillow off of which I could lift my head to kiss her.

The music didn't exist anymore. There was no movement. Only that warmth bathed me in our private hot springs.

"Hey! Do you want somethin' to eat?"

Pete, wearing a tall chef's hat, was looking over the bar at us.

"I'm frying some burgers."

Melanie wanted to help, but Pete wouldn't allow her near the frying pan. He said cooking was one of his accomplishments.

It was one o'clock, and, by the time we had eaten the hamburgers and drank more beer, it was two.

"We've gotta go," I said.

"Naw, don't leave us yet. The night is young."

"It's for Melanie's sake," I said. "Her parents are going to wonder what's happened."

"Sit down," Pete said. "Wait a while."

There was an authoritativeness in his tone which said that, since we were in his house, we had to do what he said. He would have made a good Egyptian pharaoh.

"Yes. It's too early to go," Melanie agreed.

I shrugged and reached for another beer.

"If there's one thing I dislike," Pete said, "it's a party-pooper. We haven't talked any philosophy yet. The party hasn't even begun. You ever heard of Erasmus?"

I shuddered. We were in for a dose of high-school history.

"Let's choose someone more modern," I suggested.

"Okay. Nietzsche," he said in an older tone as if he were remembering a University lecture. "I really admire him. Imagine tearing down one god and putting up another--the superman."

"It's not new. There have been about a hundred attempts like Nietzsche's which had failed to every one that had succeeded for a while."

"He hasn't failed. His ideas still live on."

"Nietzsche's idea was smoked up in the last war. But, of course, it lives on like the smog in London. But the idea existed before Plato, before Sparta, before Moses. And it is all that most people have understood or needed to understand."

"How about those writers who still talk about him and praise him and stuff?"

ROMANCE

"Most of them are like Nietzsche. They'd like to be the opposite of what they are, and damn the consequences. I know of only one superman who was moderately successful--Rasputin--and, of course, that guy in the comic strips."

"And Alexander and Caesar eh? And Alexander?"

"They were merely riding the wave of historical consequence. And, anyway, they had armies so they don't count."

Pete began to fume. He clenched his teeth and his eyes grew sharp as he searched his mind for more names in support of a theory he didn't understand but which he obviously adored.

"Peter!"

An older woman's voice broke in on us.

"Peter dear."

He went behind the bar and stood looking down.

"Yeah."

"Go to bed, dear, it's very late."

"Aw ma, not yet."

"Yes, dear. Say goodnight to your friends."

"Aw ma."

"We have a long drive in the country tomorrow and I don't want you to be tired."

Her tone was patient but quietly commanding.

He came back looking apologetic.

"My ma's got insomnia and she thinks sleep's the most important thing on earth."

"We're going," I said.

Pete and Mag stood arms about one another under the garage light while they watched us drive away.

When we were passing by a park, Melanie pushed her hand along my arm and I had to stop the car. It was after four when I put the car away in her father's garage. We said a hasty goodnight at the door because we didn't want to give her parents any chance to jump on us.

I looked up at the house from the street. In the light from the street lamp by a second story window I could make out half the form of her mother as, wrapped tightly in a dressing gown, she stood watching me.

CHAPTER 9

In the month that flew by I saw Melanie often, lost more than half of my chess matches with Maxwell and attended a few lectures at the Hall. Lectures were becoming more compulsory; students were allowed to miss only ten or fifteen percent or something like that. Some sort of threat had to be held over the heads of the students because without it, only a few conscientious worms would have attended as most professors lectured so poorly. Myself, I learn better from reading than listening. If I'm to listen to a professor hold forth on estate law, he must talk as Carlyle wrote.

Mother sent me a newspaper clipping announcing the engagement of Catherine Anne Rymal to Warren Charles Burke. When you read your friends' names like that, it's like an obituary! Subconsciously you read it twice looking for the burial times. Also, mother wrote that it would be nice if I came home for the weekend; there were so many leaves to be raked up in the backyard. So on a Friday evening after an early dinner, I caught the train for Hamilton.

It was one of those long-distance expresses from Montreal to some hole in the west, probably Vancouver. I sat in a brand new coach that the railroad reserved for us short-distance riders. But the observation car was one ahead, and I wandered up for a short one. I opened the newspaper at the comic section and was just getting settled in Pogo-land when Mr. Rymal, who looked as if he had several short ones, stopped at my chair on his way up.

"Coming with me, Tom Junior?"

We chose two comfortable arm chairs with a little black table between us. He ordered us shots of Canadian Haig.

"I'm glad I ran into you." He squinted sidelong at me. "You've heard that my daughter's going to be married."

The more Rymal drank, the more sober he looked, the more sober he talked, and the more soberly he acted. I might have been sitting with a Pilgrim Father.

"My daughter is taking a big step in marrying this man."

Rymal stared moodily at the blackness beyond the window. He could see his reflection from the sheen of the lights against the glass; the big bulky body squared in dark high grade cloth, the face fallen in moon-dog loneliness, the hair greying, the arms, having had no strenuous exercise since football days, lay flabbily on the chair-arms.

"How did you come to meet this man?"

Rymal's contemporaries had expected big things from him. All he had to do was to move into his father's shoes and sell twice as much beer. But Rymal couldn't keep a businessman's demeanour. He loved his drink, he loved his horses, and he developed a fantastic sense of humour. So now when his friends brought old John Rymal into the conversation, it was as a joke.

"I don't know what our friends are thinking of this man. He's just an upstart, came from nowhere. Taking my daughter right from under my nose. Why, she must be crazy!"

"He fought in the war and he was a hockey star," I said.

"I've been plugging those lines as much as I dare. But when you look at them close, they aren't worth very much. I don't want to make my excuses obvious."

He took a swallow from his whiskey and soda, and, as the liquid went down, I thought of weed-killer. Rymal then looked vulnerable as a fat old dandelion just before its grey fluffy top was about to be blown off.

"I'm looking for a son-in-law who can command respect. One who can move in my business and kick out those bastards who took over from me. The only experience he's had is insurance. My God! Well, I might be able to get him into the sales end."

"He's popular round town," I said.

"Oh, he's likeable enough. But you know," he leaned closer to whisper to me. "I think people expected Cathy to marry better than that." Then he reared back and boomed at me. "All I can say is, they expect a hell of a lot of you. I've just been in Toronto with a cheap guy who wants to get a horse from the States. He expects me to get it for half the price. I can do it! He knows I'm the only guy who can do it. But damned if I'll do it for nothing for such a cheap skate, so the next big race at the Jockey Club, I made him promise he'd bet five hundred bucks against me. He'll lose it all. These cheap guys don't know how to gamble."

"Only five hundred?" I said.

"Well, I was pulling a tooth as it was."

The passengers sitting near us began to chuckle. Rymal allowed a momentary flicker to crease his sobriety in acknowledging their recognition of his great natural gift. Then abruptly frowning, he spoke in a lower tone.

"Most of the people round town don't know how to live. They're so afraid of life, they chase all the joy out of it. But I know, my boy, my Tom Junior. They're trying to chase the joy out of me now, because my daughter's marrying below herself. I'm sending all my neighbors twenty yards of black crepe and the funeral oration from Shakespeare, the one that goes, 'I have not come to praise Caesar but to bury him.'"

The muscles of his face relaxed as he thought of the effect it would have. His eyes grew hazy in a sweet dream, and he nodded his head for the porter to bring two more drinks.

Swaying gently, the train clattered rhythmically along hollow sounding rails as it passed over a bridge. I looked in the dark of my shadow against the window-pane, and I saw the mucky line of shore sliding into a slate of water. I knew that on the other side, rising about us were the heights from where were aimed far out into the lake the rusted log-shaped cannons that hadn't been fired since we fought the Americans.

Rymal laid a large bill on the silver plate which the porter carried. The scene had a touch of the South to it, with the black skin, the white cloth, the silver and the greenback, and Rymal, the old-style Southern gentleman, hiding his tender grief behind the bluff of wealth.

We were in the city, under bridges and easing to a stop at the station. Rymal and I swallowed our drinks, and I rushed back for my satchel, but I was blocked from reaching it at first because passengers were lined up at the door, so eager were they to get off. I met Rymal again as he was stepping off the train, which was hooting its whistle, impatient to rush away.

"There they are," he said, and he took me by the arm.

Cathy in a black coat, a wild flower in its natural habitat, unhooked her arm from Skip's and hugged her father. Skip stepped forward and shook Rymal's hand. There was a contrast in manners: Cathy appeared to own her father, Skip appeared to be owned by him. But Skip's shy, almost subservient attitude, embarrassed Rymal, and my travelling companion, the Pilgrim Father, transformed into our host, the Laughing Cavalier.

"Skip! Glad to see you accompany my daughter when she goes out at night, old man. I'm retiring from the field. You have to take over." He punched Skip lightly on the shoulder. "Now before we take Tom Junior home, I insist on calling in at Jones's Funeral Home."

"But it'll be locked, Dad," Cathy protested.

Rymal shot out his arm and marched us grimly toward the car. He and I sat in the back, and Skip sat up front with Cathy, who whisked us through side streets to the funeral home which lay in the shadows back from the street.

"You see, closed," Cathy said.

Rymal stepped out of the car and looked at the house.

"There's a light. Come with me. I'll need you all."

We followed him to the door where he pressed his finger on the bell. We watched a series of lights go on from one room to the next, blazing a trail to the front door. The contorted face of a small, wiry man glared at us.

"Mr. Jones?" Rymal cried.

"Mr. Jones is dead." The man spoke like an angry schoolteacher correcting a child for the third time.

Rymal turned to Cathy, questioningly.

"It's the right place, Dad."

"We've been under new management for the last five years," the man said.

"Are you the manager?" Rymal asked.

The small man took a step back. "No, I'm the night-watchman."

"Good. Then you can let us in."

The small man seized the door as if to shut it.

"Hey! My name is Rymal."

"Never heard of you."

"What beer do you drink?"

The man hesitated, his eyes widened. "Is that the......"

"That's the one." Rymal pushed his way through the door and we stepped in behind him.

Five minutes later we were in a room clipping rolls of black crepe in measurements of twenty feet. The night-watchman, the only one among us who could remember the quote from Shakespeare, was set to work writing out the verse on black-bordered cards. Rymal wrote out the street addresses and pasted them on small boxes. When we had finished, we had taken care of twenty neighbors.

"It's to remain anonymous, of course," Rymal told the watchman.

The man put a hand to his mouth. "I signed Shakespeare to the cards."

"That'll fool 'em," Rymal said.

He paid the watchman for the postage as well as for the promise to send the packets on his way home from work in the morning. As we left, Rymal presented him with a certificate for twenty-five free beers.

"It's not ten yet," Rymal said to me. "You can't go home. Come with us."

We took a through-road by the foot of the mountain, and as we climbed the side of the cliff, we looked over the city lights where they lay like yellow stardust interspersed with jewels of green and red.

"What do you think of that, Skip, old man? What do you think of Hamilton now, eh?"

"It's okay," Skip said trying to sound enthusiastic.

"What kind of answer is that?" Rymal asked me. "It's more than okay. If you don't like it, why are you marrying my daughter then?"

"I like it," Skip said.

"That's better," Rymal laughed. "But I could have thought of a more gentlemanly answer, like 'because I like your daughter.' Now, Cathy, wouldn't that be more to the point?"

"Oh, stop it, father!"

"My little girl thinks I pick on her fiancé," Rymal said to me "But he knows I'm just kidding him, don't you, old man?"

"Yes sir," Skip said.

"He doesn't say much now, my future son-in-law. I wonder if he's worrying about the responsibility he's accepting."

"Not at the present moment," Skip said.

"Good! That's what I like to hear. A man who doesn't let things worry him."

"Oh father!" Cathy shouted. "Leave him alone!"

"Now, now," Rymal soothed her. "You always had a great imagination. Don't let it run away with you."

Cathy braked the car in the middle of the road.

"Shall we leave you to drive home by yourself," she said.
"Don't give me ideas," Rymal laughed. "Or I will."
Cathy threw open her door and stepped out.
"Wait Cathy," Skip said. "Come darling, don't be foolish." He scrambled out to stop her from walking away.
"Are you coming, Tommie?"

She was asking me to take sides. I didn't want to look like a traitor to them, but I also didn't want to walk home from the mountain side. Besides, Rymal had drunk too much to be trusted driving alone. Inspiration hit me.

"I'll take your father home," I said in a tone of guardian-protector.

That cooled Cathy's anger a little.

"Darling, please be sensible," Skip took her in his arms.

I got out and went to sit in the driver's seat while Cathy allowed Skip to coax her back to the car. They sat in the front seat beside me. We drove off with Rymal posed straight-backed, stiffly dignified, hand on cane, which was centred on the floor, alone in the back seat.

When I stopped to put the car into first to climb the hill to the Rymal house, Cathy turned to her father. "Skip and I are being married the day before Christmas."

I could hear Rymal's gulp.

"A merry time for all," he said.

"Tommie, we want you to usher for us." She said it as if challenging me, as if I might refuse.

Naturally I accepted with great enthusiasm, but as I drove up, I felt that the world had been turned upside down. Cathy was intending to really belong to Skip, and those feelings I had for her back in the dark part of me did a whirl, and, for a moment, I saw the front hood of the car falling on me and the roar in my ears came like the wind knocking me about on the rough edges of a star.

"Don't race the motor so, Tommie," Cathy said.

I parked the car, and we all looked over the lawn at the sleeping house. Each of us was waiting for the other to move first.

"We've got to celebrate," Rymal suddenly cried. "This is no time for mourning. I'm happy! I'm glad!" He reached forward, took Cathy's head in his hands and bent it back to look down into her face. "Your daddy's happy that you're happy," he said.

Cathy smiled up at him, and the night was warm.

"I've got champagne! And I know where it is," Rymal whispered. "Come on."

In the hall, he switched on the chandelier lights and the walls with its paintings, shields, and fancy woodwork, reflected the gaiety shot out from the hanging tree of glass.

"We'll be in the coffee room," Cathy called.

"I'll need someone to help me with the glasses," Rymal echoed. It was a hint. Cathy pointed to the room for us to enter. Small, in comparison to the other mammoth rooms, and modernly furnished with no sign of antique anywhere, it portrayed the interior decoration of fifty years hence. The curtains fell over the windows from the ceiling, while the wood about the windows was laid broadly so that when the curtains were down and rippled, the effect was of tree trunks standing in water. A brown rug wound a way between tables, which, when unoccupied, were pushed into points like small bushes. A low bar at one end seemed to cascade like a miniature falls but when we approached, we saw there were thin strips of foil accentuating the falling lines and curves in the wood which had given us the impression of movement. Along the wall was a mural of marsh land that made Monet's impressionistic sunsets over weeds and water look like a Paleolithic world in its outmodishness. Herons and cranes seemed as if assuming consciousness, not from the vibration of colour about them, as a mystic painter might picture them, but from their contrast to one another, as if each bird were a distinct personality and strove to cajole the others into existence including the weeds and rushes beside them. Yet tranquillity suffused the whole scene by swoops of blue and pink sky, while a devilish-looking Pan, with goat legs dangling, fifed on one of the swoops.

"It's modern intellectual stuff," Skip said by way of explanation. "The painter told Cathy it parodied Christian existentialism."

"What was the painter?" I asked.

"He was existentialist but no Christian."

Skip hit one of the bushes on the noggin, and it fell out flat for us to sit at. I looked at Skip, brooding, as we sat, waiting. Within the last month, his face had collected some wrinkles about the mouth that gave him a downcast expression. That happy glint in his eyes that I had seen when I first knew him, and which I remembered from the last time when he joked with Nancy at the Tammy, had been replaced by a listless glaze. When he spoke, I noticed that his tone had lost its jauntiness, a bit of that salesman's confidence.

I turned a pine-cone on its side into an ashtray. "Rymal's giving you the works," I said.

"He can't help it, I guess. He's jealous."

"Don't let him get you down," I said.

"I've been feeling sort of low for a while now, Tom. They've been tearing me to bits. You'd think I was a prize thoroughbred, and they wanted to find out who won the last prize in the family. I'm under federal investigation."

"I bet," I said.

"Sometimes I wonder if it's worth it, but, when I look at Cathy, I'm sure I'm right. And now that we've got the date fixed, I feel better. We both do."

"Is the wedding going to be big?"

"Depends on the Rymals. My folks are dead and I can't remember any relatives, none at least who took any interest in me. There's a foster aunt I had in Montreal, but it's too far for her to come. Anyway, I think she'd feel out of place with the fancy doo-da the Rymals'll have. And all my good pals were killed in the war. So I'm like a new born babe," he smiled at me. "I'm starting life all over again in Hamilton, Ontario."

"With Cathy it ought to be a nice life," I said.

"It'll be swell after we're married."

"How does Mrs. Rymal feel about it all?"

"She wishes I had a pedigree too," he said. "It would be nice to show to the neighbors."

"Aw, they'll get over it. Wait till the first grandchild comes."

"You know, I was a sergeant in the war," he said. "I feel as if I should have been a captain to marry Cathy."

I laughed.

Rymal, swinging his cane and carrying a bottle of champagne, came into the room. Cathy followed him with a tray of glasses. They were both smiling.

"Celebration, my young men. This is the best stuff drinkable." He set the bottle smack in the centre of the table, threw his cane into the corner and sat down.

"First, young Tom and I are going to drink a toast to our engaged friends. Glasses here, Cathy."

He tipped the bottle over my glass as I stood with him eye to eye.

"To the most beautiful girl in the world," he began, "and to her worthy fiancé, we wish the greatest happiness in all eternity. May their love make love around them, as we love them for their love. Drink deep, Tom junior!"

Caught in his cavalier spirit, I grasped the stem and threw the contents of the glass down my throat. The next moment, I was spewing what I could of it onto the floor. The muscles of my face stretched down and out as if I were shooting through the sound barrier. To confront Rymal's maniacal laughter, I turned the sourest face he had ever seen. He had given me vinegar.

He reached inside his coat, pulled out another bottle, and, shaking, wheezing, and exploding in short bursts, he tried to hold it out at arm's length. The spectacle of this goddamned fat man straining at the seams, holding himself to life by a thread because he had managed to put vinegar in place of champagne, was so incredibly stimulating that I burst into laughter with him. Cathy and Skip, who had gaped at me in astonishment, were seized by the lunacy too. And the four of us, repeatedly infected by Rymal's bubbling form, roared away restraint in one great release. And old Skip, good old Skip, was lying weak as a baby across the table.

Finally we reached a calm broken by Rymal's gasps for breath. Ribs aching, I took the other bottle and filled our glasses. When I drank the champagne, I still tasted vinegar. I gulped two glasses to change the taste, but to no avail. Cathy wiped her tears and blew her nose. She raised her glass to me, and we almost started again. She had a devil of a time swallowing.

Rymal groaned and said he was tired. Without touching his champagne he toddled off to bed.

I took a third glass and gave more to Cathy and Skip. We were feeling light-spirited.

"Tommie, you're cute," Cathy said. "I'm sorry I've given you such a bad time, Tommie."

"I've got to get home," I laughed.

"Skip!" Cathy cried. "Did you ever know, darling, that Tommie was in love with me?"

"No! Really!" Skip laughed.

We all thought it was a great joke. It kept us humourous till we finished the bottle and swept ourselves out to the car; till I watched Cathy's raven hair in the wind rushing through the window, flying from those opal ears, from that soft chin, and from those warm lips; till I made them let me out a block from my home so that I could walk in the November winds, leaving that gentle body to the dark hands of someone else. Yes, it kept us humourous till I saw them drive away, and I threw my arms against a tree and my head against my arms as the wind raged in the branches above me, ripping, renting, tearing, stripping the leaves from a wooden creation in anger because it lived, because it was there.

I pushed myself away from the tree and watched little brown sails sliding to the ground. Some fell at my feet, and they were yellow in the light. Others, lying like corpses in the gutter, stirred suddenly, rose like ghosts, and fluttered across the pavement into the grass where they tried to cling in the green of the life that was yet around them. Above me, a branch creaked and I saw one scratch at another. I walked, allowing the wind to shove me down the street like a small child with his wagon, and, as it whipped my hair about my head, as it dog-howled through people's backyards, I allowed my spirit to meet with it on that plain of relentlessness, and I drifted, a shell, while my core was away finding consolation, seeking adventure in the dark.

There was a roadster convertible parked in front of the house. From the street I made out two figures on the porch, and I waited till the guy had finished kissing Nancy before I crossed the lawn and greeted him as he was leaving. I caught up to Nancy at the door.

"A new one?" I asked.

"No," she said. "Just since you've been away."

"That's new enough," I said.

"Where have you been to make you come home so late?"

"I don't usually allow my sister to ask questions," I said. "But I've got news for you. Skip and Cathy are marrying at Christmas."

The door knob slipped from her grasp. The bolt slugged its socket. We heard the muffle of the roadster drifting away. It sounded fatal.

"Happy?" I asked. "Want to dance?" I asked.

Wrinkling her nose, she turned her face away and pushed at me.

"What have you been drinking?"

"Vinegar," I said.

CHAPTER 10

The first snow storm hit us a week later. I woke up late on Saturday morning, pulled back the curtains, and saw the elm frozen in veins and capillaries on the fraternity house lawn, which had risen several feet, was white, and was indistinguishable from the street and all the other front lawns as far as I could see. Some brave fellow had tramped his way out to the street and away into the white wilderness recently. Holes where he had stepped traced a track out the front walk and turned where the sidewalk was supposed to be, forming a perfect right-angle. It was an example of how people are slaves to custom. If he had cut across the front lawn, it would have saved him a lot of effort.

A knock at the door made me call out and Maxwell came in. We talked about the poor dead elm encased in skins of ice on the front lawn. Evidently death had come from one of the higher branches that had been broken in a storm and hung down on those below it. A large bump that seemed to have swelled appeared on the trunk of the tree. From there it was simple for this canker to attack the veins and strike the giant into an agony of ossification. Maxwell then related this to cancer in the human body and then to the susceptibility of such diseases to people who did not eat early breakfasts and drank only a cup of killer-coffee before eating lunch. The result was that those who slept late had small chance of survival beyond the age of thirty-five or forty. The remedy, however, was to play chess first on rising. As I threw my pillow at him, Maxwell ducked away, and I heard him thumping down the stairs on his way to set up the chess board.

ROMANCE

But I did get some studying done and, along with the time I spent with Melanie as well as other odd dates, the weeks before Christmas didn't give me a breather, so that naturally I was behind in my Christmas shopping again. I bought Skip and Cathy a pair of silver candle sticks for a wedding present. I don't know why. They are quite useless in this modern world. But I liked the design and I thought they'd go well on their mantelpiece, if they had one. Once I met Pete Miller crossing the university grounds. Wrapped in a long muffler with university colors, he was with a pretty girl whom he introduced as Mag. Her real name was Barbara but he said it reminded him of a doll, so he called her Mag. I told him it was original. He was quite merry.

Christmas decorations lit up store windows and Santa Clauses were ringing bells in the streets when I got back to Hamilton. The spirit was heightened by periodical falls of flakes. The radio stations were going all out for Jingle Bells, Winter Wonderland and Crosby. At the Rymal's house, cousins had begun to arrive for the wedding. Skip told me it was like a hotel. Poor fellow, he was still living above a tavern in the north end.

Nancy was to be a bridesmaid. The hurry and scurry of dresses and tissue papers and packages and measurements drove me out of the house. Women get so excited over weddings; they like to make that grand effort to appear like twinkling stars around the moon.

Cathy had many showers. I had to bear hearing all the trivial details as Nancy related events at mealtimes. From what she could remember of the presents, I imagined Cathy had enough intricate gadgets to make her housekeeping life miserable.

Two days before the wedding, Tim arranged for a stag party at one of the respectable hotels in town. I was amazed at the variety of friends Skip had made. Along with his insurance buddies, I met university lecturers, city employees, manufacturers, doctors, a landscape gardener, and some young hockey players. Skip was wearing his big smile, and, with chest out, he shook hands right and left vigorously. He was his old self again; the strain of the last months was gone; the athlete had bounced back as lucky as ever. We made whoopee until late in the night. There's nothing like a stag party to help a guy through the ordeal of getting married. He comes to the altar so dazed with drink, he doesn't mind making promises.

The wedding took place in the afternoon. An awning was constructed leading to the front door of the Presbyterian Church. Spectators were lined along both sides of it and into the Church, and all the inside pews were filled up to the altar. I worked like a mechanical engine when seating people, crawling up the aisle and trekking back again.

When Cathy arrived, I felt she earned the gasps of those who saw her, those who saw loveliness walking, and those whose expression of wonder rippled through the congregation, lifting their hearts in the excitement as they raptured over the raven hair against the white, over the facial beauty that awakened joy, over the slow graceful feline-like movement of the woman.

Skip was a little nervous. He had asked Tim if he had the ring half a dozen times, and, when he was at the altar, he seemed to be keeping one eye on the Minister and one eye on Tim, so afraid was he of missing his cue. Then I saw him kiss Cathy, and I knew it was done. I looked at the bridesmaids and saw Nancy trying to look bright under a dour shadow.

Then there was the reception with Mr. and Mrs. Rymal who outdid themselves in welcoming, to make up for the gap left on Skip's side. All the downstairs rooms of the gigantic house were open to the guests. And, although the weather outside was freezing, every corner in the house was warm. The guests were being fed with cocktails, cigarettes, and three-cornered sandwiches. The younger ones discovered clusters of mistletoe in convenient places. I found some and took Cathy under it.

"Oh, Tommie, no!"

"A bride has to kiss. It's unwritten law," I said.

Her lips were full on mine, and I held her until she pulled away.

"People will think we're lovers," she smiled.

"It's too early for suppositions," I said.

"Oh!" She kissed me again as if I were a bother, but not, thank goodness, a brother.

"Are you that happy?" I asked.

Several dozen of her cousins came down on us, and I found myself on the outside of the herd. Many of them were

Americans, as I could tell from the variety of accents, and, too, there was an atmosphere of indiscriminate freedom which one connects with the chewing of bubble gum.

"It sure is cold in this part of the country," said a heavily-built fellow of my age in whom I saw a resemblance to Rymal.

"I guess it's a darn good place to take a wife in," he chuckled and poked me in the ribs to help me get the joke.

He went after a three-cornered sandwich with a dill pickle on it, which he saw carried past, leaving me free to walk over to where Tim was standing out of conversation and looking pensive.

"Hi, Best man! did you forget something?"

Tim tried to smile away his frown, but the worry lay in the folds of his face and refused to budge. He was non-committal at first, but then he admitted that he was worried about Skip.

"I don't think he's as happy as he acts," he said.

"But why?"

"Because, to please Mr. Rymal, he gave up insurance and he promised to go into the brewery in the New Year. If you knew the way Skip loves the insurance business, you'd understand why he's unhappy."

"He didn't have to do that," I said angrily.

"To please the Rymals he did. And you know Skip. He wants to please everybody."

We began to walk into the next room, and I sensed how heavy was the worry in him.

"But it's such a small thing," I said. "Skip'll probably like the brewery."

Tim shrugged his shoulders.

"Here he comes now."

Skip was bringing Cathy to the table of reception where stood a tall cake set there to be symbolically cut and divided amongst the several hundred guests. When he made his speech, everyone listened intently. Since he had no relatives there to judge him by, since he could be measured only by his own six feet, he represented a mysterious type of Don Juan who had come to rule over them all with love and kisses. What he said was softly humourous, quaintly romantic. I thought he had improved since his Chamber of Commerce days.

When Rymal spoke, he praised Skip as not only the best son he could hope to find, but as a worthy successor to the family business. As a wedding present, he chose to present the couple with a house in Hamilton which would be built within the next year.

"All you've got to do is pick the spot," he said.

When they ran to their car, they were covered with confetti. We watched them drive off, and we laughed at the cupids chalked on the back and the cardboard with the crazy letters jumbled over it. I looked at the blue and green and red and yellow flecked over the white snow. There was a forlorness about these bits of paper, as if they'd been trying to look gay but were really disappointed they'd been left behind. It began to snow again. I followed the others back to the house. Oh well, there was still Melanie, I thought. She'd be at the party later on.

"Where are they stopping first?" I asked Tim.

"Niagara Falls," he said, seriously.

That evening I called for Melanie at her uncle's house in Westdale. She was dressed gaily in a red party dress with lapels shaped like poinsettia leaves. We took her uncle's car.

"He's entertaining tonight so he doesn't need it," she said. "It'll be like a mad house when I get back."

"I'm not bringing you back," I chuckled hideously, like a radio actor.

"Oh yes you are," she said.

I stepped on the speedometer and beat a red light. I began to chuckle again.

"Then what are we going to do?" she said.

"After the party we'll go to a hotel."

"No," she said quietly. "I don't want to."

"It's all right," I said, "no one will know who we are. We can pretend we're just married."

"No," she said.

"Yes," I said.

I knew we would.

The small pines on the Rymal's front lawn were strung with lights, and, from one window, the colours from a huge tree twinkled over the snow into the night. From the doorstep, I looked into the silence, and I watched the trees, weighted with thick snow, lit up here and there by the white of the street lights. Over the streets were new layers of snow through which the black of the asphalt could be seen in a fuzzy cloudiness. The bottom floors of the houses nearby were all alight. I saw a Christmas tree in one of them. In the sky, the stars were clear and the crispness of the air made the sky seem sharp. With the world so still, so well-defined, there came a docility into the night, as if it had been tamed, as if man could lie out under the stars and feel as much at home as in his own living-room. But as I stood, I became conscious of my standing and the air touched colder to my cheek.

"It's cold," Melanie said.

People were coming from behind us, so I pressed the bell and the door swung open. Melanie and I were soon laughing, dancing and drinking like the rest of our social creatures. We were two of the gang; through the high spirit of those about us, Melanie and I became closer to each other. When strangers become friends, then friends become lovers and lovers become a part of one another. Although she and I were lovers, we had never been good friends, and we had never really been strangers. Yet it was only when I held her in my arms that I knew we were lovers; otherwise, we were two companions who didn't know each other well enough to be friends but who knew each other too well to be strangers. That night, however, when she was standing on the other side of the piano, when we looked at each other as we sang carols, we were friends as well as lovers, and I felt we were a part of each other.

"Who is your pretty friend?" Nancy asked.

"Greta Garbo," I said.

"From the looks she is giving you, she seems dangerous. Watch out."

It is an unpleasant sensation when a guy's sister warns him about his girlfriend. Women have an uncanny way of reckoning members of their own sex, which a man cannot afford to overlook; and knowing this, he is never successful in completely ignoring a woman's warning. To say the least, I was disturbed.

"What are you talking about?"

"You don't want to get into any entanglements," she said.

"No worry there," I said. "I can handle her easily."

Nancy raised her brows and moved away.

I signalled to Melanie with my eyes, and we met on the way to where there was dancing. As we stepped through the doorway, she stopped and pointed to the mistletoe. In the light of Nancy's warning I didn't enjoy the kiss as I would have otherwise.

"When are we leaving?"

"Soon," I said.

"Let's go now," she said.

"What's the hurry?"

"I want to," she said.

When I started her uncle's car, she asked where we were going. Now I wasn't so keen on the hotel, at least I couldn't bring myself to say it.

"Where do you want to go?" I said.

She looked at me and blushed a little.

"It's early yet," I said. "Let's drive around a bit."

She sat close to me and put her arm inside mine as I was driving. Since we first met, we had been controlled by physical contact. So that when she sat close to me, I felt that it was her as much as I who drove the car to a small hotel on the outskirts. We sat in the car and looked at the house, old and leaning, a perfect setting for a seaside murder story.

"There are still some lights on. I'll see if they've got a room."

When I left Melanie, her eyes were glistening, but when I came back with the news that there were no vacant rooms, she looked disappointed.

"Is there another near here?" she asked.

"Don't think so," I said.

She took my arm again, and I sensed the need of finding us a place to sleep together that night; a night when her parents were miles away, when her uncle wouldn't care, a night when for once we wouldn't be missed.

We drove along the beach road where the frozen skeletons of summer circus reared grotesquely in the half light from the road. The lapping of waves sounded in the night. I heard the hollow rasp of the water slipping over stones.

"This is terrible," I said. "They don't build enough hotels."

ROMANCE

When we came to the highway, we turned back along it. There was lots of traffic rushing from one city to another. On Christmas Eve, traffic looks lonely.

"There!" Melanie said.

I saw a motel sign and turned in the lane leading to the cluster of cabins. The proprietor's cabin was the first, and he was standing in its threshold as if waiting for business.

"Sure," he said. "The end one on the first row."

He looked like an ex-truck driver who had got too big for his cab. No one would want to quarrel with him.

I signed, "Mr. and Mrs."

"Jackfish," he drawled. "That's an unusual name."

"Yes," I agreed. "It's English, you know."

He grinned and gave me the keys.

The cabin was very small but it was warm. A wood stove in the corner promised to send out enough heat for the night. And when we took off the lid and turned off the light, the red glow in the darkness was cosy.

I knew Melanie's body was beautiful; after the first time I saw her I stopped thinking of the form and recognized only the essence; but in the glow from the stove, her skin was a rosy texture that made me see her in a new beauty, and I was excited in my surprise and overjoyed with the novelty. I made her model for me so that I could see her, and, before I took her in my arms, I had a moment's reflection in which I sincerely wished I could paint.

In mid-morning, we drove back to her uncle's house. It had been the first full night we had spent together, and, although enjoyable, I found it a little too long. There was the irritation of having to wait until she woke up in the morning and then later she had wanted to just lie when I wanted us to be up and on our way. I had a particular craving to read some law cases that morning. There was a calm in the air which was perfect for concentration. And, too, I was curious to see what presents there were for me under the Christmas tree.

Her aunt and uncle were eating breakfast when we arrived so we joined them. It was the usual grey Christmas morning where the adults sit about in dressing gowns and the children scamper through fields of wrapping paper and hoot with new toys. And there was the smell of toast and marmalade.

"Late party, eh?" her uncle said.
"Fairly late," Melanie said.
"One never gets home early from the Rymals," I said.
"Oh, you were there, eh?" He seemed impressed.

That was the end of our trial. I swallowed the last of my coffee and Melanie escorted me to the door. We embraced quickly.

"What time are you coming on New Years?"

At that moment I didn't look forward to spending New Year's eve in Toronto but I knew when it came I would. "The five o'clock from here," I said.

"I'll meet you at the station."
"Don't bother."
"No, no I will," she said.
"Merry Christmas," I said.

There were no buses. It was a one and half hour walk home through the snow. But I welcomed the air. It was refreshing.

CHAPTER 11

In the middle of January I was back in Hamilton, and, hearing that the honeymooners had returned, I rang Skip on Saturday morning. He asked me to come right up to see them. This time when I approached the house now that Skip was living in it, the mansion was not so awe-inspiring. Skip's survival amongst so many rooms and so much wealth had made the house seem less grand and less private.

But I was surprised at the new Skip who opened the door to me. He was wearing a lounge suit of the latest mode, something he picked up in New York; and, with a smart, courteous wave of the hand, he accompanied me through the halls and rooms to the sports room which looked onto the garden. He strolled with more of a swagger than I remember him having, he held himself stiffly which was less becoming than before with his easy gestures and shy but intimate glances, and when he touched the furniture, he allowed his hand to caress it with pleasant familiarity, a lingering sense of happy ownership.

ROMANCE

"This, Tom, is rather fun." He led me to a corner where there was a large globe with all sorts of range finders circled about it.

"I can find the exact time in Timbuktu at this very moment, just by sliding this block along."

"It's wonderful," I said.

"Six-ten," he said, "a.m."

We sat on a divan. He reached for a carved ivory box from the table before us and offered me cigarettes about half a foot long.

"They're Bulgarian," he said. "Don't ask me where we got them."

I took one for a lark, but he took one seriously as if he smoked nothing else.

"Where are the Rymals?" I asked.

"Florida. They're wintering there." He looked relieved to have them out of the way.

"Have you started work in the brewery?"

"What? Oh yes, I spend time there every day."

"No more insurance," I smiled.

"That was a good business. I'll be getting periodical payments from the policies I sold for quite a while."

Some of the friendliness had gone out of his tone. I felt that he was beginning to look down on me as part of that life he had left behind. Now he could afford to be condescending and not nearly so friendly, not nearly so equal.

"How is the law school making out?" he asked.

He was in his realm, was Skip. While he asked questions about Toronto and listened to my answers, he surveyed the room as if he were making sure all was in order. He sunk easily into the pillows of the divan and sprawled in sportsmanlike fashion under the head of a moose. And when I spoke, he wiggled a brown felt-covered shoe in time with the rhythm of a song he kept to himself.

"I say, I'm sorry, I forgot," he started up. "What will you have to drink?"

"Nothing, thanks. It's a little early for me yet."

"But I mean before lunch," he said. "A little sherry?"

"Are you inviting me for lunch?" I joked.

"Yes," he frowned. "Naturally."

"Well that's fine," I said. "Where's Cathy?"

"Upstairs." He began to walk away. "She'll be down in a minute."

He pressed a bell in the wall. "It's a great life, married life. You ought to try it sometime."

The maid must have been nearby because she came immediately.

"A bottle of sherry," he said.

"A bottle or decanter?" she asked in a perverse, middle-aged manner.

"Well..." he paused wondering if he had made a mistake. She was making him take the mickey, so I spoke up.

"A decanter."

She went quickly, and, blushing, he cleared his throat.

"She knew what you meant," I said. "The Rymals always have it in a decanter." But I couldn't clear away a feeling of resentment that began to come between us.

"Yes, I know," he said. "It's more dignified that way."

"Dignified? I should think the dignity depends on the way you pour it. A bottle in experienced hands can look Dignity incarnate."

"Then you'd better pour," he said.

I reached for my cigarette to give me time to think of a different subject.

"How was the honeymoon?"

"Not bad," he said. He sunk into a chair across the room. "Cathy is lovelier than I thought she was. She's really beautiful. For the first week I forgot it was winter and then we got far enough south so that it wasn't anymore."

I had struck on the right subject. He began to loosen up as he talked. Cathy came like an inspiration between us, destroying ill-feeling, and giving us a ground for friendship. And while he sat there reminiscing about the places they visited, I conjured, even from his impoverished descriptions, visions of Cathy surrounded by the local fauna of various parts of the United States. Although he spoke as if they did everything together, I saw only Cathy, animated, alone, and occasionally in the company of a dark shadow that could have been anybody, perhaps me.

"Tommie, dear! What a surprise!"

Cathy was wearing black slacks which also seemed to fit in with the lazy morning in the sports room, and her jacket was yellow, making her a brilliant contrast of colour. She stepped over to where I was standing, and I took her hand. She was the same flighty, carefree, lovely Cathy, who, now that she was married, seemed bolder rather than more reserved, and just as independent as before with the added hint of a wiser look about the eyes.

"Skip was just telling me about your honeymoon," I said.

"The best part of it was the tan we got. Just look at this!"

She bared her arm and I saw the deep brown, and her face too was dark from the sun.

"I've been admiring Skip's," I said.

When Cathy sat beside me, though, I sensed more of the woman in her. Marriage had awakened a sensuousness I had not imagined she would have. When she took a cigarette from the box I offered her, I remarked a slower movement of the arm and an unexpected depth in the look she gave me. I held a match for her as her lips drew close to my fingers, and I felt an awakening in my chest as she posed there and then drew back, blowing out a thin streamlet of smoke, stretching her legs in the sexy slacks so that I wallowed in subsiding emotions, vaguely disturbed.

The maid came with the sherry and set it on the table in front of us. She ignored Skip sitting in the chair across the room.

"You are staying for lunch?" Cathy asked. And she told the maid.

"Would you like to pour the sherry, darling?" It was more of a reminder than a request.

Skip sighed and lumbered over to us. I watched him fill the glasses as Cathy talked. When Cathy was present he wasn't as much at ease. He set the glasses down awkwardly and his fingers stuck to the glass, almost spilling the drink. His hands must have been perspiring.

"Thank you, darling."

He had been on the point of handing me the glass, but Cathy stretched out her arm, that arm of social protocol, and took it. He handed me the next glass, and, when he stood up with his own, he looked relieved that there had been only three people to worry about.

"Good job," Cathy smiled impishly at him.

He, taking the humour from her glance, broke into his hockey grin, and I remembered once more those bubble gum cards I used to hang about my room.

"I didn't know a man could be such a slave in his own household," he said. "I'm at her beck and call."

"Oh yes you are," Cathy teased, and she stretched out her arms to him.

Skip set down his drink and knelt beside her. They put their arms about each other and kissed, and rubbed noses and made me thoroughly envious. When they began itseypooing one another, I got up to look out the window. The snow lay low and hard because we hadn't had a fall for two weeks. Over the white, there were specks of black from the residue of chimney smoke. Further back in the garden were gaps of ground where the winter grass was a dark deep green. And the trees on the hillside stood still and naked like scarecrows.

"Oh Skip, how rude. We're boring our poor guest."

"On the contrary," I said. "It's all very entertaining."

Cathy laughed, but Skip looked startled, as if he had suddenly realized he had dipped to a lower level, back to the old familiarity he wished now to erase.

"We're sorry," he said. "It's too easy to forget ourselves."

Embarrassed, I tried to gesture that I didn't care, but Cathy spoke for me.

"It doesn't matter with Tommie, darling. He doesn't mind. After all he's our oldest friend, aren't you, dear?" She came and put her arm through mine.

"We want an early lunch," Skip said. "I'll see about it."

"Something's different about him," I said when Skip had left.

"I know," Cathy frowned. "He started to act stiffly on the honeymoon. I thought at first it was just a defence against the demands of the waiters, you know how they try and hurry you and make you take what you don't want. But now we're home again, he hasn't really relaxed. I don't think it's very becoming in him, do you, Tommie?"

"It's not encouraging at any rate."

We sat again on the divan, and I sensed the languorousness of her body, and when she put her head on my shoulder I wanted to cry out against the torture twisting inside me.

ROMANCE

"You really love Skip?"

She laughed. "Yes, I think so. As much as I could love anybody. You know me, Tommie."

No, I didn't know her, not completely, not nearly enough.

She snuggled closer to me, and my head began to swim, my mouth went dry.

"I'll have to see about the heat in this room."

I wanted to move my free hand from off my knee over to her. It would have been like an arrow in flight, claiming its victim, unswerving in intention. But, instead, I gripped my knee until the cap ached.

She stretched her legs longly in the black slacks away from me on the divan and she settled her head comfortably on my shoulder, her raven hair grazing my chin.

"You know, Tommie, I'm in love with love. I've just discovered."

I gazed at the window, trying to see into the paleness outside, trying to concentrate on a twist of bush near the pane. "When?" I said.

"Oh, just a while ago."

"You mean you're in love with Skip?" I said.

My arm was beginning to throb from her weight against it so that I brought it about her waist, supple and warm and I had to gaze down at her breasts, rising in yellow, and I tried to freeze away my desire, to kill it with reason.

"More than that. I love the feeling," she said. "It's so full."

She sighed and bent her head back so that her lip came to my chin, and I kissed her and my strength ebbed out of me in that kiss, and I fell, my head on her lap, weak with passion. She laughed and stroked my hair until I sat up and slipped way from her.

"It's not right," I said.

"Don't be such a fool, Tommie. It's certainly not wrong!"

She settled herself comfortably on the divan and asked me to light her cigarette from a package she had placed on the table.

"Those Hungarian ones are ridiculous," she said. "They're one of father's jokes."

"Bulgarian," I said.

"Yes, Bulgarian," and she smiled like a cherub.

I flicked a table ronson and then handed her the cigarette as Skip came back. His eyes darkened when he saw the way I was lighting his wife's cigarette and I had to glance away.

"What news?" Cathy cried.

"Lunch will be served in ten minutes," he said, rather sternly. "Most of it will be cold. Do you mind?" he asked me.

"Fine!"

Cathy rolled over onto one side and, tucking her arm under her head, looked at me. "We're going to the Squash Club right after we've eaten," she said. "We'd love to have you come with us."

I saw Skip frown and I hesitated to answer.

"You can't think of a good excuse?" Cathy smiled. "Then you must come. Eh, Skip?"

It was Skip who drove now, and although we didn't arrive at the Club very quickly, we were more sure of arriving. Cars were packed bumper to bumper in the streets surrounding it so that we had to walk a ways.

"It's a big event," Cathy said. "Toronto is here to play mid-season matches."

"It'll be terrific!" Skip rubbed his hands enthusiastically. He had put on a sports vest of red plaid and now he left his coat open so that it was showing. "I'm getting fond of these matches," he confessed.

In the hallway of the club, we met Tim who was dressed in his whites ready for play.

"The first matches don't begin for half an hour," Tim said. "Let's go upstairs where it's warm." He was beginning to shiver in his short pants and thin shirt. "Some of the Toronto bunch are up here," he said as he led us into the lunchroom.

There was a lot of talking and cigarette smoke coming from young men grouped about one part of the room. None of them noticed us take a table in the corner furthest from them.

"A little noisy," Tim apologized, "but warmer."

"Heavens! You should wear those suits that runners have to keep warm," Cathy said.

Tim made a face. "They're only for sissies."

"Running's different," Skip said, as if he were explaining the difference.

ROMANCE

"Is that Pete Miller?" I nodded at a head of blond curls bobbing between the other heads.

Tim pierced the distance with a measuring look. "Yes."

At that moment, Pete looked up and our eyes met. He backed out of his chair and, tongue in cheek, came toward us.

"Oh God!" Skip said.

"Hello Tom!" Pete held his hand out.

I stood up and introduced him to Cathy. "You remember the others."

"Hi!" he clapped Tim on the shoulder and looked across at Skip before drawing in his lips and furrowing his brows like a shortsighted school mistress. "That young man, I remember him." His voice cracked high. "He was in this class last year."

Cathy, delighted, laughed, and Skip looked uncomfortable.

Pete giggled in falsetto. "I think he must like me, to come back for a second year."

Skip had to smile, and he waved for Pete to seat himself. "Where are your girls?" Skip asked. "We don't see any over there."

"I left the witches at home," Pete said. "I wanted to see what Hamilton had to offer." He grinned at Cathy. "If they're all like you, I'll be kicking myself for not doing this sooner."

"They aren't all like her," Skip said. "She's the only one, and she's mine."

"Oh," Pete inclined his head and backed away in his chair as if he were sorry for any offence. "I would never have guessed."

"Newly wed," Tim explained.

"Aha! That's it! New," Pete said. "They just aren't used to each other yet."

Skip flashed red with anger, but he sat still, allowing his eyes to smoulder.

"But we are used to each other," Cathy smiled. "You just aren't used to us." She gave him a coy look.

Pete smiled at her and made his blue eyes round. Although he felt comfortable with her, he was making the rest of us uncomfortable. "How do I get used to you?" he asked.

Cathy roared and threw her hand over on to Skip's which lay posed clenched on the table. "He's killing!"

"He'll be killed if he's not careful," Skip said.

Cathy looked sharply at him, her laughter dying on her lips. It was not the thing to say even though one may have thought it strongly. She turned back to Pete with an apologetic look. But he, still smiling, merely winked at her.

"Are you playing squash today?" she asked.

"I go on in an hour and I expect to see you watching. I'm seeded second so I need lots of luck." He reached out and took her hand. "You'll bring me luck, won't you?"

"We all will," Cathy said, flustered in spite of his joking.

"You'll have a tough game," Tim said, nodding his head for emphasis. "It won't be as easy as the last time."

"I hope not! Oh poppa, I hope not!" Pete cried. "My foot's just healing from a whopper of a cut." He balanced one leg on his other knee and drew a line across his heel with his finger. "I don't want to have to run around much."

"How did you do it?" Cathy asked, impressed.

"I was teaching my kid brother how to throw knives. He's a hell of a knife-thrower, let me tell you."

The men across the room pushed back their chairs and stood up in unison. They began moving toward the door, and one of them called at us. "Pete, let's go, boy, let's go."

"Your rallying call," Skip said in the manner of a hint.

Pete stood up. "I will see you?" he said to Cathy, and he ran after the others before she could answer.

"Let's watch him, darling. It'll be fun." Her eyes sparkled.

"Nothing doing," Skip said. "He's just a show-off."

"Oh let's." She grabbed his arm in pretended excitement.

"He'll probably lose if that heel is as bad as he says," Tim said.

"Okay. But you'll be bored," Skip warned her.

After we had watched part of one match, we moved to the court where Pete had begun to play. Cathy was not bored. She applauded winning shots that were not in any way extraordinary. Once Pete tripped his opponent accidentally and Cathy applauded; it broke the spell of an anxious moment while spectators and players laughed.

"You must tell me when to clap," she nudged me.

"When the others do," I said.

She pretended not to hear me and on the next point that Pete won she clapped harder than before.

"Not so loud, Cathy," Skip whispered. "You're making it too obvious."

"Besides, he's a Toronto man," Tim added glumly because Pete was ahead in points.

But Pete swaggered down the centre line and beamed up at her. He was not as spectacular as the time before. The tenderness of his heel made him take more care in his stroking so that he played a steadier game.

"He is good, though, isn't he?" Cathy leaned across Skip to whisper to Tim.

I saw Skip trying to look unconcerned. He must have known that Cathy was hoping to make him jealous, but, try as he might, he could not suppress a sulk that began to show itself in the lines about his mouth.

Cathy turned to me. "He's good, isn't he?"

"Whoops! He missed that one," I said diplomatically.

Since the players were closely matched, the sets ran to two even, when there was a break of ten minutes.

"Let's go down behind and see him," Cathy suggested.

Skip shook his head. "Go ahead, if you want to."

Tim had left to play a match of his own so that I went down with her.

"I'm going to see how Tim's making out," Skip called.

Cathy wrapped her arm tightly about mine for fear of falling when we were going down the steps. The cold air had made her skin look fresh and her eyes wide-awake. When we reached the level, she snuggled warmly against me, and I wanted to unloose my arm from her grip so that I could put it around her.

Pete was sitting on a stool by the court door with a blanket draped over him. He looked tired and, at first, he didn't see us, but Cathy led us to a stop directly in front of him. Then he raised his eyes and half-smiled.

"Dead," he said, "but don't tell the other guy."

"How's your foot?" She knelt beside him.

He sat with one leg crossed over the other so that his heel was off the ground. "Throbbing."

"You poor dear," she said.

He gave her a hang-dog look.

I knelt down on the other side of him. I refused to be left out of the conversation. "You're playing well."

"Where's your friend, Skip?" he asked.

"Upstairs," I said, surprised.
"Why don't you go find him?"
I wanted to tear his head off. I could feel my cheeks burning, and I looked at Cathy to see what her reaction was, but she ignored me. I stood up and looked down at them.
"Will you be able to hold out for the next game?" she asked him.
"Sure," he smiled. "You gonna be at the party tonight?"
"I don't know," she said.
"Are you?" he insisted.
She stood up beside me and smiled back at him. The Hamilton player swinging his racquet passed us to enter the court. Pete pushed himself off his stool.
"No hard feelings, Tom eh? All's fair in love and war."
Cathy put her arm through mine, and I grimaced at him. He went into the court shutting the door behind me. I took Cathy's arm out of mine.
"How many suckers do you think there are in this world?" I said.
"If that's the way you want it," she shrugged.
She walked ahead of me, and, when she began to climb the stairs, her hips swung in front or me. I reached out and held them. She let herself be drawn back against me, where she turned and we kissed in the empty passageway.
We arrived back on the balcony just as the players had finished their warming-up rallies. Skip wasn't there.
"He finds Tim's game more interesting," she giggled impishly at me.
Pete got off to a bad start, but he picked up several points in a row until we saw him limping when he couldn't reach an easy shot on time. The players spoke for a moment, but then Pete shook his head and moved back to his serving box. A fast rally followed in which Pete was being led gradually into a back corner. But falling on one knee, he scooped at a low rebound off the back wall, and, flinging his backhand wide, he made a phenomenal shot, but his racket at the tail end of its sweep nicked his heel so that, as the ball hit in a front corner, he yelped with pain. His opponent knocked the ball down the centre, but Pete made no effort to return it.
Cathy gripped my hand tightly as we watched Pete stand. Her face became slowly pale. We listened to the referee

suggest to stop the game, but Pete refused. The Hamilton man faulted his serve. When Pete moved to take a position in his service box, we saw blood where he had been standing. He won two serves by line lobs which didn't bounce when they hit the floor. He tried to do it a third time, but he hit the ball too hard and the most important rally of the match began.

"If he wins it," I told her, "he's got it."

Pete tracked blood across the floor in blotches, and sprinklings of red glistened on the white walls, but he played ignoring it. As the ball was driven more furiously and the men ran frantically crossing and re-crossing each other, falling back, and then darting for the front wall, the spectators stood in the excitement so that the slap of the ball, the squeak of rubber shoes gripping the floor, and the heavy breathing bobbed like puppets on the end of our nerve strings. The referee stood poised, whistle in hand, paralyzed to stop the rally. Pete's shoe was stained a dark brown and I saw it slip in a blotch of blood as he tried to get away from his rebound. His opponent stormed in to slam the ball but, in stroking it, he caught Pete full in the face. Cathy swooned against me. I had to sit her down.

For a moment Pete held his head in his hands as he sat on the floor. When he looked up, I saw that his teeth had broken through his lip. Cathy saw it at the same time. She was on her feet, and I was behind her running down the stairs. As we rushed into the court, we heard the referee awarding the point to the Hamilton man because Pete had got in the way, and the match, too, because Pete had to forfeit.

Cathy dabbed at his face with my handkerchief but there was little she could do to stop the blood. I turned to see Skip standing behind us.

"Leave him," he said. "There are others that can do that."

He took her arm and made her stand beside him.

Pete groaned something at her, and she nodded quickly.

"Yes, tonight," she said. "We're coming tonight."

Two fellows picked up Pete and carried him away to the dressing rooms where there would eventually be a doctor.

"Ghastly!" Cathy said.

"Come darling, we'll go home," Skip kissed her ear.

She pressed against him, and I watched them go.

"Are you coming?" he said.

"I'll wait a while and get a ride home with Tim," I said. "How's he doing anyway?"

"He's winning."

But although Tim won, he wasn't jubilant enough to drive me home. He was going to eat dinner at the Club and so I decided to join him. When I phoned home, Nancy answered with the cutest hello. She must have been expecting a call.

"Well, Tim," I said. "Here's to the winner," and we raised our beers.

"I told you Hamilton has a powerful team," he said.

The evening came upon us quickly. We hadn't finished eating, when I saw that it was dark outside the window. Tim quit me to help with the entertainment of the Toronto guests who were banqueting in another room. I sipped my beer and looked out at the darkness.

For the first time, Skip's marriage to Cathy began to take a form in my thoughts other than the images and impressions whirling about in superficial sheens of monkey suits and bridal white. Skip gave the weight to their contract and Cathy gave the meaning. While Skip served as the centrum, Cathy paraded the expressions and, although she could not go farther than a specified circumference about the centrum, she was the one to decide how the partnership was to be moulded, and it was through her actions that their love was presented to the world outside. If their marriage was to be successful, Skip had to know how much rope to allow his wife, how much running ground suited her temperament, yet Cathy too had to know how much free ground Skip's nature would allow her. I shuddered at the complications. Surely a true partnership was more simple--not a self-imposed prison where one measured the spaces in a courtyard--rather it was a unity that blinded its partners to their imprisonment. But then that was ideal and marriage was never ideal in reality. Human nature always found ways to break up a unity, and once the prison walls were caught sight of, they could never be completely forgotten.

Yet how ugly to have to think of marriage as something logically worked out, almost mathematical in its scheming! How banal! It probably suited some people, but assuredly not others. I suppose it was a matter of temperament again.

Though I didn't see how anyone could maintain a marriage for any length of time.

I killed an hour shooting pool with some guys before wandering over to where the party was in progress. A three-piece band was beating out dance numbers and several athletes were jiggling with energetic women. One of the women caught me as I walked by her at the end of a number. She pinioned me against her, and, as we jumped to the next number, I felt I was playing hopscotch with a balloon in my hand. After she had squeezed the breath out of me, and found me sexually non-committal, she let me go. "Sweet kid," and she patted my cheek allowing me to sink into a chair in retreat.

Looking around at the other tables, I saw that the people were breaking into cliques as usual. There were the Toronto and Hamilton cliques, and then there were the racquet cliques within those cliques, and then the personal cliques within those cliques until social contact became so restricted that, unless I was courageous enough to inveigle a woman away from her own group, I was going to be left alone, an outsider.

The racket-club atmosphere too had a way of shutting me out. There is nothing more exclusive than club men who wear white to play a gentlemanly sport. Racquets are an individual sport in which players get complexes about those who play them. They tend to make friends with players of their own social worth or with those who have the same idea of etiquette. Anyone who is not one of them hasn't a chance of understanding one of their jokes or of being accepted. Perhaps that's why there are rough women at their dances. They need someone to toss them around and mix them up a bit.

At that moment, however, I wasn't feeling courageous because I couldn't see a woman to be courageous about. I had just about depressed myself to the point of leaving in order to get a good night's sleep, when I saw Skip and Cathy coming toward me. They were like luck bringing happiness into a bad dream.

"She wanted to come because she promised that Toronto dope," Skip said.

"I couldn't disappoint him," Cathy explained to me with round tragic eyes.

"Nor me," I said.

She smiled and reached for Skip's hand lying open on the table. "He's cute, don't you think, darling?"

Skip said nothing. He was beginning to look on me as her friend, not his. When he spoke to me, his voice sounded aloof, and he tilted his chin up as if he were talking over a fence.

"You haven't seen this fellow?"

"Who Pete? No," I said.

"Do you think he's too badly hurt to come?" Cathy asked me.

"I don't know," I said. "Do you want to dance?"

She was good to hold. Her breasts came against me and her hips came against me; the space in-between was an enjoyable vacuum.

"I'm glad you came," I said.

"Skip didn't want to," she snickered and looked over my shoulder at him. "He's mad."

"Why are you teasing him? You know, it's not nice to have a jealous husband."

"Oh, he's not really," she said. "He's just a little hurt. I want to train him, you see, before we get on in this marriage, and really find reasons to be jealous."

"School for husbands?"

"Yes," she laughed. "What they think later all depends on what they are used to. I'm giving Skip a broad training for a broad mind."

"How broad are you going to train his mind about Pete?" I asked.

"You know I would never tell you," she said. She put her forehead on my lips.

I let her remain like that for a moment until I exchanged lips for cheek and said, "Skip thinks you've got it for me. He's been giving me the eagle look."

She laughed. "You're just feeling guilty, Tommie dear."

The band tattooed an end to a series, and we headed back to our table. Pete was there talking with Skip. He stood up, balancing on one foot and on the toes of the other, to greet Cathy. A dressing covered below his nose and up one side of his face so that he had to talk out of the corner of his mouth.

"Can't stay long," he said. "Driving home."

"I'm surprised you came at all," Cathy said. "It must hurt."

He shook his head and took the chair beside her. A heroic air haloed him. He pushed his chair back from the table and stretched his legs out, placing the one over the other. With his blond curls flopping about the sides of his head, he was a Homeric hero sitting with arms folded at a feast given in honour of his return.

"Wish I could drink," he said. "Too tough."

The slipper fell off his raised foot. Cathy bent down and put it back on for him.

One of the musicians must have wanted to mix the party up a bit because he called out a "ladies' choice." Skip was immediately dragged away by some Amazon, and I was left to cower on the shadowed side of Cathy.

"Man!" Pete said. "Wish I could dance with you."

Cathy gave him a long, sympathetic look. As a third party, I sensed an understanding crystallizing out of the atmosphere between these two. But then it was shattered as Cathy shook her head, clearing her brain of sentimental thoughts.

A girl came from behind me, and, as I was dancing, I observed those two sitting side by side, looking for any sign of affection, any give-away, any hint of the future. On the dance floor, I saw Skip watching too. Couples got in my way, and I was on the other side of the floor where I tried to make conversation with my partner, the gum-chewing girl-friend of a dentist. When the series ended, I saw Pete and Cathy sitting in the same quiet attitude, giving the impression of thought communication.

Skip had gone with his partner to another table where he began chatting with the men. We saw him sit down and become involved in the conversation. Cathy looked surprised, and she posed herself to ignore him if he should look at our table. But soon she found that he really was interested in those to whom he was talking and she began to look concerned.

"Tommie, go and see what's keeping Skip."

"Hell no," I said. "He's got enough against me now without me adding to it."

"It's rude of him," she said.

The music hit on a lively tune, and I asked her to dance.

"Not until you get Skip."

"Then I'll dance with Miss Olympia of 1934 whom I can see from here."

Pete stirred in his chair and braced both hands on the table. "Gotta leave," he said. "Long drive."

"Don't forget," Cathy said. "Anytime you're in town."

"I'll see you out," I said.

"No, you won't," Cathy said.

"Just to the car." I stood with Pete.

"Don't you dare leave me alone."

Pete and I laughed and he, hobbling, waved good-bye. The night was pleasant; it was a trifle below freezing and I could go out without a coat. I held the door of Pete's red M.G. for him until he settled himself in the driver's seat.

"Man!" he said.

I stepped back when the engine roared. I watched the lady bird fly away, fly away. I rather envied him, how he could alight on, move, and fly from the number of hearts indifferently.

When I got back to the table, Cathy was gone: to the powder room I surmised, because Skip was still with his new party and no one was dancing. I bought a beer and drank it for ten minutes before she came back, looking grim.

"Will you take me home?" she demanded.

"Wait a minute," I said.

"No!"

We saw Skip get up from his table of friends and turn toward us.

"I'm not speaking to him."

"Then you'll be the poor loser," I said.

She gaped at me as the truth of what I said slipped in like an elf to touch the trip hammer of emotion over her heart.

"Hi!" Skip smiled. "I've just been catching up on the news. I used to sell insurance with those guys. Terrific bunch!"

"That's nice, darling," Cathy smiled in return. "But it's late now."

"Sure, we can go," he said. "Your friend Pete has gone, I take it."

She faked a yawn and nodded indifferently. She saw the humour in my eye and glared at me.

"School for wives," I said.

"You are getting a ride home with Tim, are you not, Tommie dear?"

CHAPTER 12

Skip kept the upper hand. I met him on the street a few weeks later, when his tan had gone. He was very cheerful and seemed not to remember that once he might have had reason to be jealous of me. I had heard that he was doing well in the brewery and was proving himself not only a good seller, but a good organizer as well. The rumours going around town about him had changed from doubtful to good and some even to excellent. People were saying Cathy could not have found a better husband so that Skip found all social barriers falling away at his feet and with his ability to make friends, or at least acquaintances who thought they were friends, he was finding himself popular within the social unit. He was being invited into people's houses, a favour usually granted to close relatives or long-standing family friends, and he was beginning to feel very much at home in the city.

Yet when he greeted me it was with some of the Rymal bluff. He told me he had just been visiting one or two people whose names were from the upper brackets. As I was supposed to quake, I looked respectfully surprised. We talked platitudes until we got to his car when I refused his offer to drive me to where I was going.

As I continued walking, I wondered at his friendliness which was the absolute reversal of his previous distant attitude, but then I remarked that his effervescent conversation had no sign of the true warmth in it, that his goodwill was the result of a good day, that I had been talking with the salesman who spoke the same words to friend and stranger alike, until he met his own circle of confidants with whom he then traded little "me" stories back and forth, which although exaggerated and simplified, had a core of simplicity in them. I wondered then who his friends were. If he had rejected me as socially unfit, how many more of his old friends must he have repulsed. Tim, too, I suspected, did not see much of him, although he was Skip's age and had more in common with him than I. Of course, if Skip wanted to mix about in the different clubs, he had to remain friendly, but it was more of a superficial friendliness than a sincere one. It was this withdrawal of intimacy which I noticed, and which I found later that some of his other friends disliked.

It was now February, and the city was being held in a cold spell, a prison of ice and wind which snared the inhabitants when they stepped from their centrally-heated boxes into the bleak outside. In this weather, the snow was crisp, and I liked hiking for short distances into the city centre, where the shop fronts frosted, the cars coughed, and the people strode briskly, breathing small clouds and pressing muffs tightly over their ears. The exhilaration of walking quickened the blood so that, after a quarter hour, my face heated like a candled pumpkin. But then the skin grew taut, the chill clamped on the forehead, and the toes swelled so that I was obliged to step into a department store where I wandered in summer temperature between the counters until I thawed.

When I ducked out of one store, I met Nancy entering. We were on opposite sides of a swing door so that we went around twice before I signalled for her to get off the inside. Having taken a day off from lectures to come home earlier, I arrived that morning and she was surprised to see me. It was her lunch hour. She invited me to take a coffee while she bit at tiny things guaranteed to starve her into a beauty queen. We took an elevator to the lunchroom on the top floor and there sat in the hush of thick carpets and conservatively decorated walls.

I could see Nancy was eager to tell me something so I helped her get over the preliminary questions quickly in order that she could approach her story in an off-hand way.

She dug her fork into a sardine. "I met your friend Melanie at a house party last week," her eyes stared up into mine.

My heart did a hop-skip-jump. "In Hamilton?" I said.

"I recognized her from Christmas eve," she said. "She didn't know I was your sister, so she has no idea that you know."

"I saw her last night and she didn't mention it," I said.

"Are you jealous?"

"Not at all," I said. "I'm an egoist, true, but I'm also a realist. If she has time to go out with other guys, okay; I'm no star-dreamy steady; but I am surprised to hear she came all this way on a date." I thought of Christmas eve in the motel and wondered if the scene were duplicated. I felt like one of a number--as small as a digit.

"He was the tall, dark, and handsome type."

"You're making my coffee taste awful," I said.

The idea was to grow up, to reach that mature stage where you can possess without possessing. I wanted to look on Melanie as common property that I could pick up and leave without any claim. I wanted the moment to be golden only for the moment we were together, and unconnected with my life apart from her. And too, I wanted her to be as free of me as I was of her, only then would our meetings be for the sole reason of enjoying one another. There would be no drudgery of routine meetings to convince the ego that it was sought after from some sentimental need. To preserve one's individuality, this attitude is essential, and here was I being swamped with petty thoughts stemming from centuries of traditional marriage mores, and being irrationally angered by a false sense of a violation of a right to which I had no claim.

Nancy laughed. "I told you, you were getting too involved."

"Well, it's damned hard to remain detached when everyone around me wants to be attached. Women never think about what marriage really means; they want to be married period. Anyway, what am I supposed to do? Go celebrate?"

"Yes," she smiled.

"Not on your life!"

"What makes you think girls get married mindlessly?"

"Some do," I said. "They don't think about marriage until after they are married. Otherwise they wouldn't do it."

"They marry for security."

"And make the man insecure," I said.

"Oh phoo!" Nancy said. "When I marry, my husband and I will have a partnership on a firm half-and-half basis."

I thought of the prison walls again and had to admit that my sister wasn't any different from the other birds who dream of golden cages.

Hell!" I said. "Why must everything be based on a monetary system? How many '29's do we need to show us how silly it all is? A partnership is only real if it's not held together by considerations for money, laws, and other people's ideas or opinions."

"And you a law student too, tut tut," she said.

This made me impatient. "Like many people you think a lawyer supports the laws, that he's an upstanding member of his bourgeois society, but in reality his whole work is dedicated to winning his case even if he has to circumvent the laws. There is no greater anarchist than a good lawyer."

"Except in real estate," she said. My sister was a persistent arguer. She should have been the lawyer.

"A solicitor destroys as many claims as he protects. He only respects the law when he has no opportunity to bend it the way he wants."

"Still, any claim has to be decided by justice in the end."

"There is no such thing as justice. Justice means you have a better lawyer, that's all," I said. "Anyway, laws and money should not concern marriage. Yet they seem to be crucial in deciding whether a marriage breaks or not. The real danger is other people's opinions, and you have to protect yourself from having to accept them."

"So what has that to do with your attitude to Melanie?"

"No fear of marriage and not the smallest tear if I see her dining with Ali Khan."

Nancy thought all this was youth, two years younger than herself, talking. But most of it was resolve; the determination to keep myself from becoming two people, to preserve my free spirit intact.

"Speaking of tears," Nancy said, "Cathy says she tried to use them with Skip as she did with her parents, but that they don't work. Oh dear! I shouldn't be telling you this."

"How does she use tears?" I said rounding my eyes in disbelief; it was the only way to make Nancy talk, doubt her word.

"She pretends to be hurt to get her way, you know; but Skip only laughs. She says she's exasperated."

I thought of the whining fights Skip must have had to put up with whenever there was a disagreement as to where and if they were going, and all the other million petty decisions that had to be made. To be outside of it all was deliciously comforting.

"But tonight she has a plan." Nancy lowered her tone. "She wanted to go to New York over the week-end but Skip had this speech tonight and wouldn't cancel it. She and I are going to the movies while he talks, and then she's going to make him wish he had gone to New York with her."

"Where is he giving it?"

"The Junior Chamber of Commerce."

I got there about half way through the meeting, but it was time enough for me. Skip was talking about the importance of respectable drinking places in the city, especially for the sale of beer, and he related the advantages that pubs gave to Londoners, stressing their agreeableness and conveniences and how much more attractive a city became when it encouraged the opening of respectable, high-class taverns. He was being listened to with more interest than he deserved because he represented an executive of a big company. Many of his listeners were intimidated by him. Then, too, his descriptions of London pubs during the war were amusing. He accredited so much importance to beer-drinking for upholding the morale that it seemed that Hamilton's morale ran the danger of total collapse because of the ridiculously small number of taverns in the city.

When he had finished speaking, there was a short pause for questions, but for the first few minutes, the hall was silent, as everyone tried to think of something important to ask so that the speaker would not be embarrassed. Finally, some Joe stood up and asked if it were easy for the licensing laws to be altered. This gave Skip the grand opportunity to talk about democracy and the power of the people's vote. He spoke wisely, advising and suggesting rather than preaching so that he began to sound more like a top executive every minute, all of which made his argument reasonable and even enticing. And then I had to try and be funny and ask if it were true, as the official statement claimed, that it was beer which had caused the epidemic of alcoholic poisoning which had swept across Europe that disastrous winter ten years ago.

Skip blinked at me. His surprise at seeing me turned slowly into suspicion, and several seconds of silence elapsed, when a fat man coughed a laugh to break the tension and the room was filled with laughter. The meeting dispersed in a jolly mood.

"You're a fine friend!" Skip smiled when I went to meet him.

He seemed humbled, though, as if he had been temporarily knocked off the perch he had assumed, and we, more friendly than ever since the marriage, left the meeting together. He invited me to come back with him as he said Nancy and Cathy would probably be there. He told me Cathy was always interested in how well his speeches had gone. Naturally I agreed readily, secretly anxious to see what Cathy's surprise would be.

When we came to the house we could see no lights.

"Still at the movies," Skip said.

After he turned on the front hall light, I saw a white envelope stuck into the frame of the mirror and pointed it out to him. He looked at it and threw it down with a cry of exasperation.

"She says since I didn't go to New York with her, she and Nancy caught the 11.30 train and are spending the weekend there."

"That is a surprise," I said.

"But what are they going to do all alone in New York?" he said.

"If they've got the money," I said, "they can do lots of things."

"But that's desertion!"

We went into the coffee room where Skip found a couple of beers behind the water-falling counter, while I punched a bush flat into a table for us. Skip set the bottles of beer down and looked at his watch.

"Wait a minute! It's eleven now, isn't it?"

He didn't wait for an answer but ran for the door.

"Come on."

After ten minutes of hectic driving we lurched to a stop outside the station. A red-cap told us the train came through at 11.20, but when we looked at the small group of passengers gathered on the platform, we couldn't see the girls amongst them.

"Just like Cathy to be late," he said.

"Maybe they're in the ladies' room," I said.

We waited outside the door for a few minutes, where we met the blank stare of females coming and going, until Skip almost danced with impatience.

ROMANCE

"If they're in there," he said, "they're taking a long time. Supposing they're not, and they get on the train while we're here waiting for them to come out?"

I nodded my head and began to move away.

"Wait! I don't want to stand here alone. Is anyone looking?" He walked toward the door.

"Why don't you pick up that mop and pail in the corner," I said, "just in case."

He seized them as he walked by, looking ridiculously unlike a cleaner in his smart tan overcoat and brown fedora, and pushed through the door. While he was inside, an elderly woman, eyeing me suspiciously, approached the door, but when she was about to enter, Skip opened it for her from the other side. For a moment she forgot where she was because she smiled a 'thank you' at him and stepped in while he quickly stepped out, dropped the cleaning equipment, and led me in a dash. I looked back to see the woman come out, glance at the sign over the door, glare at us and enter again.

"No sign of them," he said. "I called them by name. I think it sort of frightened somebody."

The train had just come in when we got back to the platform. Passengers were climbing into one car. Skip got on too and looked through it in case the girls had boarded without us seeing them, while I watched to see if they might arrive at the last minute. Skip kept glancing through the windows to see if I had stopped them until the train tooted its departure. He hopped off before the conductor bolted the doors, and we watched the coaches pull out of the station.

"I wonder if she caught an earlier one," he said.

We asked and were told the train before had left at five.

"I saw her at dinner at 6.30."

We returned to the Rymal house with Skip feeling relieved yet mystified. Lights greeted us from the coffee room windows, but we couldn't remember if we had turned them off or not. Creeping across the lawn to a window where the curtains were not drawn, we strained to see down into the lighted part of the room where we were rewarded with a full view of Cathy as she walked over to the bar. Skip hit his fist into his palm and growled for me to follow him back to the car.

"We'll fix this little girl for trying to upset me."

"Perhaps they just decided not to go," I said.

"That would be their excuse. Don't worry, I know my wife by now."

We drove in silence until we neared my street when Skip asked me to help him.

"When they get tired of waiting, Cathy will bring Nancy home. Tell her I've gone to New York, will you, Tom?"

"It's past my bed time," I said. "But I'll do it for the lark."

"You're a pal," he said. "While she's out, I'm going to go in and surprise her when she gets back."

Half an hour later when I was too tired to read yet trying not to fall asleep in my chair, Nancy brought Cathy up to see me in the hope that I would know something about Skip.

"He caught the 11.30 train for New York," I tried to look surprised. "We thought you two were on it."

Cathy clasped her hands to her face as she sank into a chair.

"Good Lord!" was all she said.

Nancy stared in disbelief at me, as if she thought I were capable of telling untruths.

"Didn't he look to see if we were on it?"

"Didn't have time," I said. "It was leaving the station when he got on."

Nancy tried to comfort Cathy who was complaining how heartless she was and how would Skip ever trust her after that. Since I was beginning to feel sorry for her, I left them and went to bed.

It was a fiery eye I got from Nancy at breakfast the next morning. Cathy had rung saying that when she had got home she found Skip sound asleep in bed after she had spent half the night touring the countryside trying to drive away an ugly sense of guilt. In defence of my complicity, I quoted the scriptures remarking that one should not judge others before one has judged oneself.

CHAPTER 13

The print in front of me stuffed my head with logic so that I became illogical, left my books, and telephoned Melanie. I told her to meet me at Dan's. Fifteen minutes later, we were facing one another in a back booth. The youth of Toronto was dressed in mani-colored sweaters as it bent over empty soda glasses sprouting twisted straws.

"You haven't phoned for over a week," she accused me.

"Studying hard," I said. "Anyway, you've been busy with dates in Hamilton and everything."

Her haughtiness was her woman's defence at being found out at trifles, which made me think the guy must have been a favorite.

"He's a family friend," she said. "I had to go out with him."

"It's okay," I said. "Fine." I smiled but she didn't like it.

"I don't think we should see so much of each other," she said.

The turn in our shaky relationship was anticipated. How often had I taken it, seen the last months stretched out behind me, and known that the road ended just in front? I knew I would try to delay as much as I could, try to loot the last little time.

"Why not?"

"I have to study for my exams after Easter," she said.

"Ah yes, the great cram for the finals."

"And you have to study too," she said.

Her thoughtfulness was not at all convincing; nor did she want it to be. But it was too early to object so that I let it ride. I tried to think of a subject to fill the interval: something she was obliged to know that would dull her mind and weaken her new resolution.

"What are you reading by Scott now?"

"We aren't reading him this year."

"Who are you reading?"

"Shakespeare."

I couldn't discuss Shakespeare with her; she would refuse. I took a sip of my coke and glanced at the counter to see Maxwell looking at us. I waved him over as salvation.

"Here are two *corpi dilecti* looking unusually sad," he said and pushed himself against me until he had more than enough room to sit.

"We were contemplating our horoscopes," I said.

"Superstitions," he shook his head, "are man's birthright and death knoll. Personally I like to live without looking at either end--those incredible convulsions pushing us in and out of a pantheistic serenity."

"I hadn't noticed your life was serene," I said.

He set his glasses lower on his nose and peered at me above the thick dark rims. "One remarks only on the exciting stalactites dripping action into the tomb of another's existence. The walls of my cave are flat, unwimpled. Therefore, you would notice nothing but your uncontrollable childish temper when I take your queen and proceed to trap your king."

"When I've fallen asleep waiting for your next move," I said.

As we joked, Melanie's dour expression changed to one of amusement at our strange humour. She at first laughed with us not quite understanding our private language, then she began to accept what was coming and joined us by laughing animatedly, enhancing our enjoyment and at the same time drawing our attention to herself, which we tended to forget.

"Our princess is beginning to sparkle," Maxwell said. "I didn't know that I affected women that way."

"She only does that when she's angry," I said.

"It's both of you," she laughed. "You're so funny."

As if by magic a good mood had settled comfortably among us, the unpleasantness of the moments before was forgotten. Melanie and I edged closer together so that when Maxwell's brunette stepped into the store and he took leave of us to meet her, we were once more reaching eagerly for the chance to romance.

I put my arm behind her and watched her breathe deeply. We left Dan's and the public lights and, walking quickly over the broad sidewalks, we came to a dark patch in a side street where we embraced.

"Do you still think we shouldn't see so much of each other?"

"No," she laughed and snuggled her forehead against the upturned collar of my overcoat. "Only I've been worried."

"About what, honey?"

"I didn't have a period last month and my second is overdue now."

She said it so casually that for a moment I had difficulty imagining anything so dramatic as birth. Moreover, the connection between abdominal movements and the creation of a life had not quite occurred as ever possibly happening to me so that I was content just to stare at her in the hope that what she said was merely academic.

"What the heck have you been eating?" I said, playing stupid.

"It's nothing like that." She looked at the ground. "I thought it might be and that's why I waited till now to tell you. I didn't want to tell you."

"Well, that's okay," I said. "It's probably something else because we were careful."

"I'm worried. I think I should see a doctor."

"Of course, my God! You go tomorrow."

"But you come with me."

"You don't need me," I said. I tried to laugh.

There was an insistence in her tone which I could not ignore.

"Okay. But it's sort of silly, isn't it?"

"Can we go in the morning?"

"Sure. We'll find some guy who won't know us from Adam and Eve..." I hesitated and then added, "and hope it's not the original sin."

When we parted she looked happier than at any time throughout the evening; yet I felt that that was so only because she had dragged me with her under the burden of her worry. As I walked back to the fraternity, I thought of my school mates, and acquaintance of my own age, who, I remembered, married quickly only to open their arms to a child five or six months later, and how shocked and dismayed it was to the rest of us by the unexpectedness of it all. Then we imagined ourselves immune from such a fate. The strength of society's laws always stood so well by us, we thought, and we could not disguise a sigh of relief that it had happened to someone other than ourselves. If I, too, now had been caught in the trap of society's laws, then my plans for the future would be ruined: my hopes for a career in law, my love for the adventure of exploring life, my pride at being an individual to decide as I wished, all would be swept into an ocean of grief, there to drown and leave me stranded in the bleakness of my duty to mother and child waiting for me to earn their daily bread. The price of desire was too high. True, the desire was worth the indulgence; it was the supreme and absolute union between two individuals. Sacred, ecstatic, exhilarating, yes, but it should be liberating, not menacing to our lives when separated. I could live without Melanie and she without me, but that was no reason why we should not have experienced happiness now and then freely without obligations. If we were to reserve our right to love only our life-mates, we could not say we were truly living, and our desire would soon be our death. Often marriages have nothing to do with love, but everything to do with drudgery. Should marriage be the terrible price of desire? I do not think so.

The low hard banks of dirty snow clung to the lawns and my foot bounced off the rough surface, throwing white-brown sparks in the lamplight. Bleak mid-February, still freezing, lay heavy in my head, weighed low in my heart.

Although Melanie and I had taken precautions, nature had triumphed; she out-played and out-maneuvered us and came up trumps. Ah yes, nature makes gamblers of us all. The innocents have to learn from their mistakes, dig into their own resources, or into the pockets of their parents, and keep digging until they get smart enough to win. Then they keep on playing until in the end they find they have played for nothing. But I thought I was going to gamble with many partners continually for the sheer sake of the game, enjoyable when winning, and definitely not boring. Now I was the loser.

In sudden anger, I rushed at a stretch of ice, felt my soles stick on cinders, and I fell on the cement where I rolled in the thickness of my coat until I sat up, sensing the brutal shock of my fall vibrating through me, giving me the sensation of physical fear.

"Are you hurt?"

Maxwell had gripped under my arm, and, on his insistence, I got to my feet.

"Feel like a game of chess?" I asked.

"At this hour?"

We sat in the dark downstairs under the solitary light from a table lamp. As I watched the squares, I took comfort in the intellectual pastime. As we played, I warmed to the solace of friendship that was not worrying so I could plan my moves and enjoy the power of controlling under my hand the wooden figures so unlike those of flesh and blood.

CHAPTER 14

Melanie came to meet me at the Hall the next morning. I saw her waiting behind the high iron grill as I walked through the yard, the high-domed building of the Palace of Justice behind me. The hard snow was lying forlornly about me. She was wearing a black coat, too, which made our meeting more sombre.

"Do you know someone to go to, Tom?"

"No," I said. "We'll walk along until we see a sign that doesn't look presumptuous."

We walked about two blocks during which I forgot to look, when Melanie put her hand on my arm.

"There's one, and his office hours are now."

The long narrow waiting room ran up to a door, which opened every so often to allow the patients in and out. Ahead of us were older people who didn't look sicker than we, but we felt as old as they. As I sat wondering what was each person's trouble, it struck me that they too might be guessing about us. Perhaps the same thought came to Melanie because she began to fidget, shifting her position in a creaky wooden chair. She twisted her lips and began to chew nervously at them. I fetched a magazine for her but that only made her nervousness more noticeable because she flipped one page brusquely after another merely glancing at the photographs, reading none of the printing, yet industriously turning every page from cover to cover. After a few moments of listening to the crack of the pages, I wanted to seize her arm and make her read, make her be still. The room had shrunk to the two of us sitting side by side, the object of a dozen prying eyes.

Then it was her turn to go through the door. I took the magazine when she went and stared at the big black photograph of the hull of a ship tilted bow-high and sinking. A few moments later, she reappeared with face flushed crimson, a sign of having made a terrible mistake I hoped, but she brushed by me on her way to another room. A small, Slavic-looking doctor stood at the door and tilted his wrinkled balding head at the cane-toting old lady, who made hypochondriacal queries and managed to recite several dozen minor ailments punctuated by serious surmises until Melanie came back. The doctor appeared again at the door, and I left my chair to worm past him, to stand by the seated Melanie, to stare at a desk of silver and brass gadgets, tools for the human body, to wait for him to ask me to be seated in the heavy leather cushions of an old chair where I sat with bowed head, inconsolable at the thought of birth.

"Is there no possibility of having an abortion?"

"Very little possibility. The church is strong." The doctor paused to rub his chin. "They are suspicious now because many have been discovered. To be safe, you should spend the night in the hospital but now that's too dangerous. Last month two doctors lost their licenses and paid heavy fines. Now no one will risk it."

"Isn't there anyone?" Melanie insisted in a voice as pale as her face.

"There is always a mid-wife." The doctor shrugged his shoulders. "But there is the danger of infection. It's a simple operation but you should have it done in a hospital. I'm afraid it will be expensive because whoever performs it risks his livelihood."

He was a sympathetic fellow. For Melanie he was the father figure in a gown of white hope. For me, he was a hypocrite suggesting where else we might go yet not volunteering to do the job himself.

"I'll inquire for you," he told Melanie. "Ring me after the weekend."

When we went, he said, "Why don't you get married? It's not as bad as all that." He smiled.

The waiting-room went by in a blur. The hall clicked with our footsteps. Melanie's voice was still pathetically frightened and it jarred me with its shrillness.

"I can't make it out. The time when he said it happened was in the middle of a period."

I didn't give a damn. I wanted to go where I didn't have to think about it. All we could do was wait and hope. Why worry about it?

ROMANCE

"If you haven't enough money, Tom, I have some saving bonds I can cash. Mother won't know."

I didn't have enough money, really. Who has enough money at anytime for anything? I kept thinking of the injustice of such a simple operation costing so much money.

"If he doesn't find anyone, Tom, maybe he'll tell us about a midwife."

The whole rotten business stank in my nostrils as I envisaged thick slimy naked arms of a woman with a washerwoman face.

"Tom, you don't want to marry me, do you Tom?"

"No, I don't want to marry you, Melanie."

We stopped and waited for a traffic light to change colour. We were alone together in the big drab crowd. Trucks rumbled past our faces. The thumping of their chassis echoed deeply in the gray vacuum within me.

"You don't want to marry me, Melanie."

People began to move on either side of us. We moved too, and I wanted to get out of the crowd and get away from her. There was a soda bar; its glass doors showing us a haven from the street.

The waitress gave us a happy smile. She was a teen-ager hired for her figure. She brought us coffees.

"We'd be no good together," I said. "You don't love me and I don't love you."

I was as much in love with the waitress as I was with Melanie, at that moment.

"It would be better to see if we can get it done," she said somberly.

I watched her twist her tiny serviette around her finger.

"Some people get married and then they divorce afterwards," I said. "But that's not for us, is it?"

"When I get married," she spoke suddenly, almost proudly. "I want a husband who'll stay faithful to me. I want a man all to myself."

I glanced shyly away from her.

"A man I can be proud of as my husband."

I saw shiny steel scissors snipping out a row of paper men. Swallowing the rest of my coffee, I twisted in my seat to show I was impatient for her to finish.

"Phone him after the week-end," I said, "and don't worry."

"I want you to be with me when I phone," she said.

Inwardly I groaned. I hated her determination to make me take my share of the burden.

"It'll have to be late Monday," I said. "After my lectures in the afternoon."

We arranged to meet: I agreeing with her directions, she out of necessity, taking the lead. We parted in the street.

"If mother found out, it would kill her," she said. "I'm afraid she'll suspect something's wrong. She always knows. I can stay in my room and study most of the time."

Shocked, I hurried in the opposite direction. It seemed incredible that she was telling the truth about her mother, that she could be that drastic about having an illegitimate grandchild. And I resented this domination of her parents over Melanie's feelings because indirectly they dominated me. Now Melanie had succeeded in making me a conspirator against her mother's life. I didn't care if her mother lived or died; but I did care if it was I who killed her.

A street car stopped by me, and the crowd waiting at the stop surged forward to board it. Pete Miller was in it. He waved when he saw me.

"Cathy's having a party next weekend. See you there!"

He was swallowed by the doors and carried away amidst masses of overcoats. I had seen no marks left from his accident; his spirit had not been dented. He was a symbol: man's hope for survival in a world of women.

CHAPTER 15

When I arrived home Saturday, Nancy informed me that we were invited to attend a small buffet party at the Rymal's house that evening. I walked with my sister the several blocks uphill to where we found a red M.G. parked in the street.

"I wonder who owns the sporty automobile," Nancy said, her eyes widening.

"Just the man for you," I said. "You'll see."

We were ushered to the right of the main hall into a room holding a handful of guests seated about a fireplace. Cathy came to meet us, and she introduced us to three couples who were in their late twenties and thirties and three young ladies and three young men, including Pete Miller. We then joined the circle, and I sat and watched Cathy's expert hosting as she directed several conversations at once, never seeming to butt in, but very smoothly adding words where necessary to bridge a gap or to stimulate a new interest, so that soon everyone was feeling at ease and conversing with their neighbor without any noticeable shyness. Skip then made an entrance, fashionably late and charmingly delighted to see his guests with a touch of concern at keeping them waiting. I had to admire his poise and his seemingly perfect partnering with Cathy. He, however, looked more surprised than was necessary when he saw Pete. It was obviously Cathy's party with the guests selected by her.

Pete was more subdued than I had ever seen him before. He conversed quietly and maturely, concealing his boyish traits under a slight frown of affected seriousness such as a Boy Scout might wear when asked to collect dues from his fellows. I saw Nancy's eyes widening at him as they did at his car, and within a few minutes, she had managed to make him lean across the fronts of several people to converse with her. He soon was obliged to take a chair beside her where he folded his arms in a serious manner before Nancy made him smile and then encouraged him to flirt with her.

"Peter, your glass is empty," Cathy accused him while she came forward to take it. "Come, there's lots more sherry." She took him by the arm to coax him to the sideboard.

Nancy drained her glass in a twinkling and held it out to Pete with a smile. "I'd like some too, please." It was as if she were giving him a return ticket.

"I hear you're in law," a man with sharp features bent into my vision and smiled narrowly.

Trying to keep my eye on Pete's way of handling the two girls, I heard at the same time the man say he was in steel.

"Oh yes, the company," I said.

Pete was saved by Skip's intervention. Cathy had to play wife to her husband's whim and verify his statement to a disbelieving couple.

"A lot is going into that new bridge they're building. In Sales, that is my department, we're rushed off our feet at this time of year."

By the accent on "my", I knew he was the head of his department and proud of it. But I sensed that he was trying to present himself as being not only equal to everyone else in the room but also above them.

"When you graduate don't forget about our law firm. Come and see me if you need any help."

His wife turned her head on this word 'help' to smile graciously. Her face was as round as his was sharp so that her smile seemed warmer.

"Those firms are headaches sometimes," I said. "There's so much legal quibbling going on with all those strikes you have."

He looked as if I had struck him. "We don't have many!"

As this was no time to argue, I said that I was alluding to his competitors, and his wife interrupted with an observation on the rising cost of cigarettes.

"It's getting harder to get cigarettes across the border now," Mr. Daw said. "The customs are getting tougher. The last time my wife and I were in Buffalo we drove back with a load under the front seat. We almost had a heart-failure when we saw them search under everything removable from the car in front of us. It's a feeling I don't want to ever go through again. With cars lined up behind you so you can't back away, and just that little roadway with the policemen on both sides. Boy!" His mouth sunk as his description brought back his terror. "But they let us through right away. I know a fellow who goes to New York, buys a suit, and wears it back, carrying the other. That's a smart one, isn't it?"

Skip had caught on to the tail end of the conversation. "Everybody does it. Cathy and I brought back lots from our honeymoon. Everything we were wearing was new."

Mr. Daw chuckled. "They must have known you were newlyweds or they wouldn't have let you through, eh, don't you think?"

Skip refused to be condescended to. "Hardly. After a month's travelling, we'd lost that primordial freshness."

He scored with the word and left Daw like a sprawled goalkeeper who had lost sight of the puck. But Daw immediately forced a small laugh, although it met Skip's back as he walked away.

"He's been reading a lot of books," he said to me. "Primordial! think of that!"

I had no time for reflection because at that moment Cathy invited us to help ourselves from the buffet table in the next room. There was but one server, and he brought us wine, after which he went, leaving bottles opened ready for us to serve ourselves.

As one of the girls invited was presumably meant to partner me, I spoke with a brunette and held her plate while she helped both of us. My experience with Melanie anchored my spirit, so that I found it difficult to meet with this girl outside of the grayness which filled me within. When she saw my gloom, she became gayer, which accented the contrast of our moods and discouraged me all the more. Soon, attracted by the shy aggressiveness of an all-Canadian boy, she left me.

"You must eat, Tommie dear."

Then Cathy was no longer the lovely girl who wore blue, nor the feline in black slacks; she was flesh and blood that I wanted to grapple to me and hold until the dull weight in my heart and head could disappear under the magic.

"Here now, finish your wine like a good boy--and let me give you some. And heavens! Put something on your plate." She went at the call of someone, while I drank for forgetfulness.

Pete came beside me. Holding two plates, he leaned across the table, his eyes darting between dishes.

"You never said a word to me, that you had a sister, son!"

Nancy was watching us with apprehension. I gave her a sick grin to show that I wasn't in the mood to throw aspersions over her respectability.

"Where's the bloody macaroni," Pete said. "I've only had two pieces."

I pointed an index finger at a plate in front of him.

"Aren't you eating?" he said.

I watched him pile up his plate.

"Don't give Nancy so much," I hinted. "She's genteel."

"She's like all the other dolls," he said. "When she sees how much I've given her she'll get a kick out of pushing it onto me."

Confident he walked away, beaming. I saw him swoop down on Nancy, who had begun talking with Skip. Everyone was in small groups again and some had wandered back into the first room. I sensed my aloneness and wished I hadn't come. Cathy saw me again but this time she approached, accusation in her eyes.

"Don't you like my party?"

"Not nearly as much as you," I said. Impulse gripped me hard. The room with its people suffocated me. "Let's take a walk."

Smiling slightly in curiosity, Cathy led me into the hall as if she intended to show me something. We entered a room to our right where she clicked on a table lamp. Its light streamed over the jaded colours of a naturalistic painting making the canvas look like the bright fanned jewelry of a peacock's tail. She let me take her in my arms and kiss her long.

I wanted to make love to her but she held my hands and moved away.

"What's wrong with you, Tommie? What's the matter?"

I wanted to hold her close and put my forehead on the soft skin of her neck.

"Behave yourself, Tommie."

There was nothing for me but the blackness that enveloped my whole being. In one last effort, I seized her arms and dragged her against me, but she thrashed out in terror so that, disgusted with her misunderstanding, I let her spring free.

"Tommie!" she gasped. "What's come over you?"

I put my hand to my forehead and pressed against it in disappointment. "I just wanted you for a while."

"Are you mad? Skip's in the next room."

"Oh, it's not that! It's not that!"

An easy chair gaped and I fell into it.

"Well, you had better come back with me," she said roughly.

"I'll sit here alone," I said. "If you'll be so kind as to leave me."

Skip strode softly into the room. His face strained to control hints of jealousy. "What's the matter, darling? Why aren't you with the others?"

"Tommie was feeling sick," she said.

He relaxed and came toward me slumped away from them.

"Something you ate, Tom?"

"Leave me alone," I said. "I'll be out in a while "

Skip took Cathy by the arm, and I saw her look concernedly back at me as she began to think that perhaps she hadn't understood me and that now it was too late to try.

"We'll let the poor boy sleep it off," Skip's voice came back from the hallway.

But when left alone, I became more awake, and my perversity left me. The large room with its one light aroused my conscience once more. I needed companionship more than anything; and so I went back to the party where I had to turn sheepishly away from Cathy's stare.

I crossed to where a foursome was seated--three girls and a man--they welcomed me. One of the women wasn't bad. In her early twenties, she had gone to boarding school with Cathy. Soon we were on good terms, and I knew I would get her phone number before the party was over. We liked each other from the first moment, you could say.

"No, mother won't let me work," she smiled. "But I want to and father thinks I should."

"I know what you're going through," another girl sighed.

"Why don't you just get a job as I did and then tell them at home," the last girl said. "Then they'd have to accept it."

"You don't know my mother," she grimaced.

"It's a prison for you too," the young man said. "You get locked away in a house where you can't meet anybody."

"And you won't find the man," took up the last girl who had designs on the young man.

"So you'll fritter your life away for your mother," sighed the other girl, who was playing a second fiddle to the last girl for the young man.

"Oh no!" she laughed. "They want me to get married. They've even picked out men for me. How funny they are in their old Victorian ways, don't you think?"

"Funny," I said, "but vicious. Parents are a pernicious influence on the minds of the young."

"Why?" she said surprised.

"Because they lace the new generations with their old tradition. They warp natural expression."

"That's quite right," said the young man. "My father warped my natural expression. I wanted to be a concert pianist, but he wouldn't give me the money to study."

The last girl looked sympathetically at him while the other one sighed. The general mood was one of a generation being thwarted.

I invited my girl, for at that moment she was mine more than anyone else's, to fetch some wine with me. Our glasses became red and softly we chugalugged until they were transparent again. I persuaded her to drink two more with me and then, putting my arms about her, I smiled back at Cathy's disapproval.

"She doesn't like us being happy," I told my girl. "We must be respectable. Her family stays respectable by selling a liquid to make other people happy and unrespectable."

"We're being respectable," she smiled encouragingly.

Nancy and Pete stopped to talk to us. My sister was always serious about whom I was interested in at the moment; she was Bulldog Drummond looking for clues.

"Well, Tom, are you not going to introduce us?"

My girl had met Nancy at a wedding two years ago. While they roamed over the names of friends with a joy that may be called frenzied, Pete and I were left on our own.

Pete snapped up an olive and flipped it in his mouth.

"My dog does it better than me," he said.

"How old is he?" I said.

Pete held out the five fingers of his hand and then reached with them for another olive.

"Did you train him?" I said.

Pete spun on his heel. "No, siree." His motion carried him way over onto the other foot so that he flipped his arms to keep his balance. "We bought him like that."

I helped myself to an olive and listened to Nancy reciting some delightfully amusing gal-adventures with many exclamations.

"When are we gonna have that squash game?" Pete asked

"When you invite me."

"Tuesday at four?" he said. "Meet me there."

Cathy appeared. Ignoring me, she looked into Pete's eyes.

"Hi kitten," he said.

"Pete, will you help me carry in the coffee?"

Nancy left the rest of her anecdote to my girl's imagination. She turned to smile broadly at Cathy. "Tommie, will help you, dear. Pete and I were just about to take some more wine. He's very thirsty, aren't you, poor Pete?" Nancy put her arms around his arm.

Cathy then put her arms about his other arm. "But he's the only man I can really trust to do this very important job."

"Can't you trust Tom?" Nancy protested.

"Frankly no!" Cathy said.

"I'll be gone for only a minute," Pete explained to Nancy.

I saw my poor sister losing faith in herself again and giving way to that imp of a temper.

"Oh, you don't have to do what your hostess says."

"He's not!" Cathy cried. "He's doing what he wants."

She gave Pete a sudden pull, but Nancy was quick enough to hold tight before his arm got away from her. Pete's blond curls jumped with the jerk.

"Let go," Cathy said.

"You let go," Nancy gritted her teeth.

"This is my party and you have to do as I say. Now let go." She tugged Pete for several feet, and he began to laugh.

"You're disgracing us all," she glared at Nancy.

Skip stepped over to us and both girls dropped their treasure under his threatening frown. Pete continued to laugh as if he were tickled.

"Can't you stop that bloody cackle," Skip's fingers twitched with the effort of refraining from seizing his guest.

Some of the other guests noticed the drama and turned to snicker about it to their little groups.

"Come, Nancy," Skip said. "Let's not lose our tempers."

"All right that's dandy," Nancy said. "You go with Cathy, Pete. We hope you come back within the next hour."

Skip frightened and uncertain, glanced between Cathy and Pete before deciding what to say. "You watch your step, mister."

"Skip!" Cathy cried. "What a thing to say! Where have your manners gone tonight?"

He stiffened. "I'm sorry, darling."

"Come along, Peter. I need your help."

With tongue in cheek, Pete looked back at Skip as he followed Cathy from the room. Skip glowered after him, his brows furrowed in the wrath of Hercules. I turned to speak to my girl and found that she had slipped away to converse with a fellow in another group. Nancy, Skip and I, disgruntled all, came together like the Big Three to smoke peace pipes while we dreamt up our revenges.

"How did that guy ever come to plague me?" Skip said.

"Oh, it's not him," Nancy said. "It's someone else who plagues you."

Skip looked at her, and I suppose the memory of his first dates came to disturb him because he said nothing in Cathy's defence.

"What do you say we set up some bridge tables, Tom?" he said.

"Okay," I said, "if you can get me a certain partner." I nodded at the girl in mind and Skip and Nancy smiled.

Within ten minutes enough tables were arranged for card playing so that when Cathy came back leading Pete with the coffee, she met the sudden alteration of her plans.

"Bridge, everybody," Skip cried. "Choose your partners." Like the great pal he was, he guided my girl away from her new friend to where I was standing innocently eating olives, and he left us.

"Where did you go to?" I said. The only way I could play the finders-keepers role was with a sense of humour, otherwise I would hate myself.

Reddening, she gave me an excuse and came back like a dog to its master. First, I presented her with a glass of wine, which made us comrades again. And then I escorted her to a table under the watchful eye of the forsaken one, who, to my relief, was placed eventually at the far end of the room. Skip and someone's wife sat at our table and since that someone's wife was as bad at cards as I was, the game was fairly even with all hopes for a win alternating between my girl and Skip. The part I like the best in bridge is when I'm asked to lay my cards on the table; it is more interesting to see one's partner's mistakes than one's own. We all of us had our coffee beside us and then Cathy later brought around some chocolate cake. An hour or so left us in rosy comfort before I noticed that Skip was getting uneasy again.

Unfortunately at the next table, Nancy and partner were playing opposite to Cathy and Pete. My sister was a shark when it came to winning at cards so that, as her partner seemed to play well, it was not difficult to imagine why Cathy had begun to fuss.

"Man!" Pete cried. "Am I lucky. That's the first I've won."

"That doesn't matter at all sweetykins," Cathy said unconvincingly.

There was a pause in which I noticed Skip trying to concentrate on his hand so that he could pull out the best card.

"Nancy seems to have all the luck tonight, Pete darling," Cathy said. "We'll have to sit back and watch her play."

I knew Skip had always expected too much from Cathy. From the look in his eyes, I sensed that he had expected her only to 'darling' him. But Cathy was becoming something of an anarchist with her endearments. It was becoming obvious too that she didn't mind endearing Pete.

"Shall we change partners?" Nancy suggested. 'Perhaps we'll be more even then."

"No," Cathy said. "Peter and I are just getting used to each other, aren't we darling?"

"Yeah," he said, "in some ways, but not with these cards."

Skip looked round at them, but Cathy ignored him.

"Trump," my girl said and brought him back to us.

Laughter broke out from a table where Mrs. Daw's face grew as red as that of the red man with her.

"At least some people are enjoying themselves," Skip said loudly enough for Cathy to hear.

Pete then laughed so pointedly at the tone in Skip's remark that we all became conscious of a triangle that was developing with Cathy as the third point.

"Perhaps if you paid more attention to your game, darling," Cathy drawled, "you would enjoy yourself more."

I saw Cathy shake slightly at her boldness. I would never have given her the credit for having enough courage to ridicule Skip in public. And I was surprised too when Skip broke into a superficial laugh and commented that his wife was very funny. For a few minutes there was no sound save the sharp slap of cards as they were snapped onto the table.

"Trump," my girl said.

Pete took off his jacket and hung it over the back of his chair, exposing his braces that ran down his white shirt front. This action, of course, finished him with Nancy, who regarded him as if he were an ape who had just escaped from his cage, but Cathy didn't seem to mind. She looked at him as if to intimate that his making himself at home in her home brought them closer together.

"Would you like a cold beer?" she asked him.

When he nodded acquiescently before frowning at his cards again, Cathy asked Skip to fetch beers for those who wanted it. Since our game came to a stop, when Skip went, I went with him.

"A married man is his wife's butler," I said.

He grunted and held the kitchen door open for me.

"In this case a cuckold too," he said.

"You're being silly," I said. "I've known Cathy since we were children. She's always been a flirt and just a flirt. She'd never go to bed with just anybody. She's just the adventurous type who likes to control her adventures."

Skip jerked the ice-cube box forcefully from where it was stuck in the frigidaire. "I don't care what you tell me, Tom, I know she's not easy to live with. I haven't really relaxed with her since our honeymoon."

"And you never will," I said, "until you learn to give her a little free rope."

He handed me a bottle opener, and I set to work on the bottles he brought out of the lower level of the frigidaire.

"I hope they're not too cold," he said.

"You've turned into a social worrier," I accused him. "Everything's thin ice under you now."

I watched the heads form in the glasses.

"You're right," he said. "I shouldn't be so damned afraid all the time."

I tasted from a glass and smacked my lips. "Rymal's the best for your money."

"God! How I'm sick of that," he said.

"How could you be?" I said. "Look what it's brought you."

Skip nodded his head, and, looking at the kitchen table, he stood waiting to remember what came next. "When old man Rymal comes back, I'll be made a junior director. I guess it'll be more interesting."

He reached behind a cupboard and pulled out a wide tray which would carry all the drinks. We filled it up with the glasses.

"Just," he said. "Now back to Cathy's party."

When we arrived, we found that the card tables had been dismantled and that everyone was sitting in a circle in the adjoining room. We took beer around to those who wanted it and pulled up chairs on the outside of the circle to hear the red man tell a mystery story which I soon recognized as an adaptation from Poe. Consequently, I drank more beer than I should have because I was impatient for him to finish his over-exaggeration of the simple steps in the plot. I had to return for more when those who first hadn't wanted any changed their minds. In the kitchen, I had just opened three bottles when Cathy, suppressing an excitement, joined me.

"Oh! You're here," she said.

"Not afraid, are you?" I said.

She laughed. "No, Tommie dear." She had come for no purpose, yet she seemed to be waiting for something. I thought for a moment that she suspected me of robbing the kitchen.

"Are you bored with that story too?" I asked.

A toilet flushed on the floor above us. I heard the water moving in the pipes.

"Not in the slightest," she said in going out. "Everyone's enjoying it."

I looked around for some more bottles to open, and I wished someone in my family had been in the beer business. At the back of the frigidaire, I found some more and emptied their contents into glasses. When bearing my load, I stepped into the hall and saw an angry Skip confronting an angry Cathy with an indifferent Pete, who was at the foot of the stairway. Since their conversation appeared very private, I intended to slip by them, but Cathy used me as an excuse to lead them back to the others.

"Wait Tommie! Help him, Peter, please."

Skip seized her arm to prevent her from following Pete and me. I heard sergeant major tones. But then Pete went back to them.

"Leave her go," he said.

Skip glared at him in answer.

Pete grasped Skip's arm and forced it away from Cathy, who by now was looking frightened.

"Let's not get ridiculous," I said.

"Our husband here is the only guy who's ridiculous," Pete said.

Skip hit his jaw sending him on his back, but in throwing his whole weight, Skip had counted too much on the support of his poor leg and he had to grab the banister to keep from falling too. As Cathy rushed to kneel down beside him, Pete sprang up ready to revenge himself, but Skip easily blocked his blows, and, furious, he seized his shoulders and threw him against the wall.

"Get out of the house."

"Whose house do you think this is?" Cathy cried at him.

"It's okay," Pete laughed suddenly. "I'll go."

"Don't go," Cathy said.

"It's a long drive home," Pete said. "Will you get my coat for me?"

Swallowing hard, Cathy went into the room to retrieve his jacket while Pete looked in the hall cupboard for his overcoat. Skip stood biting his lips while Cathy helped their Toronto guest into his clothes, and he watched her step out to accompany him to his car. Up to now I had forgotten the tray, but it suddenly seemed so heavy that I had to put it down.

"A fine mess!" Skip said.

We went to the window together where we watched Cathy and Pete embrace by the side of the car.

"Damn it!" Skip said.

I shrugged my shoulders and returned to pick up the tray. I had enough worries of my own. When I got back to the round circle, Mr. Daw was reciting "The Ballad of Sam McGhee," and the young man who had turned my girl into his at one point in the evening had now taken advantage of my absence to sit on the arm of her chair which he rode like a knight of yore in the saddle. Discouraged by this double deflation to my optimism, I quietly set the beers down and left the room.

Cathy came in the front door as I was leaving. She was furious.

"Where's Skip?"

I looked toward the stairway because that was where I thought he had gone.

"Just like him to leave me alone to do the entertaining," she said. "But you aren't going?"

Her dismay at hosting three girls without males made itself known to me in that question.

"I'm sorry," I said. "I'm feeling sick."

I sensed her swearing never to invite me to another party. But Nancy came from behind us, and she was obliged to wear her mask of enthusiasm, to receive my sister's gushing compliments, and to wave us a friendly good-bye.

"Wasn't it awful!" Nancy said when we were a block away.

"It wasn't very lucky," I said.

"You weren't either," she smiled.

I didn't think of the girl at the party, though; instead, she made me think of Melanie's taut, anxious face searching for me on Monday afternoon.

CHAPTER 16

"I've been waiting half an hour," she said.

"I'm sorry," I said. "Our Prof. was keen on his subject and didn't want to stop. I've never known it to happen before."

There was a vacant phone booth standing near the corner. She stepped in and held the door for me.

"There's no room," I said.

"Yes," she said. "I want you. If I faint you'll have to catch me."

I stepped in and squeezed the door shut behind me. Her fingers found a strip of paper in one of her pockets, and then I watched her dial.

"Hello doctor, this is Melanie."

At first his voice sounded gruff while he proceeded to disappoint us, but it softened when he heard the dejection in her own as she asked him again about midwives and any other hope, any other straw in the wind.

When we left the booth, I sensed how hopeless, how desolate, how unhappy she was. Her face to the sloping lines of her body was weighted in gloom. It seemed that no matter how hard we hoped, we were destined to drown in the ocean.

"What did he say?" I asked.

Her mouth twisted in a rueful smile. "He plugged the marriage line again."

We walked for the sake of walking, not knowing where we were going, nor caring. Melanie wore an expression of indecision. I found myself in a barren land where there was nothing but rocks, and where there was nothing to search or know what to search for. And although we feared, there was nothing in the landscape that was really threatening to make us afraid. As if in a dream, we moved uneasily in our indefiniteness.

"I don't know what to do," I said quietly.

I shouldn't have spoken because I brought tears to her eyes. There was a small park on the corner. It had been one of the city engineer's afterthoughts created out of the extra space left over when squaring up the streets with private residences. We turned along the pathway and found a bench between two firs. There was no one else in the park as it grew dark in the late afternoon in February.

"We've got to do something," Melanie cried.

I glanced about to make sure there was nobody. I bent closer to remind her not to speak loudly.

"I've read about girls going away to have babies," she said. "But I couldn't do that with mother."

"No," I said, "you can't do that."

I thought of a kid of mine growing up thinking his parents were dead while I, the coward, pretended not to know of his existence.

"But we haven't much more time," she said. She lowered her head. "I'll be getting bigger and mother will notice." She began to swoon so that I sat against her and put her head on my shoulder.

After a few moments, I said, "Don't you think it better that we have the child?"

"Why?" she said quietly.

"Because it is sort of denying life, you know, Melanie."

"No," she said. "It's just fluid now. It's not a being. If we do something right away before it takes shape, it's all right."

I felt as if I had been ushered into a surgery room where my white-aproned confreres were discussing limbs crushed on the table before them. Melanie's voice had become as sharp as one of their shiny steel instruments. In the half light I shivered and my stomach was empty and raw.

"Besides," she added, "I just couldn't tell mother."

I put my arm about her, and, pressing hard against me, she gripped fiercely at my shoulders, and I felt the strength of her fear. We were players in a drama which was throwing our wills against the will of nature: a drama which had a Shakespearian symbol, this time a ghost of a mother.

"If we got married," I said, "would she care so much then?"

"It'd be better," she said.

"Maybe we should get married."

Melanie took her arm away and leaned back on the bench.

"What do you think?" I said.

"If we can't get a mid-wife," she said.

I sat very still. It was the first time I allowed myself to think that she didn't love me. I wondered if now she didn't hate me. My feelings for her were those of indifference. She was a body undergoing a biological adventure which was linked to me only by conscience. I felt no affection for her and if I had any sympathy it was not for her but rather for the situation in which she was caught, in which we both were caught.

"Don't worry," I said. "I'll find someone to help us."

"I'm sorry, Tom, but I just don't want to have a baby on my hands. And I don't want to ruin your career as well as mine. You probably think I'm heartless wanting to get rid of it."

"No, I don't," I said. "I want to get rid of it too."

"And my family would be disgraced and I'd have to quit college and I'd never be able to face any of my friends again."

"Yeah, I know," I said. "Okay, we'll get rid of it."

"An abortion is not a sin. Married people even have them."

"Sure," I said. "I know it's not a sin. Now don't worry."

I watched her twist her fingers in her hands while she sat rigid and looked glassily at the wet green of the winter grass.

"When can you find someone, Tom?"

"I don't know. In about a week, I guess."

"I hope."

I smiled weakly at her pitiful little misery. I liked her more now because she could easily have turned all her troubles onto me. I liked her because she didn't like me enough to marry me.

"It's getting dark," I said. "We should go."

"I don't want to go home," she said.

"Okay, phone and say you're having dinner with me."

As soon as I said it, I was sorry. She was going to be a nuisance who wouldn't go home after dinner and who'd want to stick to me as if I were her flotsam. I had too much studying to do and wasting my time with her would only make me think the more of what I should have been doing. And too, she was a reminder of what we were to each other now.

"Oh, mother's having friends in," she said. "I can't."

"That's all right," I said, with relief.

We stood up and stepped along the asphalt of the walk between small fir trees and blank flower beds. The street was bare of traffic and people. We noticed that the lamps burned feebly in the gray as if they were cheap ornaments for the street. The darkness was settling into the trees, and, by the time we had walked a block, it had slipped down to us. The houses behind their lawns began to show lights in the windows as their owners arrived home from offices. The dampness in the ground and pavement reflected the ochre from the lamps and made me yearn to be where it was dry and comfortable with happy people around a roasted dinner. I accompanied Melanie to within a few blocks of her house where we stood by the thick trunk of an ancient maple.

"It's getting colder," I said. "It might snow."

"We won't have anymore storms," she said.

I sensed that she didn't want me to go, yet we had nothing to say, and it was wet and cold.

"I don't want to go home," she said.

"But why? You've got nothing to be afraid of."

"I'm afraid I'll tell mother."

A car turning into the street flashed its headlights across us.

"Do you want to?" I said.

"No, but I'm afraid I will."

"Look, don't do that, Melanie, don't do that. Whatever you do, don't tell your mother. That'd be the end, that'd be the finish of both of us. Do you understand?"

"I don't want to," she said, "but I'm afraid I will."

"Well don't! I'm telling you, I can't do anything for you. Just keep control of yourself."

She bowed her head. "I'll try."

"'Cause if you did that, well, there'd be no way out of it for us. And anyway, I thought you were afraid of shocking her."

"Yes," she said. "I'll try not to tell her."

"Just hold on," I said. "I'll phone you at the end of the week."

"Can't I see you before then?"

I paused to swallow the irritation that had salivated in my mouth. "But there's no reason. Besides, I've got a lot of work to do and so have you." I remembered when she had said that to me, and I sensed the colour rise above my eyes when I realized she would think it was a phony excuse.

"When will you phone?" she said.

"Friday, before I go home."

"Aren't you even going to see me Friday night?"

I couldn't see her face clearly but she seemed to be between anger and tears. Her tone was accusing.

"All right," I said. "I'll phone you and we'll go out Friday night."

We said good-bye from three feet apart. When I had walked a ways, I looked behind me to see her disappear out of the light far down the street. I wondered if she really would be able to keep our secret when confronted with her mother's prying eyes. To me she had become a girl different from the one I had known. She had become a bundle of nerves. It was ironic, I thought, how when we could make as much love as we wished without fear, I couldn't bear thinking of her naked body without repulsion.

I resolved to ask Maxwell for advice, although I didn't know how he would take the news. Maybe we had played our last game of chess together.

CHAPTER 17

Between the high square pillars and from the front door frame of the medical school, the students streamed out from a lecture, all stooping under the weight of the words they had just heard. Maxwell was among them, and, when he saw me, he made the frat sign of salutation as he came to meet me.

"I looked for you last night," I said.

"I was in the thralls of a late date. Have you ever been mauled by a sexy brunette?"

"No," I said.

"Neither have I," he said. "Last night I was mauled but she was about as sexy as a moose. One of those over-grown red riding hoods from private school, you know."

"Again!" I said. "You have a mania for that type."

Maxwell, taking off his glasses, looked down his nose at me. "I beg your pardon," he said.

"What I mean is," I said. "You like those young creatures on the free weekends they get after being locked up with their sex dreams for three or four months."

"Yes, it's a pity," he sighed, settling his glasses back on his nose. "One has to keep the poor things under control. And they're so young too." He rolled his eyes looking like pin balls within the dark frames. "And so beautiful," he drawled.

"Sometimes," I said.

He sighed, and tucking his books under his arms, he sunk his hands in his pockets. "Well, what's your problem, Horatio?"

"Problem?" I said.

"When a lover of the fair sex admits that they are not all beautiful, he has a problem," Maxwell said.

"Where are you going now?" I said.

"Back to the frat."

"Walk by the U-grounds with me, will you? I've got to meet a guy."

We passed along a quiet avenue instead of the noisy main street.

"I got a girl in trouble," I said.

"Good going, Horatio, I always knew you were a man."

"Yeah, but I don't want to marry her."

"Naturally not."

"There's nothing I can do about it."

"I know the situation. I can see it in my crystal ball. She was tall, blonde and beautiful. Her name was Melanie and she would have been a happy piece for anybody."

"Cut the joking," I said. "I'm damned well worried."

"I know," he shook his head sympathetically. "You just don't want to see her go through the rigours of child birth."

"I'm only asking you because I wondered if you knew of any doctor or anybody who could help us."

"You have found, then, that the law, which your profession connives to throw over us, is a tough one, eh? You have discovered how faulty are the beams that hold up our so-called civilized society. You want me to be one of those guys, who, instead of blowing the ridiculous law out of existence where it belongs, sneak around it so that we can all still point to Church and State with pride. And all the time, we're too stupid to face the truth. The law is unnatural, but so fundamental to our hypocritical society that to change it would mean the rearrangement of the whole system, and that's too much like hard work--although the spirit in which the law was written is in danger of being found out for its very treachery. Not all of us suffer from it, but that's okay, not all of us suffer from cancer either. Tom, I don't like the idea of killing a life before it pops its head on this side of the world anymore than anybody else does, but unfortunately it's got to be done."

"Melanie said it wasn't really a human yet," I said.

"If you catch it within the first three months, you've got nothing to worry about. Anything could have happened to it. And if a natural accident happened would you say the blame was on the woman? Hell! You know your history. The layman's been fighting the Church since the Middle Ages on this idea. You know that, at one time if anybody mixed anything in test tubes, he was burned at the stake? Bloody superstition!"

"I didn't say it was wrong," I said.

"I know. I'm just explaining why I'll do it for you," he said. "And why you don't have to feel as if I'm doing you a favor."

"Can you?" I said.

"Officially no. I'd be thrown out of medical school if anyone found out."

"I don't want you to do it then," I said.

"Don't be stupid. You won't find anybody else unless you're damned lucky. If you do, you'll have to pay them. Those dregs of humanity live like blood suckers from the unhappiness of others. I feel like setting up an office with a big sign in red letters, 'Abortions Free of Charge', just to run those termites out of business."

It was comforting to listen to Maxwell rave. He lured the bitterness out of me by expressing it aloud. He gave the answer to my worries very simply and reasonably. His help was as great an event as Melanie's pregnancy because it was decisive.

"When do you think you can do it?"

"I'll have to find a place," he said.

"Melanie's nearly out of her wits."

"Next week," he said.

We were near to the squash courts, and I saw Pete approaching us.

"Here's my man," I said.

Maxwell turned aside and cut down the street to our right. I saw him hike his books to his other arm as Pete came close enough to wake up from a dream and recognize me. He bridged his hand over his eyes and peered at me to parody a sailor at sea.

"You ought to beat me. I'm short-sighted today."

"To tell the truth," I said. "I don't feel like playing."

We managed to establish that it wasn't because I was afraid of losing but merely an upset stomach that prevented me from racing him about the court with a series of brilliantly played shots. Pete too was glad to have a rest from his everyday sport. He admitted he was suffering from love-sickness, which, he said, I already knew something about because I had seen the lady to whom he would later refer. I replied that I had seen several ladies to whom he might be referring and that, as far as I knew, love sickness was harmless, never lasting for more than a week. He invited me to take a coffee so that we might discuss this delicate problem.

"If it won't hurt my stomach," I said.

When we were huddled over coffees, Pete explained that he was in love with Cathy, but with she being married, their position was difficult. He wanted me to tell him about her past and about the relationship between herself and Skip. I wasn't anxious to encourage his appetite for her because I knew that, if he plunged into their affairs, he'd be like a hippopotamus in a swimming pool causing a huge splash whereas the most that should happen should be a ripple caused by a child's sailboat tossed by warm understanding breezes. If Cathy wanted Pete, she'd have him whether Pete wanted her or not so that I became non-committal about the happily-married Burkes who were settling down respectably

ROMANCE

like seemingly faithful lovers in Hamilton society. Pete was convinced that Cathy liked him more than she did Skip. He'd liked her from the first moment, he said. He wanted me to suggest a way out of the predicament. I said to keep on going to see what would happen. If Pete and Cathy really loved each other then they'd prove themselves to be above marriage. On the other hand, their feelings for one another had a good chance of petering out when faced with the difficult issue of Skip, once they began playing around seriously.

"I'd tell you to stop seeing her," I said, "if I knew the power didn't lie in her hands."

"But to stop seeing her wouldn't prove anything, would it?" He opened his big innocent blue eyes at me.

"It would prove your candidacy for entering the Benedictine Order," I said.

He smiled and turned to watch a couple of young women walking by the window. A newsboy broke through the doors, and, hoisting his bag above his knees with one arm, he held a paper at us with the other. Peter paid for it.

"Then I'll just sit tight, man, and wait until she hollers for me. But I'm not going to her place to get socked in the jaw again."

Holding the paper below table level, he leafed through it before he halted at one page which he spread out for me to see. "An article here by my Minister," he said. "He sometimes writes things for the papers. He's smart."

I saw the unexpected yet peculiarly apt title, "Is miscarriage murder?" After what Maxwell had told me, its sudden appearance seemed uncanny.

"I'm Anglican," Pete emphasized. "He heads my church."

"Do you agree with what he says here?" I asked.

"You bet. He's smart. You can't go wrong by agreeing with him."

"Still, isn't murder a pretty strong charge?"

"Well, that's what it is," Pete slapped his knee. "If life has already started, then, according to the law, we shouldn't interfere with it. If it's called murder, then it's murder. Why some boobs are always questioning the law, I don't know. They all ought to be locked up in the hoosegow."

I felt meek beside him just then. When he spoke in such a way, he represented a mass of people, ignorantly powerful and ruthlessly determined. Beside him, Maxwell suddenly looked extremely insignificant. Since the subject had no interest for Pete, and too immediate an interest for me, we dropped it, finished our coffees, and agreed to play squash at a later date.

When I returned to the Frat house, I found a letter from Cathy for me. She must have asked Nancy for my Toronto address. I opened it with a curiosity heightened by presentiment. Her writing was of the thick squat girl-school variety in which the letters pushed up in round stubby formations from an imaginary straight line. It appeared that since the coming weekend was a long bank holiday, she was going skiing in the North and, since Skip couldn't ski with his bad leg, would I go with her? She was motoring through Toronto and would bring my ski equipment with her. We were meeting a party there. It was the last good snowfall of the year there.

At first I groaned because I had planned on getting a lot of law reading done over the weekend. I was far enough behind to start feeling stupid in some of the lectures. But I thought of how she would look in her ski costume and what a great chance it was to travel alone with her, and, after all, since her note seemed rather insistent, perhaps the invitation wasn't just platonic.

CHAPTER 18

About five that Friday, Cathy stopped her new blue Nash in front of the Frat house. From my window, I saw her step out of it. With the close-fitting ski slacks and smart-cut jacket, she could have been modelling for a magazine advertisement. Some fellows coming in the front walk turned round and gaped; only one of them had the presence of mind to whistle. I knew that when they saw me meet her, my prestige in the fraternity hierarchy would be considerably heightened. I began to wonder which would be better: to go directly down and meet her or to wait until she asked for me. By honking the car horn, however, she decided for me, and filling my pockets with the small last-minute things like money, handkerchief, and comb, I prepared to meet my lady love in as unaffected a manner as possible under the undoubtedly envious gaze of my student brothers.

When I reached the front hall, I caught her asking the houseman for me. She turned when he nodded at me, and our weekend began auspiciously with a bright blossoming smile. We walked to her car in high spirits, she telling me about the slippery state of the roads and of an amusing mishap she had had, so that I didn't remember to telephone Melanie until I was about to sit in the car. I excused myself with forgetting something and contacted Melanie with the hall phone. She had been waiting for my call because there was but one ring before she answered.

"It's all right," I said. "I've got somebody."

"Good?"

"As good as anybody," I said.

"Where shall I meet you?"

"I can't see you tonight, honey." My excuse sounded weak against the strength of her determination. If I hadn't explained that I had one foot in the automobile, she would have protested vigorously but as it was, the immediacy of my flight surprised her into a hopeless acceptance. When I was about to step into the car again, I saw Maxwell watching me as he approached from down the street.

"Private school?" he called.

"No; graduate," I answered.

"Hot dog!" he said.

Cathy whisked us along through streets where she paced our speed so that we broke through on green lights. Although Toronto seemed an endless series of districts, we eventually came to where the road dipped in a stretch of wild grass and young trees, a sign of the outskirts and a promise of the countryside to come. Snow still lay in patches, but the skies for the past week had been clouded, and the barometer had been quivering about freezing point in the expectation of a plunge.

"Tommie, we're in luck! Did you know it's been snowing where we're going? I heard the skiing was wonderful!"

"It was a great idea of yours," I said. "I haven't had a chance to ski all year. What made you think of me?"

"Who better for a safe, understanding escort?" she said.

"You've got me wrong," I said. "Nothing safe about me."

"Oh, but understanding," she said.

I was beginning to wish I hadn't come. All that effort of climbing hills and getting wet in the snow and dry in the clubhouse wasn't worth just a smile. I thought I would have to look forward only to the joy of skiing if I was to keep up my spirits, but then my spirit was too wet and dismal like the weather to foresee any joy in it. My thoughts must have expressed themselves across my face because Cathy began to laugh.

"I love you because you're so cute. Now cheer up."

"How can I when you expect me to be so unfriendly as to become understanding?"

"Darling, you can be as friendly as you like." She stretched her hand out to take mine and glanced back at the road in time to spin the steering wheel so that we missed another speedster shooting over the crest of the hill in the middle of the road. Fortunately the shoulder was strong enough to hold us until we got back on the asphalt. "We've always been friendly, but you must remember that now I'm married, and I want to be a good wife."

"What do you think I am?" I said. "The devil?"

"Of course not, darling. But you are dangerous, you know."

"I was under the impression it was the women who were the dangerous ones. They work it out so that it seems as if the men were making the advances when all the time they are the ones doing all the seducing."

"Tommie dear, I keep a pocket book on Freud in the dashboard compartment in front of you. Why don't you take a look at it? It might help you."

"Touché," I said. "That'll stop me generalizing, which is fine because I wanted to get more personal."

"Let's not talk about it, shall we? We'll see what happens."

"There you are, you see, you prove my point. If you're not going to seduce me, I can't make any advances, that is, safely."

"And we are now ten miles from the nearest town," she said. "So my darling, you be good!"

She switched on the headlights as it was getting difficult to see in the darkness and mist in front of us. The occasional

ROMANCE

farmhouses squatting darkly distant in the fields with only single lights glimmering from them gave the aspect of quiet hearths and lonely prayer meetings. The car lights at full range lit up the tall naked trees grappling in the air. By the roadside, cold stones glinted bleakly.

Our flight into pleasure was also an escape for me. That sordid world which had strangled me like a snake in Toronto was being left behind, and now I was free for three days of enjoyment when my conscience could rest morphined with the finer air. Decision could wait for my return, but, until then, the world had stopped turning, all obligation was dead and, most important of all, Melanie no longer existed.

"Tommie, will you light me a cigarette?"

She brought a package of king-size from her pocket, and, when I touched a match to the end of the white, the flavor cut inside at the roots of my nostrils.

"Look," I said, "you don't have to smoke to keep awake. When you're tired, I'll drive."

"Not a bit tired. But we won't stop for dinner. I've stocked sandwiches in the back seat."

"Say, you are practical," I said. "Why didn't you wait to marry me? I need a wife like you."

"Cause I didn't want to be a middle-aged bride."

"You think I'm not the marrying type," I said.

"Tommie, you won't get married until you have to."

I looked at the road being eaten up in front of us. "Not even then," I said.

It seemed strange to be sliding through the night with Cathy miles from anywhere. It was as if we were like souls flying over the earth and commenting objectively on our past life. I had a strong impulse to tell Cathy about Melanie, as if I were to make her my confidante, as if it didn't matter what I said because we were so alone and cut off from the problem itself that the time of the present floated in isolation from the time of the past and of the future, as if her reaction would be indifferent instead of vitally personal, and not that of the inhibited female shrinking from a monster who had violated her sex. But the impulse passed, and, remembering reality, I saw only her raven hair, her lovely profile, and the life that pulsated through her body.

If before her marriage Cathy had been fresh as the petals of a rose, now she was the rose itself in full, sensuous, mystical, all-compelling bloom. A summer rose she was, who would not fade for decades, I thought. If, before, she had acted with confidence, now was added the assuredness of experience. She was one of the gifted who could weather the ravages of life and show few scars. Sitting at the wheel, she could easily have been my pilot in many things. But she was two years my senior and far too beautiful.

We raced by roadside-houses strung out like little prisons, and I sensed the freedom and comfort of the car by contrast. At a crossroads stood a restaurant, small and dingy in its isolation. Cathy stopped there.

"Let's get cokes."

I ran over wooden planks sunk across puddles of ice and frozen mud until I reached the paint-peeling door which stuck then swung wide open to reveal shabbily dressed farmers sitting awkwardly round a table and playing cards. A small gray-haired woman fumbled with the icebox handle, so unaccustomed was she with my hurry. I was back swinging my cokes across the boards into the car where Cathy waited, then twisted toward me and embraced me for minutes which shocked me with the suddenness and force. We lay back limply, and, with the tips of my fingers, I played with fringes of her hair. Presently she sat up straight and grasped the steering wheel.

"Tommie, can you reach the sandwiches? I'm hungry."

The motor cleared its throat and we turned into the road. I saw the restaurant fade through the back window until it climbed into oblivion. The sandwiches were meat and cheese, travel fare on railroad lines. There were oranges too. I found the bottle opener low on the panel beside me and held the wheel while she took a swig. If affection was not allowed, at least there was tender communication as I held the wheel when she drank.

Now the ground was completely covered with snow. Small banks of white bordered the highway and sweeps of crystals lay across the black of the road. A round, red sign spelled the Indian name of the town which was common on the lips of city dwellers when the weather got hot and two weeks' holidays were merely a calendar month away. Cathy slowed the car to take the curves which I remembered from brief summer visits when I and other teenagers strolled with tanned limbs in white shorts and red sweaters under the pines. Cathy and I shot over the narrow bridge into the main street which was now deserted and where once ice-cream bars swarmed with holiday makers, and penny arcades jukeboxes blared out rhythms to the tastes of long-haired, pinball shooters. A cement platform stretched out into the lake. Where once dinghies would bob on short lines moored to it there was now a lone lamp beaming over the bleak emptiness. Our Nash picked up speed, and we left memory behind in a swirl of snow.

Two hours later, Cathy was tired. I stepped into the night, cold against my chest, and walked around the car. With the skis strapped to the roof and their ends pointing over the hood, the car looked like a spaceship waiting for its captain to blast it off to its destination. The feminine co-pilot was worn out. At first, she tried resting with her head on the back of the seat but, admitting that the position was uncomfortable, she lay her head on my shoulders and caught forty winks to re-assemble her forces of endurance against the unseen enemy of the future. Cathy stirred and nuzzled my neck.

"Oh Tommie, I'm sorry." Her sigh quivered deep with meaning, striking at chords somewhere within me but playing no tune that I could recognize. "I'm such a stinker."

"No, you're not. You're wonderful," I said. I rubbed my chin in the strands of her hair and felt their softness slip over the smooth warmth of her scalp.

"I wish things could work out for us, Tommie."

The steering wheel seemed glued to my hands, and linked as if only supernaturally to my body, as I seemed to float up and look on at myself, gasping with unbelieving joy. I dared not to turn to park because I knew the moment was not right and that I would only ruin that exhilaration I felt at the time.

"But I'm silly, aren't I? Just a silly dreamer who doesn't know what she wants."

"Why won't it work out?" I said.

"Oh Tommie, do be quiet and let me go to sleep. You're like an alarm clock with such serious questions."

Within an hour we arrived at the log lodge looming large in the dark. Leaving the car, I unstrapped the skis and Cathy pulled our cases from the trunk. A round, merry-faced woman smiled sweetly at our tired approach. She took Cathy to her room while I sat below watching for milk to boil. When Cathy came down again, our hot chocolates were ready.

"A group arrived over an hour ago," she said excitedly. "I've asked her to bring the register to see who they are."

When she had the ledger in her hands, she slipped her finger quickly down the names. "Not come yet," she breathed.

"Who hasn't come yet?" I asked.

"A lot of people," she blushed. "There are lots to come yet."

"Oh, I thought you meant someone special," I said.

"Tommie, how could you?" She looked a faked hurt at me. "Finish this, darling. I'll see you in the morning."

As I watched her climb the stairs, intuition told me I was being used. Her cup of chocolate was half-empty like her words to me. But taking it, finding some comfort in that it had belonged to her, I swallowed from it.

Under warm blankets in the fresh air of low mountains, I slept deep and awoke quickly. A pale sun rolled along the white edge of one of the hills as I dressed. Downstairs sat a group of eight woollen-dressed youths, rosy-cheeked over white porcelain, and laughing in unison as I approached. As I knew no one, I lingered about feeling that I belonged yet not quite to their party. We were waiting for breakfast, mine to be served separate, perhaps with Cathy, if she would only come down and save me from the curious eyes inspecting my person, as if my aloneness were evidence that I was socially an outcast.

"Uh, the young lady coomin' soon?" the red, round-faced white-aproned woman inquired. She put two cups steaming on the oil-cloth, and I rose using this excuse to retreat up the stairs.

"Walk in," Cathy's muffled voice said. She was dressed sitting on a stool and combing her hair in front of a mirror. Her beautiful femininity transformed the bare board-plaqued room into a bright colorful spectacle made delicate by the fragrance emitting from the bottles on her dressing table and gradually filling the atmosphere.

"I'm being iced out downstairs. I need your introduction."

She jumped from the bureau, and eyes twinkling, held out her cheek for me to peck. Taking my hand in mock solemnity, she led me to near the foot of the stairs where,

ROMANCE

stopping, hand upraised, she addressed upraised faces--surprised, bemused, waiting.

"O low, coarse, vulgar ones, plain ignorers of true Roman virtue. Here is your king!" Amidst the laughter, we descended to meet her friends who now greeted me in excessive welcome.

None of them were over twenty-five, none were married, and none came from Hamilton. Jack, Jane, Alice and Paul, Ottawa, Toronto and Montreal. Gordie was short, thick, and otiose, the son of a banker. Ted looked eager, alert, full of loud hollow laughter, a representative member of his family's advertising company. All of them seemed as if looking for that right connection that meant more parties, more drinking, more women, more life, more money, a good balance in the bank account. Their hearty camaraderie was based on the promise that it might pay in the end, one never knows. Who was I? To them I might be the son of a Texas millionaire, and schooled in Switzerland. I might be the Hero of the weekend so that they could say later, "Did you know, we met this fellow Davis--Tom Davis--living in Toronto now."

Cathy and I squeezed together in front of scrambled eggs and bacon. Our hot coffees were brought to join us, and, through the wide window, the sun stared scarlet on the winter scene of white snow. Outside, we clamped on our skis, and I watched Cathy trek quickly to the forefront, the sportswoman on the lookout for dares. A tow rumbled, sounding like empty oil cans disturbed in the back of a shed, and I grabbed a handle to be swept up along the ski tracks, my toes stirring to keep me straight, away from the valley soon to sink in the distance. Copses of pines huddled on the hillsides, quiet in the peace, then I let go, my arms raised above me, as my handle and I obeyed different forces, horsepower and gravity. The shoving of one ski in front of another until a short climb, herring-bone style brought us to the rise among rises where we could choose among the paths for our descent, one as impressive as the other.

One after another, the skiers stood against the cirrus sky, and pushed against the snow to plunge circling below a crest. I watched Cathy go, her body-beautiful taking the rises, the sudden dips with an easy grace, a sharp style, colorful against the white. Too soon it was my turn. I kicked fine flecks from tanned slats and, moving, slid through masses of twinkling crystals first blurred then clearly wide-stretched to follow Cathy's trail, who was abruptly accelerating in her love for thrill and dodging away to overcome new crests, to elicit every inch of pleasure. The wind whistled past my ears, as excitement alerted me to what lay beyond the next jump or turn. Woods rushed by, a dead branch to leap, steep fall away to the right through a gap, and up, then bank, and down and on, pursuing the woman just ahead but out of sight.

She was waiting, twisted round to watch by a tall pine, as I swung in to the last dip and felt my muscles relax in the slowing comfort of having won an experience. My weight brought me easing to a stop beside her, and I saw humour crinkling around her eyes.

"Do you know what I've done? I've stolen you away from the others. That last high incline was irresistible and so here we are five minutes from the tow."

"I'm fagged," I said "Let's sit before we walk."

There were some rocks against the base of the tree, their ray-white faces poking above the snow. We half-sat half-lay, our skis forcing us onto one side so that we faced one another, propped on our elbows, skis overlapping.

"Speaking of fags," Cathy said. "Do you have one?"

I uncramped and stretched back to reach in my pocket, and felt a warmth created by the movement under the face of the sun. I watched her blow out smoke and follow it as it swirled away. But I couldn't touch her. We were on two different planes with no meeting point of kindred souls or spirited animality.

"It's too bad Skip isn't here?" I said. "He'd like this."

"Thank the good Lord he's not," she said. "I planned this trip to get away from him. He's been getting on my nerves."

"What!" I smiled. "The office man bitching for his supper?"

"Oh no, not Skip. He doesn't bitch about anything other than poor little me. That's the trouble. He's so damn cool and collected that only by making him jealous can I make him a little human. The rest of the time he's the man of iron just like the ad pictures you see of those handsome ex-athletes, fame resting on their shoulders, a pipe in their mouths, the ideal man. Goodness, I should have hired him to shovel my coal instead of marrying him. Oh Tommie, you don't know what you're saying. You want him here to put a blight in the landscape and a weight on my heart?"

"For Christmas' sake, Cathy!"

"Disappointed? You think I should be the happy homemaker? I'm not. I'm a better home-breaker. Oh Tommie, I'm like you. I'm not made to be married--or if I am, my husband will be one in a trillion."

"Look, this is just a stage," I said. "All married couples have to go through it."

"Well, they're not all me, Tommie. I can't be pushed through the same slot that everybody else goes into."

To argue was useless. I was making her more adamant, driving her further into an exaggeration of her feelings. She drew deeply on her cigarette and flicked it high so that it spun end over end to crash ash-first in the snow.

"Coming?" she said.

When we rode the tow up again, we saw some of our gang waving us to follow them onto another set of hills where there were trails blazed through woods that covered the slopes like mats of green burrs to where human dots moved a mile away.

"You go first," I said. "I think I'll say my prayers."

The steep grading to the timberline looked long and desolate after she disappeared into the trees. I stood looking down it as at a black hole, imagining perils, and glancing over the green, wondering if I might glimpse her or where she might be. The minutes passed, coaxing forth reasons to worry which tortured me to action yet glueing me common-sensibly to inaction. When it seemed she had fallen for certain, a black dot moved from out of the trees, strangely mechanical in its movements; she was safe.

I pushed off straining to see into the dark from out of the sun, racing between trees with faith only in the path beneath to guide me until everything jumped into perspective. I scraped against barks on close turns, dropping and rising again, with fear lightening my brain, and I swearing, as I came into the safety of the sun, never to do it again. The smells of cedar and balsam added to the thrill of danger and hung in my nostrils like sweet spice as I approached the others who were practicing turns on a small slope. Like energetic bugs, black against the snow, we climbed up the slopes to ski down in meaningless repetition, made merry by companionship and made interesting with delusions of self-improvement.

At two in the afternoon, we straggled home to lunch. Cathy had gone ahead of me, and I saw her skis leaning against the building when I arrived. More cars had come so that I imagined the party was complete. A couple of M.G.s were parked amongst the bigger cars. In the dining room, sitting together at a table near the window in front of its picture panorama of snow, hills and sun, were Cathy and Pete Miller.

"Yowza, look who's here," Pete said not without a slight blush.

"I'm from Texas," I said. "Have we met?"

Thinking I was angry, Pete frowned, but Cathy said. "It's his little joke. He's travelling on a glorious reputation."

"Did you bring your skis," said I, finding room at the table on the other side of Cathy, "or are you here for treatment?"

"We're going skiing this afternoon. You can come with us," he said generously.

The others arrived, and our conversation altered course, sailing with the balmy breezes of high-strung optimism. When the soup came, it tasted bitter. That afternoon I read until Cathy and Pete came back before dark. They didn't bother me for a while, letting me sit in my chair and look blankly at a printed page while listening listlessly to the chatter. I felt as if recuperating from an illness so that any moment I expected them to wheel the sad invalid away to his room. But Cathy came to me.

"Tommie, don't be a party-pooper."

"You knew he was coming."

"Yes," she said. "But I didn't think you would care this much." A smile flickered like flame across her features.

"That's fine," I said. "Then I should stop caring."

Getting up, I put the book away and sat beside a girl whom I noticed was attractive. By concentrating my attention on her through dinner and about the log fire afterward, I forgot Cathy and Pete. We sang songs and watched the wood crackle. Someone had brought marshmallows to toast, and we made hot chocolate. She was fun but only half the personality of Cathy. I tried not to feel gypped.

ROMANCE

The next morning, when the snow fell in big fluffs screening the out-of-doors and keeping us inside, Cathy and Pete acted like love birds. I saw him play with her fingers while quick smiles, the nervous laughs, bounced back and forth like a beach ball. Someone had turned on the radio obliging the nearest person to switch channels at program changes to keep a continuous grinding of inane music flowing from its inner tubes. At one point, a husky female voice, singing as if the woman were swinging her hips and mastoids in alternating emotions, gave out with "Can this be love, dah dah dah dee, dah dah," giving me a most peculiar feeling of revenge on the whole lot of them. For a married woman, Cathy was acting like a fifteen-year-old virgin, and Pete, hustler extraordinary, looked like a child surrounded by toy automobiles from the enjoyment that lit up in his face.

I tried talking with the girl from the night before. Her name was Alice. She won every game of ping-pong we played. She was exceptionally accurate at darts. She had a good figure. But she thought the difference between the sexes was merely to give people a variety to look at. It was this frigidness towards anything to do with sex, or jokes or friendly intimations that must have discouraged so many male hearts, that made her an extra at the party, and explained why she was brought by her brother. Like an experienced thief, I kept telling myself that the most valuable safes were the hardest to crack. But after she had beaten me for the fourth time at gin-rummy, and clouded at the mention of strip poker, I gave up.

By mid-afternoon, the snow fall had let up enough so that we could ski. The odd flake caught to our clothes and melted. The skies were dark, making the snow gray, although the new fluff kicked up a light protest against the gloom. Night fell early, driving us back around the fire where Cathy and Pete were still happy together, and where I recommenced operations upon Alice. I could have been trying to make love to an iceberg. It was like banging one's head against the icy wall. Later, she loosened up enough to allow my arm to go about her. After most of the others had gone to bed, we sat looking at the fire. I suppose she thought it was engendering up some spiritual communion between us. I hoped her half was coming through; mine crackled static but plagued her frigidity. When alone with the lights out and only the flickering orange from the fire by which to see each other, we reached the high point; she let me kiss her lightly. The drums could beat, the trumpets blow, but all she felt was that she was on the way to hell below. She went to bed instead. I sat in the firelight for a few minutes longer. I felt I was trapped in a square box anchored in the shadows of nowhere.

The immediate past swam in my mind. There was no future because I couldn't think any further than the here and now. There was no comfort in the darkness yet there was no hostility. The fire was indifferent, burning itself out. My state of mind was neutral. I could have been killed then, and death would have made little difference to my soul, if I'd had one. The weekend, instead of being a swirling instant of a good time, was an eternity of boredom. Disappointment had come and gone. There was only penal servitude left. I had to stand aside and outwait Pete so that I could drive back with her. Then, her little fun finished, she'd be the same again, my friend and Skip's wife. Come gay little girl, let's finish your game and go. But one more day, one blue Monday, and that would be the end of Pete. I wished Cathy had chosen someone other than me to shield her caprices. Skip probably thought I was the safest man on the earth to send her with. But he need not have been worried about Pete; Cathy would keep him in the somersault-stages of playful admiration. But even that thought was pleasant, almost insanely rare, when contrasted to the cold-blooded Alice.

A glow burnished the wood of the railing winding snake-like to the above. I climbed slowly, loath to sleep, but tired from sitting too long in the nowhere. A door opened down the corridor, and I, thinking it was Alice, concluding that an internal revolution was bringing her back, nightgown and all, stopped, but when I made out the figure moving stealthily over the creaking floorboards in the faded orange that tinted the skin of his naked chest and arms, and in flashes touched his blond locks, I recognized Pete. Swiftly he slipped near by me and entered a room into which I had once looked where bottles and boxes of feminine accoutrements extended to embrace the visitor and swoon him in lovely delights into a bed where blankets came up and over sweet young limbs. I wanted to rattle the handle and smash at the panelling and yell, "You goddamn whore, get the hell out of there!" But I didn't. I really didn't care. I went into my room. I took off my clothes. I lay in bed and tried to breathe in a way it wouldn't hurt.

At breakfast the next morning, I broached the idea to Pete that he allow me to drive his car back while he drove back later with Cathy. He was only too agreeable. He was all for it, man. I was not playing cupid, though. I was tired of idealism. I wanted to get back to Toronto and to good old realism.

"But Tommie dear, why are you leaving so early?" Cathy, concerned, said when she heard.

"I'm wasting time here," I said. "If you know what I mean."

She was glad that I was helping her to escape that guilt-ridden ride homewards, which we both dreaded, but she was disappointed to see one of those irons she'd stuck in the fire go out. "Don't be angry with me, Tommie."

"How could I be? You sweet thing you," I said.

Alice was as perversely disappointing as ever. I tried to persuade her to drive back to Toronto with me, but her scruples would not allow her. Since she had come with her brother, she intended to return with him. There is a thin line dividing what makes life meaningful and livable and what kills it by being over-moral. The latter know it, but are afraid to dare to live, as some people are afraid of the water.

The sun was attempting to wink through clouds when I left the lodge and pointed the red nose of Pete's car to the south. Fate was drawing me back. It appeared that I was to have no girl but Melanie, and since that were so, I was to be by her side. I felt that I should not have left Toronto, that too much had depended on my staying, that one reason why I could not enjoy myself at the lodge was because I was avoiding duty, rather white-starched and puritan, but still, duty. By running away I had escaped nothing, merely a small segment of time.

For the moment I was like a cork in a sea that was calm but, as Conrad said, ever threatening. On the horizon was a piece of land onto which I might drift, but now it was smaller than when I had first seen it, now it was less of a miracle, now, at this perspective, Maxwell appeared like an over-exaggerated hope. And the skies gave signs of darkening for a storm. Being a cork, I had no fear of drowning, but I didn't relish a smashing about. I accelerated in Pete's speedster to diminish faster the distance between me and those palms.

That afternoon I came into Toronto. It had snowed but the flakes had mostly melted in the city streets. The crowds downtown moved in furs and overcoats against shop windows. As usual, pedestrians were not looking where they were going, and the other drivers were having difficulty keeping their eyes on the road. But finally, without accident, I reached the Fraternity House and left the car in the street where Cathy could drop Pete to retrieve it. Maxwell was sitting alone in the lounge. He had fallen asleep over a magazine; and pictured on the page opened on his lap was a photograph of a brain. He awoke when I slipped the mag away from him.

"Don't lose my place," he said. "I am studying the mechanics of how some people think around here."

"For instance?" I prompted.

"For one, the President of our little group. An arts man, he stopped all subscriptions to scientific reading with the disgusting excuse that we are inexcusably ignorant on subjects of real culture. He's ordered all those damn drama, stage, screen, and juvenile literary digests with the latest pictures of some ham-actor in a role too big for him, and essays on whether George Eliot subconsciously adopted that name as a prognostication of another literary figure two centuries later with the initials T. S.. Mysticism, the writer suggests, was one of George's fortes; communication, then, with the yet unborn T.S. was not at all unlikely. This argument is further strengthened by the writer's connection which he sees between *Silas Marner* and the *Waste Land* both, of course, being vitally Christian and vitally moral. Thus, he says, that the pre-existent spirit of T.S. tapped out, in a heavenly Morse shall we say, his message to George to get the ball rolling in ideas which he will complete in his poetry. Now, everybody knowing poetry is superior to prose, and she, in deepest gratitude at being thus selected, chose his name Eliot--all embryonic spirits know ahead of time what their earthly names will be and can communicate this to the chosen through mystical revelation. I spent over an hour reading that crap and that is why I fell asleep trying to read something as simple and insignificant as an article on the intricate structure of the human brain, without the mystical spirit."

"I suppose he's stopped the *Ontario Bar Review* too," I said looking at the covers ranged over the tables.

"It's all right: it's his last year," Maxwell said. "We can begin building for the next."

The gloom of the day faded into the darkness of the room about us as we, sitting, stared at one another in one of those pauses when thought jams, refusing to carry over to the next idea, comment, triviality, nonsense, to escape the inevitable topic.

"Are things fixed now?" I said, at last.

"Nope." He pulled at his earlobe. "The only thing we can do is to take a hotel room for a night. Preferably a hotel where there isn't a detective."

"Does it have to be for a whole night? Not just a couple of hours? I don't know if Melanie's parents will let her go."

"She'll have to go and give them an excuse afterwards, bonehead. Being sent to bed without her supper is better than supporting a child for the rest of her life."

"I'm phoning her now," I said. "When can we arrange it?"

"The end of next week. I'll reserve a room."

"Are you sure you can do it, Maxwell? I don't want anything to happen to her."

"You sound as if you've been reading Faulkner."

"No, seriously."

"Would I suggest it if I couldn't do it?"

"I'm sorry. I'm being silly."

The telephone rang a long time at Melanie's end. I was on the point of hanging up when I heard a voice answer.

"Yes, it's Melanie," she said slowly, expressionessly.

"Look, can you sneak a night away for next week? Say Friday, eh?"

"It's too late," her empty voice monotoned. "Mother knows."

From somewhere above, I felt the heavy, wide blade of a guillotine slip down and crash against the back of my neck. Irrationally I sensed the spectators' silent shock.

"How?"

"Yesterday, I told her. I had to. She wouldn't let me alone."

"That's okay! We'll do it anyway," I said.

"Oh no, not now," she breathed. "Oh no, you have to marry me."

"But I thought we decided against that. I don't want to marry you for God's sake!"

"Mother says you have to. You have to come to dinner on Wednesday. She'll tell your family if you don't."

"She doesn't even know who my family is." The thought that that woman could bother my family, swagger into their lives with a threatening billy-stick under such a sordid excuse was sickening.

"Shall I tell her you're coming?"

"Yes."

"I'm sorry. Tom, I just couldn't help it." She began to cry, quite unexpectedly, as if that hard shell of a woman had exploded finally throwing destruction all about it.

"God damn you!" I said.

I didn't go directly back to Maxwell. I stood looking at my hands shake. Then I went to the men's room. As I washed my hands under hot water and felt the warm current, I thought of a stuffy little prison rectory where people solemnly stood in freshly pressed clothes. "I now pronounce you"--ten, twenty, thirty forty years of life imprisonment.

"Well," Maxwell said.

He took the news with a laugh. "When you go to dinner, take flowers with you, Romeo."

"Seriously arrange it for Friday night, will you?"

Maxwell shrugged. "I'll let you know."

In my room, when I tried to read my lecture notes, I found that every sentence was ending with an invisible Wednesday Night.

CHAPTER 19

The car belonging to Melanie's father was standing darkly revealed by open doors in the garage when I passed to ring the doorbell. Melanie's father opened the door and, surprise of surprises, smiled at me.

"Well now, Tom, it's been a long time since you've been to dinner," he emphasized as if I was in the habit of dining there but had missed the last couple of weeks. He took my coat and directed me into the living room. Melanie's mother smiled from a stool near the grate that glowed behind her.

"Good-evening, Tom. It's nice to see you again."

I took a chair near to her, and, while the father bemusedly stood by the mantel place, the mother and I chatted about things of interest to Toronto society: the dog show, the Winter Fair, the Mexican jumping horse entries and plans for the extension of one of the large department stores, until Melanie entered wearing a wow of a new dress styled to make her look so smooth and elegant that I rose with a step backward. No tale of sorrow was etched in her face. She flashed a smile at me and I found myself standing beside her, facing our older generation in the attitude of a new one springing up to eventually take its place. Sherry was given round by a maid, who slipped away again, and the spots of dark red colour seemed like rubies against the light which gave the atmosphere a precious and secure feeling. Melanie moved voluptuously onto the sofa, and, I, sensing a round spot left vacant for me, sat beside her. The parents then directed the conversation at me, which resulted in the confirmation that I was healthy, happy, and free. I tried to distract attention away from the obvious by suggesting that I missed the little sister. She had been given an early supper and sent to the movies, although they said 'Went to the movies,' so that it would not cast a dark shadow of a suggestion over the pleasantness in our spider's parlor. But for the next five minutes until dinner was announced, I prolonged the deviation by spouting complimentary remarks on the cleverness and resource of that child with the help of reminiscences of my own childhood and encouragement to the parents to find similar incidents from their youth.

At the dinner table, however, it became difficult for me to direct conversation. When I tried to do so, there were often no answers forthcoming, so it seemed I was carrying on a monologue which made me self-conscious. Yet the party was friendly with intimations that I was being taken for granted like a visiting relative.

"Make yourself at home now, son," said the father looking professionally about at the glass dishes containing various colored foods. "If you see something you like, take it." He chuckled then and winked. "That's a rule of life for you."

The missus laughed. "Now don't you give him ideas, Jack. You are the worst influence a young man can have."

"Girls are a worse influence than anyone," he said. "Don't you agree. Tom?"

"Yes," I said and tried to laugh. It seemed as if my chair were chained to the floor.

"Especially the good-looking ones, eh?" he winked.

"Jack!" the mother said.

"Now mother, I wasn't referring to you," and he roared with great good humour before he gagged himself to a stop and said obviously, "but I could have meant Melanie, though, couldn't I, son, eh? Couldn't I?" and his laughter trailed into the great beyond.

Melanie looked down at her plate; her long blonde hair falling like a willow weeping. There were a few silent moments during which I pretended not to notice the pressure of regret that was being ejected by wicked goblins into the air.

The mother cleared her throat and squared her large fanny on the leather seat of her chair. "Tom, we have heard what has happened from Melanie, and we are terribly sorry. It was a blow to both of us and quite a shock to me, I must say." She glared sharply at Melanie's downcast features. "But we are aware that such things do happen, although I could never have imagined it happening to a member of my own family. It was quite a shock." She accented 'quite' and looked again at Melanie. "You must remember that our family is very well thought of in Toronto and anything like this would be a disgrace among our many friends here, and I doubt very much whether we all won't suffer from it. Your family too is of good old stock, and I am sure you don't like to blot the good name it has had for so many years, do you?" She waited until I thought I was supposed to answer when, nipping my first syllables short, she began again. "We know Melanie is just as much to blame as you are and for that reason we don't want you to feel that the whole burden is falling on you." She looked at her husband who was sitting arms folded, head down, judging his table napkin. "Father and I have been talking it over and we have decided we can help you a little financially until you are through law school. I'm afraid, though, that Melanie will have to stop college and work after the baby comes. It is not a very pleasant prospect right now, but I am sure you won't regret it in the long run." She laughed a little to lighten her heavy role. "You can look back at many happy years of life and joke about this someday."

At first, I didn't know what to say, and, when I looked at Melanie, she ignored me. "I don't think Melanie and I are in love."

The parents, startled, sat up in their chairs. Melanie's father glowered at me. He was a man of swiftly changing emotions.

"You mean to tell us that you don't want to marry our daughter?"

"I'd marry her if we were in love," I said. "But the love we had wasn't of the marrying kind." I felt foolish trying to explain a simple truism to people who, I knew, were not willing to understand.

"Listen here, young man, you aren't going to sneak out of anything, do you hear?" His face had become red and his eyes had begun to blaze.

"I'm not," I said. "I just know that Melanie's got an idea of the man she wants to marry, and I've got an idea of the woman I'd like to marry, and we haven't met them yet, and maybe never will."

He threw his hands in the air. "What books have you been reading?"

"It's true," Melanie broke in. "Tom's right."

"You be quiet." Her father then turned directly on me while Melanie's mother sat finger-fidgeting with the silverware in front of her. "You may have had that choice once, but now it has been eliminated. Now you have no choice. God! where's your sense of decency, of moral obligation? I don't have to tell you this! Is the youth today so mixed-up it doesn't know what morals are?"

"I only know what's right," I said. "And it isn't right for us to marry just because other people want us to."

"It's not because they want you to, it's because you *have* to."

"The Church says we don't have to if we don't want to," I said.

"The Church? Who's talking about the Church? That's only where you get married!"

"If it's a question of helping with the support of the child," I began.

"Now, look here! You're going to marry our daughter, do you understand that?"

I was on the point of losing my temper too. I wanted to yell at the bastard and tell him to stop trying to ruin two other people's lives for the gratification of his social pride. I had no intention of going under to keep him high in the social register. Let him mix his own cocktails.

"But, Tom, think." The mother moved forward to lean across the table. "Melanie will have to go through this all alone. She'll be the only one to suffer. Is that fair?"

"She'll be the only one to suffer whether we're married or not," I said. "A natural event like birth has nothing to do with a man-made law like marriage. Anyway, I know I wouldn't make her any happier by living with her."

"But, Tom, what about the child? Have you thought of that?"

"Melanie and I have thought of abortion. I know someone who'll do it."

"That's the last straw! That is the last straw!" Melanie's father jerked himself away from the table and turned angrily on Melanie. "Is that what you brought home to dinner? Why he's suggesting murder! Young man, if you attempt anything like that I'll have you and your accomplice locked up for manslaughter. Why, you'd probably kill Melanie too!"

It was then that I realized there was no remedy. I would not put Maxwell to the risk of being caught. This man might be bluffing for the moment, although he might take his threat seriously after the operation was done out of revenge. It was better to have an illegitimate child than to see Maxwell imprisoned and perhaps myself with him and perhaps Melanie and God knows who else. There was, of course, the chance that once the operation was over he would keep quiet for fear of a scandal, to protect his beloved social standing. But the risk was too great.

"Sit down, Jack!" The missus was losing her temper too. "You are only making matters worse."

He took his chair while glaring at me as if I were a badly polished cuspidor. Melanie was staring again at her plate. Her eyes were rounded largely as if she were imagining some horrible danger she was about to meet.

"Tom, I think it only fair to tell you that if you don't marry Melanie, I shall make sure that everyone will know that you are the father of her child." Her mother spoke sharply with an anger that backed up every word with emphasis. "Your family won't be pleased with you, and I shouldn't be surprised if the law school does not allow you to continue your studies next year."

I let the strength of this threat echo unchallenged in the dining room. My position seemed minuscule now. Society so tied a man down that in the long run he had no free will. By sidestepping one of its commandments he had to flee them all, and when he did exchange one society for another, he left behind those innocents who would have to suffer for him. Anyway, as for changing the rules of a society, an individual couldn't do it alone; society had to alter itself.

"Okay," I said. "If you want me that badly."

Melanie's father flushed red again but, at a warning look from his wife, he subsided. I was determined to live my life as far apart from these people as I could. Only then, I knew, could Melanie and I find any basis of understanding.

Her mother rang a small pink bell and the maid came in to clear away the dishes. I sensed that the kitchen ears had not had to be very wide open to hear us because the maid circled the table and looked admonishingly at me as she left the desserts. When she had gone, the silence she brought with her remained behind while we spaded with teaspoons in small round bowls.

"Tom's not the only one who doesn't want to get married," Melanie spoke up, her voice shuddering high, betraying her hidden hysteria.

"I don't want to marry him, and I don't want to have his baby either."

"Melanie, it's not his baby, it is yours!" said her mother in exasperation.

"I don't care. I don't want any baby."

"I'm afraid there's nothing we can do about it so will you please shut up," said the official head of the family. "You've caused your mother enough trouble without adding to it with your useless whining."

Melanie left the table and ran into the living room. I followed her, leaving the two elders staring irresolutely after the desertion of their congregation. On a wide thick-armed easy chair, she sat crooked over one elbow and choked despondently. Walking uselessly about her, I muttered sympathetic but superficial catch-words. We had never had a brother-sister understanding, or any affectionate or consolatory relationship. Whenever we came close to each other, we were overwhelmed by physical desire. It was a tyrannous compulsion that drove out all other feeling even as we lay recuperating in an unsettled aftermath. Then we turned on ourselves for being beasts, and at the same time shrank from softer emotions in the fear that they might entangle us again in the bestial. As her parents were leaving us alone, I ventured to sit on the arm of the chair, and throwing my arm along the back of it, I bent over Melanie whose sobs had weakened. She turned her stricken features to look up at me, and I, drawn to her, slid to sit beside her, seized her, and our bodies twisted against one another under long hard kisses which knew no point of satiation, only exhaustion.

We felt like banished goods, condemned to be dumped away from the expensive niceties of a bourgeois living room. That fear, that our lives would be only that, dominated us.

"We can try it, can't we?" I said. "In the end we can always get divorced." The incongruity of our position suddenly made me scream with silent laughter; I felt the pain within my skull. I thought of the Hollywood movie stars with starched black hair, their loving hands cupped at the end of long graceful arms rising over their flowing evening dresses and embracing. Final curtain.

"What about the child?"

"I don't know what about the child! We're just caught and that's all there is to it. We'll get married, you give birth, and we'll see what happens."

We heard footsteps and sprang apart turning to face each other standing on opposite sides of the chair. Melanie's colour faded at the entrance of her mother, who looked hesitant as if she didn't want to disturb us.

"We've decided we'll be married," I said.

"Oh! I knew you would." Her relief was genuine. "Oh, Melanie, I knew you would!" She took her daughter in her arms. "You'll be happy, you'll see. You'll find it's the right thing to do. You'll see that we're right. We parents know what is right. You'll see, you'll be happy."

I turned away from her empty assurances. The moment they were uttered, they revived my insecure feelings and made me regret what I had said. But suddenly the situation appeared ludicrous to me. The exaggeration of the importance of our decision was farcical. The whole idea of marriage as a serious solemn step is in reality insignificant in the face of the great drama of nature. We live, we eat other animals and plants, we copulate, and whether we did it under an officially signed paper or not didn't matter. Our procreative act is merely a reflex of nature fulfilling its one important function: the continuance of the species. Why then all this fuss?

Melanie's father, hearing the good news from his station in the hall, now stepped into the room. He was transformed back to his old bemused self, the man who had opened the door for me at the beginning of the evening. He stepped forward to shake my hand.

"That's the spirit, now," he chuckled. "Fooling us all the time, eh? You know were getting too old to be worried like that. Here, let's celebrate this occasion, this big occasion with a big cigar. You smoke them, don't you, Tom?"

I watched him reach onto the mantel piece from where he brought a carved wooden box which he opened below my nose. Although I couldn't pretend to be very jolly, I could at least throw myself into the stream of his good humour. We lit them, he beaming at me, and I palely reflecting that beam. Melanie and her mother were arising from the stage of consoling one another, and they went together to bring us drinks, Melanie being coaxed quickly by her fast-stepping mother.

When they returned, almost at once, we drank to the health of marriages generally and to the long life of ours specifically.

"What do you think about the end of next week?" her father suggested. "We can unite you in the United Church," he chuckled.

"I'd like to give my family time to digest the news," I said. "But if I mention it this weekend it'll be soon enough."

"Good! Then shall we say Saturday? A small service?" he raised his glass as if to clinch it with a toast. I envisioned him on the morrow running to his temple with instructions.

"We should wait and see what Tom's family will say," Melanie suggested quietly.

Her father cleared his throat in an attempt to dismiss his anger. "Perhaps you're right. Yes, perhaps you're right."

"I'll tell you Monday," I said.

"Fine, Tom," her mother said. "We are so glad that you and Melanie see your way right now. Please forgive our tempers at dinner time. You know we didn't mean what we said. We think Melanie's lucky. We are very proud of our new son-in-law, aren't we, Jack?"

"Indeed we are," he said. "We are indeed. And now about finances and so forth you know, you see me after the wedding and we'll see what we can arrange."

I left them, my cigar still smoking in my fingers.

Melanie accompanied me to the door and held my overcoat while I struggled into it. We kissed quickly and with the muffled slam of the door I walked away, striding in the street, flicking ash onto the snow, mellowing in the opiate of the cigar yet uncomfortably conscious that for the last part of the evening neither Melanie nor I could look the other directly in the face.

CHAPTER 20

By Sunday afternoon of that first weekend in March, I had not yet found the courage to tell mother or Nancy that I was to be married at the end of the week. Although I had rehearsed how I would phrase it, no matter what I said seemed awkwardly out-of-place and too sudden for an announcement. They would think me either joking, if they were in a charitable mood, or stark raving mad.

Since the weather had turned warmer for the last few days and the march winds had not as yet begun to blow us into Spring, I retreated into the out-of-doors where my problem didn't seem so immediate. Within fifteen minutes, I was strolling along a mountain path climbing through skeleton trees, which caught at the sun dimly warm in a cold blue sky. Most of the snow had melted, but clumps of ice still clung to the undersides of the cliff-side, where tiny streams filtered through clumps of black earth and trickled over stones across pathways down the steep sides into the cement troughs by the roadway which was visible through the trees. The humming of cars from the distant roadway rose and faded into inaudibility. Below the roadway were the thick trees, now naked, and further below were flat stretches of long grass where couples used to start in surprise like young deer lying under the warm sun. But now the ground was wet and puddled. I followed a trail upward leading over loose stones that gave under my feet, and, tumbling over the ground, I kicked a few of them and heard their descent resound hollow-like in a tin-can. On reaching level ground, I found a small falls splashing in a bath-tub of rocks twenty yards below. Surrounding the rocks was a ribbon of snow, which I gathered, packed into balls, and threw at the naked trees. Just above, sitting grandly near the edge of the cliff and overlooking the Western half of the city, were the ruins of a mansion burnt to its foundations with only a few charred walls sticking out. Being next to the mental asylum, and in the forlorn, bleak winter light, the whole scene appeared like something out of a gothic novel. Veering left, I came to the Asylum's grounds. I crossed the sodden lawns, bordered by desolate flower-beds and sensed my being watched from behind the forbidding thick walls of the squat hospital buildings. I recalled when as a boy, I used to hear the terrifying endless screams in the late afternoon, the naked man shaking at the bars and shouting from a third storey window, the thin lady calling to me, pleading to me to come below her window so that she could give me a note to take to her sister to rescue her, and my being half-convinced and frightened, as I vaguely sensed she was lying. A driveway led me straight, like a long aisle, to the road. I passed by houses on the mountain brow, unprotected from the cold winds. These houses were old, compared to the new housing-estates springing up behind them. I glanced at the city below and across the plain to the Bay waters beyond.

Lake Ontario was steel gray now. Inlets of water cut into the shore shaping the small curves of coastline. The Bay was a darker gray, and lay still, laden with the refuse and the slag from the city industries. The city reached out of sight to the East, and looking to the West, it ended in a series of houses trailing out over the dull green earth. Founded over one hundred years ago out of an Indian valley, the city was now merely an adolescent compared to the cultivated ancient and mature cities of Europe. Hamilton was a city that lacked culture or a distinct cultural identity.

The sharpness of the air, the clearness of the view, and the solitude of my position led me to contemplate on my immediate predicament. I thought of the biological cycles, of the muscular movements accompanying the reproductive urge, so natural, so vital, so necessary that it was inconceivable it should be penalized. I thought of the city and its social customs which trap and tamper man's natural impulses. To toil endlessly and stupidly for money, home, wife, children without any other goal in sight was all that was required to be a good member of society. That the real "I" wanted more, wanted freedom to explore the meaning of life, to give expression to other urges of creativity besides that of procreation, was not to be. I was to be suffocated by the demands of an artificial system devised imperfectly by my species. I had performed well by it in perpetrating my species, but it cannot be accepted or recognized as natural unless sanctioned by a ridiculous piece of paper that would ensure my eternal material and spiritual bondage, in order that that social machinery could function.

And so, if I were to enter the social order with wife on arm I had to prepare myself for the disappointment of choking my dreams, those such as only an independent man can make come true, and settle down to the business of feeding a family. Already I felt that the money in my pockets didn't belong completely to me; when I jingled the coins, the sound was an unhappy one for it reminded me of duty. But I knew that somehow my mind would have to develop free from my circumstances, that I should keep it ever on the outside of daily routine. I had to conform to the ideas of my peers without being subject to them. Only then could I hope to save myself from the monotony of existing for the sake of material progress alone.

There were consolations supposedly, I was told. A wife to a monogamous man was indeed a comfort, and a child to a doting father was indeed a blessing, but I, being neither doting nor monogamous, would likely find both a bore. Yet still, my marriage at the end of the week might not be as bad as it appeared: Melanie would go her own way eventually, and marriage would ensure that the offspring would live. That was after all the crux of the problem that bothered the conscience. Although the biologists believe that the embryo is still at a spiritless stage, there was the knowledge that it would eventually develop into a human fetus, and that it had every bit as much right to life as I. Perhaps it would grow into someone far worthier than I. And who was I to play Father Providence? Whether a boy or a girl, it was enough that it should live through the sorrows and joys of being human, that it should be allowed to shape its own destiny. The breezes blew colder on my face as I realized with relief the importance of my decision to marry Melanie and to go ahead with the birth. For a moment I was almost happy that I was to be married. But again I was confronted with the reality of my circumstances and became apprehensive. Irrationally I grasped at wild arguments to support my terrible fear. Wars, accidents, and diseases caused death, why should abortion be regarded as different? I tried to rationalize. Societies killed criminals because those men proved inconvenient to society, why should not unformed embryos be washed from wombs when inconvenient? If all males refused sexual intercourse with women, would not that mean the mass deprivation of millions of dormant cells from developing into human life? If so, would not that make all virgin men, including priests, willful negators of life? Would not that mean that all users of prophylactics and devotees to birth-control were murderers too? Come now, Tom Davis, let's have an answer to these. Shall we fall weakly back on the perennial religious precept of predestination? If we do, there is little sense in pretending there is any independent choice is there? Can we accept that our life and death are predestined, but that for the rest we can exercise our free will? Such vague teachings that determine societal mores leaves man in a really ridiculous situation. When man sets to work eliminating an inconvenience, it can be assured that what he does not eliminate is convenient. Eliminating the inconveniences seems to be the rule of life. Nations rid themselves of their inconvenient enemy, society of its inconvenient criminals, the sick man of his inconvenient goitre, the housewife of the inconvenient ants in the kitchen, the gardener of inconvenient long grass, and the unmarried couple of its inconvenient pregnancy.

 I stood up, kicked a rock into the trees below, and listened to the sharp retorts of the wood. Perhaps life was unjust because all objects have their own life, in other words, forces, which refuse to be pushed aside by other forces, like the rock that plummeted into the trees. In history, there had been many other souls like Christ's, and they were all individuals; they too had their central forces but they were eliminated like Christ because the masses refused to put up with their inconveniences. Although my marriage to Melanie was, aside from the social implications, an inconvenience to her parents, I saw last Wednesday evening that I had lost the battle. Their force was stronger than mine. It was immaterial to me now that I had belonged to the weaker. I was resigned to accepting my fate, but, like everyone else, I feared the change to my life's direction.

The sun had sunk low in the sky, where it was a pretty picture instead of the source of light, as I followed the road winding down the side of the escarpment. Cars moved slowly in the traffic jam. The slowest car honked its horn and pulled to the side of the road in front of me. When I reached its window, I found Tim Lake waiting composedly. I got in and we set off in slow descent again, he fixing his eyes on the road, ready to avoid any reckless driver.

"I've got bad news," he said. "Cathy left Skip last week."

A rumour that Cathy was having a good time with Pete had come south with the party and reached Skip's ears. They had had a violent quarrel which decided Cathy to leave the house and go to Toronto. Skip evidently didn't know where she was staying, but he was sure she was meeting Pete.

"He was wanting to talk to you."

My position was difficult, but since I had messed up my own affairs, I didn't mind helping to mess up other people's.

"I'm dropping by to see him now," Tim said.

After we were let into the Rymal house, a maid led us back to the sports room where Skip was sipping afternoon tea alone under the bear and moose heads. He looked up wanly and I saw that his eyes betrayed nights of sleeplessness. They had lost all power of expression. He stood up, greeted us, and pulled two arm-chairs closer to the couch he was sitting on.

"Tim's told you, I guess," he said.

"A bit of it," I said.

"I want to know what happened up there."

"Cathy had just planned on spending the weekend with him instead of me," I said.

"How do you mean, spend?" His eyes narrowed.

ROMANCE

"Well, they were talking together all the time and stuff."

"What?"

"I don't know what they were doing," I said. "They looked like two dopey kids spooning in a parlour."

Skip whacked the arm of the couch with the flat of his hand.

"But they were just kids all the way," I said. "Nothing like that will last."

"It's gone pretty far," Skip said. "Too far, I guess."

"Not too far yet," Tim said. "I think Tom's right. If you take it easy, she'll come back."

"That doesn't solve anything." Skip drew his hand down the side of his face, handsome now in profile, grievingly handsome like a movie actor in an old film. "Unless something happens to change her inside, we'll always be having this kind of trouble. Do you guys want some tea? Help yourself. Wait a minute!" He walked over to the wall bell and came back to sink heavily onto the couch. When the maid appeared he asked for two cups. "This bloody system is a nuisance. It takes too long." He passed us sandwiches.

"When are the Rymals coming back?" Tim asked.

"This month." Skip smiled slightly. "They'll just love this!"

"It's not your fault," Tim said.

"When they get here, it will be," Skip said.

"Tell them to jump in the lake," Tim said with unexpected forcefulness.

"I've got too much to lose."

We knew what he meant. The rich interior decoration on the walls around us was enough to convince us of that. And it was not every house that had a sports room.

"Keep it quiet though, Tom," he said. "Don't tell your sister or the whole town will know."

"This town will find out without me telling it," I said. "It hears by mental telepathy."

"When you get back to Toronto, Cathy'll probably get in touch with you. Do me a favour? Tell me where she's staying?"

"Do you think that's wise?" Tim said. "Why don't you just leave her stew? You're her husband, not Miller. She'll have to come back to you."

"She's stubborn," Skip said. "She has to be persuaded nicely."

"Huh! Isn't the legality of the wedding certificate enough?" Tim straightened his glasses, looking primer.

"Not to her. She might sue for separation if I don't go after her."

"True," I said. "She'd out-legalize any law if she wanted to."

Skip looked closely at me. "You know her, don't you, Tom? You've known her longer than I have and maybe even better. Can you persuade her to come back?"

"Sure Skip, I'll try. Is there anything special you want me to say?"

"Since we were married I haven't been able to think up anything special for her," he said. "Maybe that's one reason why I failed."

"You haven't failed anything," I said.

He shrugged his shoulders, and the maid entered carrying two tea-cups which she set on the tray. She had taken so long, we had forgotten about her. Then I saw the baffled look in Skip's eyes as he watched her go, he powerless to reprimand her, and I sensed the reason he thought he had failed.

Tim and I left him a little while later and Tim drove me home.

"It's that beer business at the bottom of it," Tim said. "He has to work so hard to prove that he's more than just the son-in-law of the owner and to redress the bad impression that old man Rymal left on the firm that he works all the time and gets sort of cranky and nervous, and naturally he quarreled with Cathy. He would have done better to stick to insurance."

I was just on time for dinner. As I sat down at the table with mother and Nancy, I decided to withhold my news of nuptials until after the town exploded with the scandal of Cathy and Skip, when the surprise of my little event might be drowned in the noise of an agitated society marching to war against more important foes.

CHAPTER 21

Sure enough, as Skip surmised, when I picked up my weekend mail at the fraternity, I found a note from Cathy amongst circulars about business college and what the smartly-dressed young man was wearing that spring. She asked me sweetly to meet her for lunch on Monday, "please do come," and, "darling, don't worry, I shall pay the bill." Since I intended to attend my first lecture in the late afternoon, a leisurely meal in attractive company greeted me like a good omen for the day.

About ten o'clock, I pushed my books off the bed and went down to breakfast. My promise to contact my future in-laws condensed like a cloud over my head when I passed the telephone; it grew blacker as I looked at my coffee. To prevent any threat of a downpour I ducked back to dial Melanie's number. I wanted to speak to Melanie first to see if she would agree to be married quickly by a Justice of the Peace with a couple of witnesses excluding the families of both sides. By leaving the arrangements to her father, I felt that I was being pushed into marriage, which I was, of course, but I didn't want to feel it. If a man were going to pretend to enjoy what was happening to him, he should pretend it is his own idea out of self-respect if nothing else. And too, my family might have been disappointed if Melanie's parents were present and they were not, although the very thought of the latter's presence was unlikely and pure fancy on my part.

"Tom, I've got news for you," Melanie said immediately. Her voice bounced through the receiver in high excitement. "I've had an abortion!"

I was kicked into space where I mulled over the meaning of her words, and returned to earth to begin a gay little tap-dance.

"Natural?" I gasped, knowing it could be no other.

"No," she said softly. "Can you meet me this morning? I don't want mother to hear."

We decided to meet at Dan's in an hour; I would have agreed to five minutes. I went back to my coffee and methodically ate three servings of toast. Any flight into ecstasy was hindered by feelings of forebodings which marred my mood of relief and pleasure. Melanie might have risked infection with some careless mid-wife, or she might be found out and have to answer to the law. Yet the feeling of release was real and had to be recognized.

Maxwell, stripping off his overcoat, came to my table. He picked up a paper, and, beginning to shake it nervously, he asked me if bridegrooms usually affected their best men that way. I said ex-best men and told him why.

"I feel deprived of my only chance for distinction this year," he said. "Although I offer congratulations at your astoundingly miraculous escape. And so timely too," he warbled.

"Yeah," I said. "Golly! I haven't been giving Melanie all the credit she deserves."

Fifty minutes later, after I had met her outside of Dan's and listened to her explain what had happened while we walked toward the university grounds, I would have repeated that praise gladly.

"It was carbolic soap in water. A girl at college told me what to do. I tried it several times but it didn't work, so I was surprised on Saturday night when it finally did."

"Did it hurt?"

"Oh Tom, did it ever! The movement began about nine and by twelve I could have stood on my head with the pain, but I remembered my friend said not to call anybody because a doctor could save the baby at the last moment. Then I blacked out and woke up in the early morning when it was all over. And, Tom, you know it did have a definite shape. It gave me a shock. I'd left it too late."

"Have you told your parents?"

She nodded, the tassle on her college-colored toque rolling round to the front. "They think it was natural."

"I guess they don't want to see me again," I smiled.

"No," she said.

"I guess you don't either," I said.

"I don't think we'd better," she said.

We took a side path over the campus where there were flower beds, some trees and benches.

"You wouldn't touch me with a ten foot pole," I said.

She smiled wincingly. "It's too dangerous. I don't want to ever go through it again."

ROMANCE

A bend in the path led us to a bench hidden from view by tall bushes. We sat down and clung like leeches, we kissed, thrilled and happy to be free to embrace and to be together, yet we felt the weight of sadness underlying our moods and we pressed a little harder and longer to make this last meeting a memorable one. We finally got up and were ready to go in different directions. At parting our finger tips of our outstretched arms touched, and she, with an uncertain smile, and I, with zero of regret, saw each other for the last time.

It was half past noon when I reached the street and the time to meet Cathy. Since I knew she would be late, I took my time arriving twenty minutes on the wrong side of the clock. She had chosen a plushy restaurant in which to wine and dine me. I found her sitting in a smart gray suit in the foreroom where thin red-upholstered chairs tempered an elegant atmosphere. Her long black cigarette holder blew curling strands of white away from her lone figure, so aloof and grand in supreme sophistication. But when she saw me, her smile raced over and invited me toward her.

"Tommie dear, you're better late than never. How are you?"

When we walked into the restaurant proper, she looked so beautiful beside me that I straightened my back in an effort to make it appear that we might reasonably belong together. The morning's events had left me light-headed so that I reared back in such an attitude of pride that all of the diners, the prim spinster-looking ladies, the pasty-faced cane-toters, the expensive-looking females, all halted their eating to stare at us. Cathy, of course, was overjoyed with the success of her new suit.

We were invited to sit at a table on a higher level by the window overlooking the street whose traffic swarmed on the other side of the glass. When the waiter showed Cathy the wine she nodded condescension at the label, and as the glasses were filled so was I with admiration. With her prompting I chose several fine-sounding names from the menu without worrying about the price column. When we were left alone, Cathy shifted her blue orbs into mine.

"You know why I'm here?"

"I've seen Skip."

She made a face and looked down at her wine. "Toast with me, Tommie--may he drop dead."

I laughed. "You don't hate him that much?"

"I've told you already what I feel about him so it's just doubled."

"You'll never find anyone better," I said.

She laughed, pooh-pooing me. "You're loyal, aren't you?"

"He'd be a hell of a lot better as a husband than Pete."

"Now you're jealous. Oh Tommie, dear, you're jealous!"

"Jump in the lake," I said.

"Come, don't be angry with me. I want to keep all the friends I can. In the next few months I'll lose most of them."

"Why?"

She smiled waiting to be laughed at. "I'm in love with the man you think would make a hell of a poor husband."

"He might make you a good one," I said. "You're a special type."

"You're turning against me already. I thought you'd be different, Tommie."

"Look, don't be silly! What do you expect me to do? A tango?"

We were silent as the meal was laid in front of us. Green beans lay at the side of roasted meat, some fancy cotelette. I watched her eat before I began. She was lucky I thought. She could afford to be preoccupied and not notice what she was eating. She was accustomed to expensive meals, never having eaten worse, except perhaps at boarding school where, however, there was always the fear that she might complain.

"I was thinking you would do something," she said. "You could keep me clued on what Skip's up to. I don't want him to know where I'm living or what I'm doing."

"I've heard of double-agents at war-time working for both sides," I laughed, "but they usually got paid for it."

She was uncertain of me until I promised to be neutral, not to work for either side.

"He wouldn't hire a detective," she said. "It was just people like you I was worried about--especially you." She looked happy now.

At first, I could not believe that her leaving Skip was anymore than a lark. Even though I had witnessed some of their quarrels, their marriage had seemed deep-rooted since that afternoon when I saw them kissing for the first time. When Cathy had spoken disparagingly of Skip, I thought she sounded petulant, as if momentarily irritated, but now I realized that there was something in her manner that was decisive and that more was to come. The happy times I had seen her with Skip now seemed passing dreams, their wedding and marriage a myth. The bond of their marriage had never really existed. It was taken for granted that it was there because, from the first moment, they seemed secure and established in wealth and position that would guarantee success.

"What do you plan on doing?" I asked.

"I don't know yet, except that I want to be free from Skip."

"I'd wait a while before I did anything," I said.

She smiled then. "One has to wait long enough for a divorce as it is."

"Oh Cathy!"

"What's the matter? Am I breaking up your little dream of the perfect marriage?"

"I have never thought marriage could be perfect," I said. "But I think it deserves more thought than you're giving it."

"Tommie, I make my decisions quickly. Once made, there is no use delaying things by thinking them over and over. If Skip had a little less pity for himself and more for me, he would see how necessary it is that we separate too. We never belonged together, and we should never have married. It's mostly my fault, I'm afraid. I didn't really love him. I know it's an awful thing to say, but I married him out of curiosity. Don't you ever repeat this! I was curious to see what it would be like, married to him."

"Curiosity killed the cat," I said.

"Thank you for the inference, Tommie. I'm afraid I can return the compliment remarking on your canine attitudes."

"Damn you! Do you think I ever cared for anybody but you, really deep down?"

She paused then, flattered slightly, reminiscing on the sweetness of a few minutes before. "I believe you, Tommie."

I felt a fool again, opening my heart so that she could look in and laugh. "Platonically, of course," I said.

"That's sweet."

I turned away from her smile, kind, affectionate but superficial, and shifted uncomfortably. Her mind was far ahead of her expression; I could tell she was considering a proposal.

"Will you help me to convince Skip to give me a divorce?"

"No," I said.

"I don't really need your help," she said, "but I thought you would want to."

"That's sweet," I said.

For a moment, I thought she was going to hit me. Her eyes blazed; her jaw jutted to one side sharpening the lines about her mouth. She braced her hands on the table but she controlled her temper. Sinking back on red leather cushions, she pouted miserably at me. "Why do you treat me so cruelly? What have I done to you?"

"Cathy, I don't want to, but you make me."

"Then why won't you help me with Skip?"

"All right, I'll talk to him."

The pout was gone. She sat up to receive the waiter with our desserts--prunes on red jelly camouflaged with a squirly white paste, specially prepared, one dollar twenty-five.

"He'll listen to you more than to me. Tell him that Pete and I are in love and want to be married."

"He won't listen to that nonsense."

"It isn't nonsense. You'll see." She squared her jaw like a little determined girl.

"You're fooling yourself if you think Pete will marry you. I bet he calls you Mag, doesn't he?"

"Yes, for a nickname. How did you know?"

I laughed then, relieved. "He won't marry you."

Cathy took out her cigarette holder, and immediately she seemed older as if the length of her black holder made her automatically adopt a pose of a mature, sophisticated woman of her upper class. Casually she offered me a cigarette, and I could not escape the scrutiny of her eyes, which testified to my younger years by two and to my degrading unsophistication.

"When are you going to grow up, Tommie dear? I would never have told you that, if I didn't know Pete was crazier about me than I am about him."

"His mother wouldn't allow him to marry a divorced woman."

"If he was the one that caused the divorce, she would," Cathy smiled.

"Why do you want to get married right away? Once, I should think, would be enough for a while."

"Because I'm sure Pete's the one, and I am not unaware that he is hard to catch."

"Like you were with Skip," I said. "You'll be out with a lassoe."

"But this time, I'll get the right one," she said.

I made a moue, and she glared at it.

"Come out with Pete and me some evening and you'll see."

"No thanks," I said.

When we parted, our friendship was extremely unsteady, and I was sorry, but at least I had thrown some doubt into her mind to mull over. I showed her that wedding-bells with Pete would not stir any fuss in the world, that the only time she would win the limelight was when she separated from Skip, and then she would become an easy target for people to throw things at. Of course, I could be wrong about the reaction of society as I was wrong about their marriage. Perhaps if she could hook him, Pete might make her the best husband she could ever find.

CHAPTER 22

Because I had a great deal to study, I stayed in Toronto until Easter when I went home for the holidays to prepare for my exams. Although, naturally, law was the only study I cared about, there were parts of it which I didn't like and which now had to be thoroughly stomached to make up for the special diets I had allotted to them during the year. I thought it unfortunate that the final exams should be held at the end of April and the beginning of May when the atmosphere was transformed from the heavy, despairing bleakness of winter to the exciting awakening of oncoming Spring, when the March winds howl the approach of their resplendent visitor, who when she appears, is greeted by the young fresh grass and the wafting perfumes of the budding array of colours shooting up in the sunshine around her. To stay indoors and look at books week after week in Springtime was the real test, the real ordeal. The actual written examination, where professors asked convoluted questions with ambiguous meanings ,were merely tricks to trip up the geniuses who had worked too hard, the unlucky ones who didn't, and those who didn't want to continue studying in the next year anyway. It was with resolve I returned to my bedroom library, notes in briefcase, and locked my door to all distractions, but unsuccessfully. Nancy, imagining she would surprise me, told me about Skip and Cathy's separation when she first saw me.

"Hamilton knows all about it," she said. "Cathy's been sleeping with any number of different men. Poor Skip!"

"What about Skip and his women?" I said.

"What!" she said.

"I'm not sure about it," I said. "Ask someone."

But I learned not to joke about such things because Nancy thought I knew more about it than she did so that for the next quarter hour I wriggled through a pestering test that finally brought me up against swearing ignorance of the whole affair in language that was unmistakably forthright.

The next day, Skip himself dropped in to see me. He was looking better than when I last saw him, having had some sleep in the meantime, I suppose. He had become used to living without Cathy, and although he missed her terribly he said, he looked healthy. The big smile had disappeared, however, as if it had been only a trait of his youth, that happy time of irresponsibility. Now he was submerged under the weight of heavy responsibility; family, business, money. The side of his mouth turned up when he greeted me, and I thought that his insurance days were well over.

"The Rymals came back last night," he said as a starter.

"Do they know about everything?" I said.

"They weren't supposed to come home for another couple of weeks."

"So the old man is hopping mad, eh?"

"He's nice to me, though," Skip said. "So far. Cathy has got worse reports than I have, and he's heard all the bad ones. Mrs. Rymal is even sympathetic."

"Do they want to see Cathy?"

"They want to know where she's living. That's one reason I'm here."

I put up my hands. "Pete's the only one to tell you that," I said.

"They want you to come around for lunch tomorrow, if you can."

With that invitation my studying day was halved, with a big piece chunked out of the middle.

"I don't see what good I'll be."

"You can at least help me squelch these rumours about her. It'll console them," Skip said.

"How about you?" I said. "Are you consoled?"

Skip laughed bitterly, shortly. "At first, some people tried to be nice about it and said it wouldn't last long, but, you know, when a thing's a rumour most people become two-faced, and, pretty soon, you find yourself facing a lot of hypocrites until you turn away from them all. I know everybody feels sorry for me--that's the first part of the chorus--but I can't stand the song because I know they don't mean it."

"At least they're pretending to be on your side," I said.

"One big trouble," Skip said, "is that they forget this is a private argument. Everybody wants in on the drama without playing any roles. Since this thing happened, I haven't been invited out once. I get nothing but far-away looks from those persons who used to ask me to their dinners. At first I didn't mind because I didn't feel like going anywhere, but after a while, you get to notice how cold the atmosphere is. Can't blame them too much I guess. They don't want to be seen associating with you. They get sort of scared of scandal and the only way they can pretend not to be afraid..."

"Is by sitting behind doors and giggling," I said. "I know. Real life is unlike the radio soap-operas in that it doesn't have the same success in winning sympathy for its sufferers."

Skip gave me a half-smile again. "I'm not suffering, and I know Cathy isn't. I don't think anybody can suffer as much as those radio actors."

"Aren't you in love with Cathy?"

"Sure, but I'm not going to let it be ruined by worrying because she doesn't love me. It makes me a little mad and I can get jealous damned quickly, but I won't be miserable. I'll just keep trying to get her back until she proves she likes someone better than me."

"Don't you think that someone is Pete?"

"I would hate to think so."

"She told me she wanted to marry him."

Skip grimaced. "She told me she was going to."

"She may be a spoiled girl," I said, "but she's strong willed."

"Yeah, but I'm sure she doesn't like him anymore than she does me. I think she loves me, Tom, still. He's just a passing flirt."

"She's doing more than flirt with him," I said.

"Don't tell me." Skip put his hands to his ears. "I don't want to hear any of that stuff and it won't do me any good."

I glanced out the window to see a newspaper blow across the front lawn with the paper boy in pursuit. The wind dropped, the sun came cheerily out from behind a cloud, the boy reappeared folding his paper while walking slowly back across the lawn, and the sharp window rapping of the old lady downstairs tattoed an aggressive complaint which nettled our nerves with its insistence.

"You're right," I said. "Every extra reason for complaint just aggravates the situation, like the old bag below who probably now will get that paper with pages missing."

Nancy walked into the room and started with surprise when she saw Skip. Self-consciously, she found a chair and sat down smiling uneasily at Skip because no doubt when she had now come face to face with the gossip's hero, she was feeling guilty about her part in fostering the rumour-mongering.

"Do you mind my listening in or is it terribly private?" she said and smiled at Skip, that irreproachable smile.

"Gosh no," Skip said. "You might help us. I guess you've heard about Cathy."

"Yes. I'm sorry." Her eyes looked it.

Skip glanced at his shoes. 'Maybe you'd know where she might be staying in Toronto."

Nancy shook her head sympathetically and then brightened suddenly. "Have you thought of asking Pete Miller?"

She got the reaction she wanted: Skip went red and choked out a negative. Now that she had rid Cathy from the conversation, she had to bring herself into it.

"Pete is such a fool, he wouldn't know, I suppose. What I saw of him, I didn't like," she said.

"Especially when he preferred Cathy," I laughed.

"That's not nice," she said.

ROMANCE

Skip stared intently at her. "He made a big mistake," he said with a seriousness that made us pause.

Nancy preferred to overlook any personal overture. "But I didn't like him." Yet seeing Skip trying to wither a disconcerted look, she added, "Like I did some people."

He smiled. With Nancy he looked for approval and then joked about it when he received it. With Cathy he was the First Lord of the Admiralty, but with Nancy he acted first mate. Nancy, too, would have liked him in that role if the words had had any literal value.

"You two can reminisce in the cutest way," I said, making them both acutely embarrassed, and then becoming embarrassed myself as if sensing that we had all become conscious of the other's secret life.

"Where's your sense of humour, Tom?" Skip laughed. "We're only joking, eh, Nancy?"

"What else?" she said simply, smiling at me. "Skip and I finished with each other ages ago."

"Beaux ago," I corrected.

"And the only thing we have in common is our joking." Her smile sharpened fiercely, as if she were grinning through pain.

"Wait a minute," Skip said. "I like you as much as I ever did, Nancy. Just circumstances are changed, that's all." He seemed struck by a fit of bad conscience which Nancy was deliberately eliciting from him.

"I know, Skip," she said, winking back tears. "I understand."

From where I was sitting, the scene looked uncomfortably melodramatic, and Skip unwisely staged. As I watched him talk with my sister who was getting him more involved in a friendship which at that time could possibly do him harm, as I watched my sister take advantage of his poor pummeled ego which lay in a wretched state after Cathy had finished with it, I realized that for what seemed a long time Skip had stopped being a hero for me. When I saw that he found difficulty in adapting himself smoothly to his social position as Cathy's husband, he began to fall in my estimation, and now that he was the cuckold, he was on the bottom floor in my house of admiration.

"But," he was saying, "it was just a little tiff between us, and Cathy's running it to extremes. You wouldn't do that, would you? You have too much common sense."

"If I'd had," Nancy said, "I wouldn't have let her marry you without a struggle."

Skip laughed, pleased. "It's hard to say where a guy'll be the happiest. Maybe I made a mistake."

"It is beginning to look like that," she said.

"If I let Cathy do whatever she wants, give her free rein, maybe what's supposed to happen, will."

"Why don't you?" Nancy said.

Skip took a deep breath and let his eyes focus far beyond the brass ash-stand he was looking at. "I guess it's because I love her."

For the moment Nancy was checkmated so that I came to her aid. "But it takes two people to make a real love." Then I hesitated, when I saw how low was Skip's morale and how rotten it was to play games with his feelings, how helpless they were in their betrayed state. I muttered something about fetching us all a drink.

In the cabinet in the dining room, in the section hidden behind a walnut door, I could only find gin and a little soda. When I came back to Skip and Nancy, they were looking serious and were leaning forward as if about to hold hands. Skip didn't stay long. He left with a reminder that I should come at noon the next day. Nancy took him to the door. I heard their voices drift up the stairway.

"Yes," she said. "I will."

"Then, the middle of next week?"

Nancy came into the room and, dreamy-eyed, trailed her finger over the top of the cabinet.

CHAPTER 23

"Well," Rymal said, "our Skip has been setting us a record of sales and everyone wants to make him a director, isn't that right?"

Skip nodded. There were four of us sitting in the April sun between showers, behind tall windows in the sports room. Mrs. Rymal graciously supplied us with buffet food, graciously prepared in large gracious platters.

"I think he deserves it, too. Wouldn't you say so, Tom Junior?"

"Yes," I said. "He has a remarkable capacity for the job."

"He must have," Rymal confirmed. "I feel lucky with him as a son-in-law. He's proved himself now. The only trouble is that, although I can be as happy as I like with him, my silly young daughter suddenly takes it into her head to pretend she's not happy with him. Always," he hit his knees, "we've had this trouble. She against me, me against her. It's inane! Whenever I come round to agreeing with her, she jumps onto something else and hi ho Silver! She's away again and we are back to where we were before; at loggerheads. She just won't like anything I like."

"This has nothing to do with the problem, dear," Mrs. Rymal said. "We are all old enough not to believe that she left Skip because you and she don't like the same things."

"Oh no? You don't think it's true? There's more than a grain of truth in that," he said. "She and I have an uncanny way--a sixth sense--of knowing what the other likes and dislikes. She instinctively disagrees with anything I agree with without any trouble whatsoever."

"Then she inherited it from your side," Mrs. Rymal said, "because I know nothing about it."

"Yes," Rymal said proudly. "She inherited it from me."

We took a bite of food! Mrs. Rymal to stop from retorting, Skip to stifle a denial, I to avoid the duty of replying, and Rymal because he was hungry.

"But there's more to it." Rymal sipped his beer and smacked his lips. "And that's what we want you to tell us, Tom Junior. Now don't be embarrassed because Skip's here. He wants to know too. Now tell us from your own opinion why Cathy has left him. Can you do that?"

"I don't know," I said. "I think it's because she likes someone else more than she does him."

The Rymals gasped. "But why should she leave him?" Mrs. Rymal said.

I looked hopelessly at Skip.

"She left me because she liked another guy," Skip said. "She doesn't need any more of a reason."

"But that's not our daughter," Mrs. Rymal said.

"No," Skip said, suddenly angry, "that's my wife." He returned their stares evenly, almost coldly.

"She doesn't change overnight," Rymal growled.

"She's the same as ever," Skip said, "and always will be, but as I've told you, I still love her."

"You think Cathy would leave you just for the sake of another man?" Rymal asked.

Skip nodded.

"Then you've got a poor opinion of our daughter."

"Cathy's no different from other people of our age," I said. "We've got different ideas now. If one doesn't love his mate why stay with her when there's someone else one could love and be happy with. Marriage ceremonies still insist on saying 'till death do us part,' but no one takes that oath seriously anymore, no one gets married with that point in view, which is mediaeval, to say the least, although many think they do. The world's changed so that divorce and separation have become common occurrences and thought no more of than Edison and electricity. Your generation agreed to adhere to such vows, but we, growing up, needed only to see our parents or their friends switching partners legally, instead of illegally like our ancestors, to desire a freer atmosphere with no guilty feelings to consider, in which to live. Of course, society frowns on our generation's style, but really we are more honest, more frank than your generation in the past when it would have to continue committing adultery and hurt their betrothed more than would a divorce. Cathy's behavior is not strange. It's the expression of the free person who has managed to throw off clerical or civil restraints, because she is capable of living freely her own life without any institution or communal organization to tell her what she ought to do. Cathy is typical of our generation. She is an individual, the twentieth-century woman with a free will, who might accept advice, never orders."

"Good lord!" Rymal cried. "Our problem is solved! Cathy leaves Skip to marry someone else and then leaves that someone else to marry someone else and so on. Think of all the son-in-laws I'll have! I can put them all in the Company. What the devil are you saying, Tom?"

"Don't worry. Cathy will stay in love always with someone even though she runs around with others, and I agree with Skip when he says she loves him," I said. "If we leave her alone to follow her own will, she'll come back to him."

"Meanwhile, she is causing a lot of noise in the city," Mrs. Rymal said, spooning me some potato salad. "We think she's inconsiderate not to have thought of that."

"Damned if I'm going to sit still waiting for her to make up her mind," Rymal said. "This generation is very strange. You give women credit for having minds. We didn't ever make that mistake."

"Women suffrage," Mrs. Rymal smiled, reminding him.

"That was a formal concession--we weren't admitting anything except that women could throw rocks."

Mrs. Rymal looked at the plates in front of her hopelessly stymied, yet, like a good sport, she was amused at her husband's words.

"Since she is my wife," Skip spoke up, "I'd like to handle the situation in my own way."

"Since she is my daughter," Rymal said, "I'm going to handle the situation in my own way."

"You see, Tom," Skip said, "this is why I needed you."

"You'd need a lot of people if you want to convince me to sit still while my married daughter is playing the vamp."

"That, she is not doing!" Skip spoke angrily, colour suffusing his cheeks. "You don't seem to understand. Cathy thinks she's in love with Miller. We have to persuade her she is not--but gently, not with a whip; you know how obstinate she is."

"Yes," Rymal smiled. "That characteristic comes from her mother. I remember now having the same difficulty trying to persuade her to come back when I was about your age."

"But I didn't leave you for another man," Mrs. Rymal said. "You and your drinking were too much for me, and they still are. I don't know why I came back."

There was a pause plunging us unwillingly into their troublesome past that we had not suspected, and which was not yet healed but thinly covered over. We were both slightly shocked and slightly embarrassed.

"Sometimes I wonder why you did too," Rymal said. "But here we are," he brightened, "together like apple blossoms from the same stem."

"Sour apples," Mrs. Rymal said.

"Huh! That's what Cathy is not. She's sweet, isn't she, son-in-law?"

Skip refused to answer. He walked over to a low table and came back with a box full of cigarettes which he offered to us. It seemed as if he were signalling his independence by not answering Rymal.

"What did you want me to tell you?" I said. "Skip mentioned..."

"The truth," Rymal broke in. "Has Skip really been treating Cathy well or has he been rotten to her since we've been away?"

I laughed. "As far as I know he's been good as gold."

"Because it takes two to make a quarrel."

"Three in this case," I said.

Rymal unlabelled a cigar. He was unwilling to blame his daughter for the separation, yet logic would not let him blame Skip. He wanted to find a middle way so that he could sympathize with Cathy, because he was her Daddy.

"And you have never seen Skip being unjustly rude to her?"

"What do you want?" Skip said sharply. "A signed declaration of my innocence? I tell you this is an affair between Cathy and myself. People will tell you that I haven't mistreated her. I don't see why you can't believe them. In fact, I'm at the point where I don't care if you do believe them. But just for the sake of reason, give it up!"

Rymal lit his cigar.

"Skip, we are not doubting your word, dear," Mrs. Rymal said. "But we have to know where we stand. We just can't sit by and watch Cathy ruin her life."

Skip shrugged his shoulders and moved his athletic frame to sink like lead into the flaccid cushions of his chair.

"Now, Tom, tell us," she said, "if you contacted this Miller boy, could you send us Cathy's address?"

"To you, I suppose I could. I promised her not to give it to Skip. But she'll contact you when she knows you're home."

"We can't wait for that," Rymal said.

"I'm not going back to Toronto until after the holidays," I said.

"Two weeks!" Rymal cried. He blew a large cloud of smoke at the moose staring majestically over our heads.

"Phone him now. It's early afternoon. He ought to be at home. Who is he anyway?"

"His father's a broker," I said.

Rymal slapped his forehead. "I know him. So she's wound his son up like a toy, trussed him up like a baby." He began to laugh while pulling me by the arm to a phone in a nearby room. "We'll get long distance."

It was Rymal's study, small, comfortable, clean, surrounded with shelves of leather-bound books, authors in complete sets, the modern classics, Kipling, Stevenson, Irving and Shaw, with the not-so-handsome volumes of Meredith and Trollope beside them. French, German and Indian translations stood in a special section. Below them were bound volumes of old newspapers, track journals, jockey club issues, magazines and almanacs of sport history. I thumbed through a Philip Gibbs while Rymal contacted the Millers in Toronto.

"Here, quick," he said.

I left Gibbs and took the receiver. Pete was called to the phone. He sounded like a kid of fourteen, and when he heard what I wanted, his reaction was very much that of an adult stalling, confessing his uncertainty, and finally telling me Cathy's address which I repeated aloud as Rymal scribbled it on a desk pad. He then asked me to wait a moment. I heard voices near to the phone, and he told me Cathy had just arrived.

"Tommie, I hate you" she said. "You promised me not to spy!"

I imagined Pete getting real hell about ten times as hot.

"It's for your father," I said. "Here."

Rymal was too eager. He forgot he was supposed to be angry with her or at least disapproving. His voice rose to an affectionate joy. It took them ten minutes to decide anything. The Rymals would drive to Toronto the next day to meet her and Pete.

"I'm positive there's a lot behind this," Rymal said after setting down the receiver. "It's not all her fault."

"It's not anyone's fault," I said. "It's circumstances. They were caught in something they couldn't handle."

"Okay," Rymal said, leading the way back to the sports room, "but why can't everybody realize that instead of blaming Cathy?"

Skip and Mrs. Rymal were standing together looking through a window at the sun on the green lawn. There was a strange sense of loss about them, which had not yet made itself felt. They sensed that an outside force was about to threaten and deprive them of an up-to-now comfortable and reasonable smooth-sailing life. The Rymals liked Skip for a son-in-law as would any couple who had not had a son, and Skip liked them as substitutes for the parents he had never known, so that the three of them were locked in affections which had seemed stable but now seemed too flimsy by the uncertain whims of torture. Skip took the news of his exclusion from the rendez-vous set for the next day with indifference. He had not expected Cathy to ask to see him with the Rymals, and he seemed to be aware that the attachment between daughter and parents was so great that it was he who would become the subject under discussion. Resignation had become an attitude of mind with him, when he was dispirited over Cathy. It was probably a defence against the hurt he must have felt. Pained as he was, he controlled the muscles of his face in front of company, and perhaps relaxed only when he was alone.

"The day is so lovely," Mrs. Rymal said. "We're driving to the Golf Club, and we'll stay there for tea. Would you like to come with us, Tom?"

I took the hint offered in gracious tones and formed a gracious negative. Skip saw me to the door.

"They're only going to make things worse," he said.

I didn't say that things couldn't be worse. His confidence was the only remaining trait which still held my admiration. All the rest, the glorious hockey star, the seasoned veteran, the sharp businessman, the hero had disappeared into the ignominy of his position. He was like the dazed ship-wrecked sailor who wouldn't give up his raft to board one of the rescue ships for fear of drowning.

"Cathy's not the only woman in the world," I said. "But I'm glad to see you think so."

Skip smiled widely then in imitation of the melon rind he used to form so spontaneously in the past carefree days.

CHAPTER 24

Gossip was on the run, rampaging the city. Everybody was *au courrant* with the latest. In the cafeteria, groceteria, and drugstore it seemed that wherever two people were together, the subject was the Rymals. But by everybody, I mean only those in society or who pretended to be, which meant some of the foot-of the mountain set, some of the Westdalers, and the odd East-ender who was still upholding the family coat-of-arms among the plebeian clerks and workmen. The large stretch of the North-end of the city had never heard of the Rymals except when his dollar bills were distributed before elections for their support of Rymal's choice of a Federal candidate. The people of the North-end had their own gossip and were not concerned with what happened in the south. Yet "the people who mattered" were now discussing extensively the character of the Rymal family. Cathy and Skip's scandal provided them with ample opportunity to express their grudges and hate with fanatic vehemence. Overnight, the Rymals' reputation fell from the respected-family part of the city leadership to the level of immoral aberration. Skip was presented as the victim. Cathy was Delilah, Judith, and Salome rolled into one. I heard several versions about why they were separated; none of them near the truth. But, then, no one was interested in the real story; all they wanted was the fall of the house of Rymal. They wanted it not because they seriously thought society would be better without the Rymals, but because they wanted excitement. The pleasure of seeing power slip on its backside was a reward to those who had taken second and third place to Rymal's first in social esteem. While some of the city's elite drew into themselves, remained reserved and secluded, Rymal threw open his doors and made his personality as big as his house with success. The signatures in "Rymal's visitor's book" were international whereas those in that of the other Hamilton patricians were largely inter-city.

But there were other scores, which people wished to settle with Rymal. He was a winning bettor so that in every sport from curling to horse-racing he had enemies. His life seemed to be lucky too because he had escaped the normal share of hardships, which was helped along by his unfailing sense of humour. His practical joking, too, had gained him more enemies, who wanted to see him miss out for a change, to see him suffer from a joke of fate. The revelation of latent evil among the overwhelming number of his fair-weather friends was astounding.

Nancy reported some of the stories to me, and we couldn't help laughing over them. In one, Cathy was supposed to have been previously married and had now returned to her first husband, a high-school teacher in a Toronto public school. In another, she was mixed up with a French-Canadian lover, a hired man on a fruit farm. Whatever was current, Nancy was sure to hear. She saw Skip and told me what was happening between him and Cathy. Although she still liked Skip, she saw that he was too in love with Cathy to think of her, so she spared her efforts to win his confidence and his sympathy. When it came to love, my sister had a head on her shoulders, but she was always being out-lucked. It was as if she were in a game where she had all the moves figured beforehand except for the last fatal one. The reason for her failure was never really understood by her. I suspected that she was as afraid of marriage as I was.

With Skip already married, she had no fear. She offered herself as a consolatory companion, and she and Skip found a platonic relationship of value to them both. While Skip had found a sympathetic listener to his worries about Cathy, Nancy could preserve her idealism of a communion that demanded nothing more from her than companionship without sexual involvement.

It didn't take long for Nancy's name to be connected with Skip's in the gossip. Friends stopped me on the street and, smiling, asked me the truth about Nancy, some among them her ex-beaux, so that I wasted a lot of time denying the reports and a lot of effort trying to look honest while doing so. But as long as my questioners kept smiling, the whole affair remained on a humorous basis, as if I were concealing some general joke which everyone was obliged to make me confess with so many pokes in the ribs.

Nancy was not looking happy about it. Being talked about made her furious and she adopted a disdainful look for streetwear. Although the suggestion of her part in the affair was brutally insidious, and horrified her when she stopped to think of it, the effect was to encourage her to react against it, and see all the more of Skip, in public, as if she were exonerating herself of any pettiness, which, she implied, lay completely in the minds of her gossipers. Unfortunately, she wasn't aiding her reputation, and the slights she received were inflicted on mother and myself as well. We had to convince her that if she must see Skip, their meetings would have to be more discreet. The gossip was not doing Skip much good either, but he didn't show any more sign of giving up Nancy's friendship than she his, yet I think they were both glad to have the welfare of her family as an excuse to stay out of the public-eye, which, in Hamilton, meant to refrain from entering public eating places together or going dancing, although the cinema was all right as movie-houses were dark enough to go unrecognized. Once I went with them to a film, and there was a small line-up at the ticket booth. They made me buy the tickets, while they went ahead and waited for me in an obscure corner of the lobby.

"How long is this going to go on?" I said to Skip. "You're going to have to marry my sister if you're not careful."

Skip thought it was funny. "Not a bad idea at that. She's the only one who's kept my spirits up for the last few weeks."

He was right, of course. Nancy had dragged him out of his doldrums. The sad longing which had hung in the lines of his face was gone. The memory of Cathy periodically fell on him, dampening his spirit, until Nancy held his attention again, and he would only think in the present and enjoy the life about him as much as we.

When we came out of the movie theater, we met a group of young people about my age, the girls among whom had tongues like reporters' typewriters. We knew that once again many people would be conjecturing on the moral state of the city and on how strong was the bad influence of Nancy and Skip on society's youth. For a moment, I felt slightly notorious merely by being in Skip's company, but I managed several strained hellos to some of the boys, who nodded coldly in return as they stared at what they concluded was adultery and hence a great sin.

"Now we can be seen anywhere tonight," Skip said.

"I've given up caring about it," Nancy laughed. "It's hopeless in spite of all precautions."

We drove a short way out of the city to a popular highway restaurant where there were sure to be people who'd know us. Sure enough, at one table sat a small party of businessmen and wives from the foot-of-the-mountain set. Smiling, Nancy led us to them and, they, surprised, welcomed us with a nervous spontaneity that left them gasping for something congenial to say.

"Well, well, well..." said the young vice-president of some small firm while strongly pumping Skip's hand, and calls of 'Nancy darling!' 'Fancy meeting you here!' and 'Hello!' rose in a disjointed chorus from the women. Since they were dawdling over coffee, they invited us to join them, explaining that their outing was in celebration of a birthday party, the honored one being a woman who looked young enough to still celebrate birthdays.

"I saw Cathy last week," a thin wife said. She rolled her eyes at the sudden attention, while her husband stared without a flicker of expression at hearing his wife's stale official news bulletin for the umpteenth time. "She was shopping in downtown Toronto with a blond-haired man. Quite good-looking." She rolled her brown eyes at Skip slowly enough to take everyone else's eyes with her.

"Her valet," I said. "He's a Swedish merchant-seaman who was ship-wrecked on Lake Ontario."

There was a pause of startled astonishment until Skip sneezed in laughter, and his sense of humour, which had been absent for the past six months, showed signs of returning. The thin wife lost countenance and the women reneged on the dramatic seriousness of her story.

"Your young brother could be a danger," an older man said to Nancy.

"He tells the best stories of anyone," Nancy said with a warning look at the honored one who was whispering to her neighbors.

Some of the women began to slowly gather up their belongings as if to say that the birthday party was over. The leave-taking was saved from any awkwardness by the arrival of the Rymals, who pushed through the doors on their way back from a week's stay in Toronto, so that we left the table to greet them, and, crying the birthday party a friendly adieu, we retired with the Rymals to another table, from where we could see the party-makers casting curious glances at us as they went out the door.

The Rymals wanted to know what was happening between Skip and Nancy because they had heard the rumours in Toronto.

"And the first thing we see, by George, is you two together," Rymal said. "Even before we get into the city proper."

After we had explained that there was absolutely no truth in what they had heard, the Rymals were still frowning.

"We don't think it's a good idea for you to be seen together whether it's perfectly innocent or not," Mrs. Rymal said.

"If you had had to listen to all the nonsense I have, you wouldn't see each other for the rest of your lives," Rymal said. "So many people have been warning me about what's been going on while I was away that I was half mad with the thought that everything about me was getting out of control."

"Show them some of the notes you received, dear," Mrs. Rymal said.

Rymal pulled a packet of letters from his coat pocket and slipped an elastic band from off them. "I'm saving these because someday I'm going to find out from whom they came."

He showed us the first letters, which were the usual crankish nonsense. But we saw a pattern of similarity emerging in them, that is, the suggestion that Rymal was a failure in the bringing up of his daughter just as he was in business.

"Probably from an ex-employee who was fired for drinking too much of the product," Skip said.

"Sure," Rymal swept his hand to the side. "These things don't matter so much as those who ought to know better. We've been snubbed by so many friends lately, we're afraid to speak to anybody. We were invited out to dinner in Toronto before our host had heard the news, but by the night of the dinner, he had heard, and our reception was the coldest I've ever known. We planned to see lots of people, but they weren't home when we called. Oh no, Brother, were they busy! So now I'm pretty mad, and tomorrow I'm going to get a little of my own back on the people I think have been spreading these nasty little stories." He stared at me. "I'm lucky to have met Tom Junior tonight because he's coming with me. Someone's got to drive the car, and I'm not going to be in a fit state to do it, d'you see?"

"Now be careful, dear," Mrs. Rymal said.

"Will ten o'clock tomorrow morning at our home suit you, Tom junior?" His eyes sized me up as if he were appointing me to the royal guard.

Smiling, I nodded and thought of the volumes of law I still had to read through.

"How is Cathy, Mrs. Rymal'?" Nancy changed the subject.

"She's fine, dear, but I have to admit she is acting foolishly about this Miller boy. Neither of us like him very much."

"He's a dope," Rymal said.

"But does Cathy know it?" Skip said.

"I think she does, Skip dear," Mrs. Rymal said, "but she won't admit it, even to herself."

"Typical," Skip said.

"You didn't persuade her to come back?" I asked, feeling precocious talking over the private concerns of parents whose daughter was older than I.

"Skip and you were right," Rymal said. "We didn't do any good. The more we insisted, the more she was set on doing the exact opposite."

"But I think she does miss you Skip. I can tell from some of the things she said," Mrs. Rymal smiled sadly. "And then a mother always knows her daughter."

"I knew she would miss him," Nancy said quietly as if to herself.

Skip smiled wryly. "Hope so."

With the Rymals, there was an undercurrent of optimism, which affected their immediate company, and which made them invaluable in times of stress. Now that they were with us, our meeting with the birthday celebraters was no longer unfortunate, rather just amusing, and the rumours directed at Nancy's reputation seemed no longer serious.

"Perhaps it would be better if we didn't see each other again until something definite is decided," Nancy said.

Skip opened his mouth to protest but then closed it again when he saw the sad, decided look on her face.

"That will make things so much better," Mrs. Rymal smiled.

Between Nancy and Skip, I sensed the knowledge of the end of something, perhaps the giving up of a striving after something that they knew could never be realized, or perhaps the recognition that the something had come and gone and now it was too late to reclaim it. I stared at the brown grains anchored to the white china bottom of my empty coffee cup and the forlornness of their broken companionship seemed to be reflected there.

When we parted for our different cars, Rymal heartily clapped me on the back. "Remember now, tomorrow morning. We're going to have us a wow of a time!"

CHAPTER 25

At ten o'clock, Rymal opened the front door of his mansion to me and led me down through the underground passage leading to his garage from where we appeared in a long black car. I drove with a sense of power and pride as if I were now a ruling aristocrat. The day was cloudy with April showers falling at intervals of sun which lit the water drops like tinsel on trees and houses. At this time of year, often it would rain while the sun was shining. Through one of these periods, we drove to a coal company where I accompanied Rymal into the head office. It was a glorious entrance, both of us walking under an umbrella through the sun until we came to the door that Rymal rattled open. He strode up to the main desk where a clerk, with papers in hand, stood nervously waiting for him, while I snapped shut the umbrella in the still pause between Rymal's stern look at the clerk and his first words.

"You have followed my orders?"

The clerk nodded, his 'yes sir' catching in his throat like a lump of coal.

"Send the truck load now, and I'll sign the cheque."

I heard the scratches of a wood-handled pen.

"And here's a little extra for the driver," Rymal gave him an envelope. "Make sure he does a good job."

When we marched into the sun again, it had stopped showering.

"I'm settling complaints," Rymal explained. "I remember one fellow complaining about the price of coal and lately he's been complaining about my daughter, so I thought I should help him out in one of his troubles. It's the least I can do."

The next stop was a lumber company, and I went with Rymal to the head office where a clerk and he went through the same procedure.

"Every time anybody visits this guy," he said, "he complains about his back porch being in terrible disrepair. Today, when he and his family are out of town, I arranged for a crew of wreckers to clear the porch away and build a small one after my own design in its place."

"What guy is this?" I said.

"Oh, he makes paper boxes or tin cans or something," he said.

I drove him to a pet shop. The owner was tall and muscular with an intelligence distinctly animal but with an instinct for easy money that was distinctly human. Although he himself was huge and could have been mistaken for one of the more athletic creatures of the jungle, his pets were on a much smaller and tamer scale.

"The fellow I'm now fixing up has a wife who loves cats. He hates them like poison. Every time he sees her pink-ribboned favorite, he throws something at it, with the result that there are some rooms in the house he never enters and some rooms that the cat never enters."

We followed the owner along by a row of cages in which were varieties of sleek-looking cats.

"Kittens're more pop'lar," said the owner, excusing himself for not having more of the full-grown vicious-looking kind.

Rymal stood back from the cages and waited until we stood back with him before pointing his cane in selecting the animals he wanted to purchase.

"Three of those yellow and white striped ones; about five of those tabbies there. They're cheap, aren't they? Then a couple of those brown-looking things with the black faces-- look like they've just drunk the blood of a Chinaman. And oh yeah! there're some nice black ones. You must've got them out of the back alley, didn't you? Beautiful symbols for death in the dark, eh, Tom junior? How about a few of those things you call Cheshire? That's what I mean. They look like they're settling down after a full dinner. When this guy sees them he'll think they're staying for life. Throw in one of those great big Persian specials with all the hair. Boy! look at the murder in those eyes. If you were a fish, you'd be gone, uh? Now this guy comes home for lunch about 1.30, so if you deliver them about two o'clock.... Do you get me, two o'clock?" Rymal held up two fingers in front of the owner's eyes, which were dazedly trying to see the total amount in dollars. "You'll catch him half-way through his meal. It ought to give him indigestion for the next ten years, if he doesn't die of fright on the spot."

As we left the shop, he called, "You'll have enough men to help you, won't you?"

The next stop was the last. "It's noon now," Rymal explained, "and I want to be watching when my old pal opens his door at two."

We stopped in at an office building in the centre of town and took the elevator to a stock broker's office. Rymal went into a private room in conference with a thin, smiling man whose hair was prematurely grey. He wasn't gone long because I had just time enough to read a short magazine article on the danger of inflation and necessity for investment in gold when he strutted beaming, swinging his cane toward me.

On the elevator he spoke in low tones. "One fellow doesn't know I own a lot of shares in a company that he's depending on, so I've transferred my shares for 36 hours, and we'll see how strong his nerves are when the floor falls out before I put them back."

"What did he do to deserve that?" I said.

"I overheard him say that Cathy was typical of the modern housewife--she carries on all her activities outside the house and outside the husband's knowledge. That made me mad!"

Rymal's face was pale, and his movements were increasingly nervous now that his business for the day was finished. Although I had smelt a faint trace of liquor on his breath in the morning, it had been at least two hours since he had a drink. Rymal was not an alcoholic in the sense of not being able to stop until drunk. He was rarely drunk, but he was always drinking, a paradox explained only by his strong constitution and his slow, deliberate method of taking strong liquor. Although he always had a strong drink at meal times, he limited himself to one only. And when he drank during the day, he didn't follow one drink with another, until he was sure that he could take it; consequently, one could not call him an alcoholic, he said, except that his taste for drink was incurable.

We went to one of his clubs for a quick lunch, and I took a rum and coke. We were in an oblong, thickly-carpeted, cushioned room, at one end of which the bar retreated from large conservatively furnished reading alcoves on either side of the room, cheerfully lit by the sun's diffusing beams through tall windows which were careful not to disturb the quiet atmosphere of the club by shining too brightly. There were a few other gentlemen, but I couldn't hear them talking. They provided the foreground to an old oil painted mural. Over the bar, there was an oil painting of a clean, smartly-dressed jockey sitting on a brown horse, which looked startled as if at something in the room, perhaps the bald head of one of the members.

The waiter brought us toasted cheese and ham sandwiches when we had finished our drinks. Already Rymal was more at ease as if his club were his home and a tranquil oasis which the chaos of the outside world could not disturb.

"I've seen the days when I didn't leave this building for weeks. They've got bedrooms upstairs, you know."

He was the father of a beautiful girl, and I supposed he must have been good looking when he was young, but now it was hard to imagine how he had looked. Too many whiskey-evenings had lined and strained his features early in life so that now, when he was past middle-age, he already looked old, yet his spirits remained young, even juvenile. His energy was fired by an enthusiasm for a good time, it sparkled up like the last few small bubbles rising through a glass of stale beer to puncture the surface and fizzle out. When he was amused, he looked his youngest. Now that he had set into motion an afternoon of practical jokes, his spirit was getting younger, and his face beamed with expectant humour. If it is true, as the ancient Greeks have told us, that the gods make sport of men, then Rymal was a god, rubbing his hands eager to see his plans in action.

"I'm sort of sorry to have to do this to these fellows this afternoon, but in this game everyone's on his own. You sink or swim depending on how you fight back. I'm going to swim, Tom junior."

"You've never been sunk," I said.

Rymal rounded his eyes and mouth. "Oh ho! Don't say that! I've been sunk many times, but I've been lucky and people haven't noticed. But this time it's different. When people attack me through my daughter, I give no mercy. Ridicule is the most merciless weapon I can think of."

We left the club and drove to a stop on a street at the side of a large house whose garden, surrounded by a high board fence, ran for a block in depth. A gate had been opened in the fence, and when we stepped into the garden, we were met by a carpenter-foreman, who spoke with us while we watched his crew build a porch.

"You work fast," Rymal said.

Hitching a thumb across the strap of his overalls, the foreman smiled with pleasure. "It's a lark for the men, sir. We're using the wood from the old porch and this here new one's easy to make."

Rymal's design, which the foreman held in front of us, showed three cubic blocks on top of one another leading to the house door. The letters A B C were to be affixed each one to a block, and, on the top block, was to be laid a new broom, and a sign was to be fastened to the wall of the house, "Please Keep Clean."

"The trouble is, sir, a fellow has to sorta climb from one block to the other."

"Put a rope down the centre then," Rymal said. "Although the owner is a small man, I know he is fond of reading about expeditions in mountain climbing."

When we left and were out of sight of the workmen, Rymal, putting his fist to his lips, began to giggle. We sat in the car, and his body shook until he burst into a series of short coughs, while I sat smiling, trying to glimpse into his mind and figure out how his imagination with its peculiarly comic insight worked. But his world was out of reach, and I had to wait until he came back to mine, which he did abruptly by glancing at his watch and gasping that it was almost two o'clock.

The house, in which the man who hated cats lived, was near by. We had no sooner parked the car than we saw three men lean into a van and gather an armful of cats. When all of their arms were packed solid with fur, the men stepped to the door of the house where one of them wiggled his small finger free to ring the doorbell.

While they waited for someone to answer, I admired their power of command over the animals. I supposed it demanded special understanding to be able to handle them so quietly and efficiently because the cats had allowed themselves to be packed like sandwiches in rows of four and five. Pussy faces stared calmly in greens, browns, blacks and yellows over dangling hind quarters of corresponding colors. Even the gray Persian monster declined to cry out against being dangled by its neck for a two minute wait, although the glare from its eyes clearly expressed how great was the insult to its noble nature. The door opened, and a young maid gaped at the men as they stepped inside. Rymal grasped his thumbs with his fingers and keenly watched the closed door. A moment later, the men appeared again and hurried to their truck. Rymal rocked with glee, and I was excited too. The truck had begun to move down the street when the door was flung open and a man in his sixties rushed down the steps into the street where he stood shouting furiously at the disappearing van. I glanced at Rymal to see him bunched in a hysterical ball bouncing below the windshield, and I slid down in the seat to avoid being seen. For a few moments, we heard only the exasperated roars of the man in the street and our stifled laughter. Eventually, a woman's voice sounded from the door and we pushed up enough to peek over the edge of the window. The man's wife was standing blissfully cradling the Persian and looking with opal eyes over the murderous gleam from the animal, which seemed to have taken immediate dislike to the man in the street. He stood deserted by the tempest of his anger and trembling in attention to the woman.

"Oh Harry!" She sighed, "Isn't he beautiful!"

I let out the hand brake, and, unnoticed, we slowly coasted down the street leaving Rymal's pal stranded outside his house while Rymal grasped his middle with both arms in a frantic effort to hold still his jiggling stomach muscles shooting pains in complaint at the most outrageous exercise.

As I loosened the clutch, the motor kicked in, and I directed us toward the Rymal mansion. He was too weak to move himself. I had to help him out of the car, and, with one of his arms over my shoulder, I guided him into the house to a comfortable chair in the hallway from which he waved me an exhausted farewell, a light of appreciation glimmering over the pink of his face.

As I strode down the steep slope of the avenue, it started to shower again, as a reminder that the gaiety was over. I wondered why Rymal had chosen me instead of his chauffeur to drive him about that day. Perhaps he thought I would appreciate his humour more or perhaps he wanted a sympathiser, who could understand his revenge, who would know he was doing it for Cathy, and who then would be in agreement with the method he used.

As I passed a corner house, I looked over tons of coal heaped on the front lawn. The residential atmosphere of quiet respectability hovered about the mound. The soot, strewn black over the green grass, was splattered across the sidewalk into the road. The rain had carried some of the dust away in gray rivulets pushing over the pavements and forming large puddles looking like long charred pan-handles. The frustrated efforts of the rivulets to reach the sewers reflected my own at seeing Rymal's pathetic attempts to revenge himself. Without him laughing beside me, I could see no real humour in his jokes; I felt only the slight humid heat in the air and smiled mildly at the thought of the plight of Rymal's stingy 'Pal' on receiving coal for the summer time.

As I walked on, I thought of how similar Cathy was to her father in wanting the last laugh. It seemed incredible but it might be conceivable that her affair with Pete was provoked by a desire to pay Skip back for such things as giving her a worrying night that time when she had failed to fool him with the New York trip. Her imagination could quite easily have been inherited. As I thought of this, I determined to see her the next time I was in Toronto.

CHAPTER 26

One exam was scheduled a week ahead of the others. When I went to Toronto to write it, I phoned Cathy's hotel after I was finished. It was early afternoon, and fortunately she was in her room. She asked me to come by.

Plush was the name for her surroundings. Her rooms looked extremely comfortable. We sat by a rubber plant with thick leaves behind us and looked over roof tops of the city. Since there was a warm sun that day, as always when one writes exams, she had been sitting on the small balcony leading off from her sitting room and playing old jazz and Dixieland records. The first thing she did was to play a Bessie Smith. She had found it at the bottom of a dusty pile in a second-hand store for fifteen cents.

"Luck is where you find it," she laughed.

Bessie's deep sexy voice could have sparked danger between two young people alone in an apartment but Bessie became the more important topic than her torrid voice as we relaxed and discussed her personality which must have been big, black, and warm.

"How's Pete?" I asked when the record was finished.

"Haven't seen him for days," she said.

"I haven't seen him for weeks." I said. "How is he?"

"Why don't you ask him yourself if you're so interested?" she said.

"Don't you like him anymore?"

"No, Tommie dear, I don't like him anymore."

"Doesn't he like you?"

"He never really did like me." She stretched her body over the floor to reach a record, and the soft forms of her figure were revealed in all its grace and beauty, and it might have been deliberately seductive had I not realized that she was absolutely unaware of how compellingly attractive she was.

"Oh, I don't believe that," I said, mistrusting the joy beginning to jump in my chest.

She put on a Bunk Johnson with wheedling off-beat combinations so that the rhythm made us stand and do a crazy dance, springing our knees, hipping our shoulders, softly tapping fingers in palms, swinging our feet, moving slowly round each other, back and forth to bob and weave and show-off how extravagantly individual we were. When Johnson died out on his horn, we were against each other and I put my arms about her. My nose went in her hair and I breathed.

"I want to go back to Skip," she said pushing up her face against the side of mine.

"Oh hell," I said. "Don't tell me you love him again."

I dragged myself away to a chair, and she came and sat on my lap and played with the fringes of my hair.

"He's my husband and I've been away long enough."

"What happened with Peter?" I asked.

"It was just one of those things, and anyway he's always had other girls."

"He believes in numbers, I guess."

"No," she said and moved away to get her cigarettes. "He just needs them. But I only want one, and now I know that that's Skip."

Her voice floated out of the distance on the other side of the room. A match scratched and I heard the exhale of breath so feminine in the soft wind.

"He's been going out with Nancy hasn't he?" she said breezily, pretending disinterest.

Then I knew that she really did love him.

"So you want to run home and rescue your treasure from the fire, eh?"

She brought me a lit cigarette which surprised me. She was getting more thoughtful. Before she wouldn't have remembered to offer me one let alone light me one without being asked.

"Rescue my husband, Tommie, dear?"

"Ah, yes! Every little girl's dream of security," I said. "Once it's threatened, you gotta run home and bolster it up."

"Oh Tommie, stop talking nonsense. Help me go back to Skip. Does he still want me?"

I was recruited. I came back in an hour and found her packed ready for the return.

"Don't you think you should phone Pete?" I said.

"We'll drop in at his place on our way. I want to say good-bye to his mother. She's sick, so I should."

The large white house with its Corinthian columns looked less mysterious in the daylight, and the green of the long lawns surrounding it enhanced the pillaring effect of the white so that it rose with the grandeur of an ancestral seat brought up to date. Cathy parked in the circle by the garage, and I followed her to the door for which she had her own key. We came to the games room, and I saw the countryside slide in soft slopes into the city all along the opposite wall.

"Isn't the view wonderful?" she said. "This is the only thing I'll miss, sitting here in the day and in the night. It's corny romantic at night."

I sat in an easy chair facing the window and glanced through a magazine while I waited for her. It was like May outside, although the calendar hadn't got that far. Bright sun encouraged blossoms on the trees in whites and pinks, and they had filled out with leaves. All was still, yet there was a promise of renewed life and freshness in the air, as if any minute now a party of nude picnickers might suddenly appear and lie on the green lawns in gay embrace before a feast of wine and kisses.

A door closed, and I saw Pete in tennis whites swinging a couple of rackets with a tall blonde girl. He was explaining a backhand stroke and, stopping her, he stepped quickly to one side to illustrate what he was saying, his form moving easily in masculine grace. He saw me when he pretended to see where the ball had gone.

"Hiya, man!"

His girl was called Mag, naturally. She was terrific looking with heavenly blue eyes smiling under a cluster of golden hair.

"Pete said tennis is good for the figure," she said. "So I'm learning."

Any improvement in her tennis would have been superfluous, but I supposed it was the only way Pete could persuade her to go through the preliminary training in order to keep her with him. He was diplomatic with women, but I was curious how he would manage the situation with Cathy and this new girl. Before I could explain my presence, a voice broke in on us. Pete went behind the bar and spoke down.

"Yes, ma."

"Cathy is here, Peter. Come right away, won't you?"

"Yes, ma."

When he had left us, the blonde took the chair beside me. Her tiny white shorts marked one end of her gorgeous long legs. I wished that there were picnickers on the lawn outside and that we could have joined them.

"Who is Cathy?" she asked.

"A friend of his mother," I said.

"His mother is awfully strict with him, isn't she?"

"She bosses him."

"More than that," she said. "Pete told me she's the only person he's ever really liked, and she's always sick and cranky and takes advantage of his sympathy. She made him take me to see her the first time I was here. He says all his friends have to meet her."

All his girl friends, I thought.

"I think she's horrid!" The blonde crossed her legs and shifted sulkily on her shanks.

We heard voices raised in argument coming our way. Cathy pushed through the door in a flurry of throw-away gestures while Pete followed immediately behind her. They stopped shouting when they saw us. Ignoring the blonde, Cathy approached me.

"Tommie dear, we've discovered a star for our new Canadian theatre. At the moment he is playing Othello with a frightening sense of reality. All he needs is a Desdemona. There!" She arched a finger at the blonde. "There you are, darling. Strangle her."

Pete's face was wrenched grimly between stopping Cathy and still keeping the blonde. I expected to see him wither away in indecision, but, when it came to women, he was a genius. Striding for the blonde, as if he were intending to strangle her, he kissed her instead, passionately. The poor girl was like a moppet in his arms, but Cathy stared in disbelief slowly giving way to jealousy. When the kiss was finished and the blonde was holding to Pete for support from what she must have experienced as a lightning transformation from hate to love, Cathy was frantic for some way to make an impression before she left.

"Bravo, Peter! I haven't seen you kiss like that for over a week. But I see you won't get out of practice when I'm gone."

Ignoring her, Pete whispered comfortingly to the girl in his arms. Cathy was angry enough to throw something. But she whirled on her heel and struck out for the door.

"Wait!! Wait!"

At the door I glanced back to see Pete with one arm around the blonde and the other outstretched toward me, his fingers vainly grasping at the air, distress and pain showing in his face. I shrugged my shoulders hopelessly at him and galloped down the stairs across the driveway, to open the car door and jump in just in time as Cathy drove off. We sped over a country road kicking up dust and stones which beat the fenders in imitation of her anger. But suddenly, she jammed her foot on the brake, and I went arms first against the windshield. She looked at me as if realizing there were other people in the world besides herself.

"What a silly goose I am! He means practically nothing to me, Tommie, nothing at all! He's just a part of my vanity!"

"Wow! Are you changing! What book did you get hold of?"

She gave me a pleasant smile, and we moved forward in low gear. "Living alone, I've had lots of time to think."

"You have changed," I said.

She hit me with one arm, and I seized it. We wrestled for seconds while the car slowed down and stalled to a stop. I held her back against the seat, my lips close to hers.

"How much have you changed?" I said.

"Enough to allow one kiss and then I'm going back to Skip."

I thought of saying 'I will collect it later then,' or 'Then it's no use wasting our passion,' but I did kiss her, and we did start the car, and we did go back to Skip.

When we arrived outside the Rymal house, Cathy was afraid to go in.

"I just can't walk in as if I'd never been away," she said. "Skip will want some explanation and I don't want to have to give him one."

"No, he won't," I said. "Anyway he'll still be at his office."

She brightened then, and, with me carrying her suitcases, we approached the house in the mood of a confident female prodigal, who although expecting no fatted calf, was at least glad that no one was about who would stop her from entering. A maid answered the door and looked more pleased than surprised, fortunately, so that Cathy jumped the first hurdle of reception with ease. Mrs. Rymal met us in the hallway, and in her pleasure she looked the expression of relief.

"Cathy! At last dear! You're back!'"

I dropped the cases and followed the women, their arms encircling one another's waists, into the sports room at the back of the house.

"Skip went with your father to see the construction on your house, dear. They ought to be back any moment."

"Oh, mother! I'm so happy to be home!"

"I know, dear!"

Mrs. Rymal put her arms about Cathy who had pushed her head onto her mother's shoulder. It was a scene which made me uncomfortable looking on the way I was, outside of their feelings, as if I were a part of a theater audience watching the actors on stage, except that I was not a part of the audience and they were not acting. We heard men's voices approaching along the hallway and both women, startled, shot anxious looks at me. I stepped along the hall and met Skip and Rymal. They had seen Cathy's car in front and been told by the maid of her homecoming. Skip was striding swiftly, his face in one huge smile while Rymal hurried behind him. Feeling completely impersonal to Skip's happy glow, I winked him an okay as if I were glad that he was going to be happy. Mrs. Rymal caught Rymal at the door as Skip rushed into the room. She led her husband and myself back down the hallway. We were not to intrude.

"So nice of you to accompany Cathy," Mrs. Rymal said.

"Yes," I said.

The big door of their house thudded dully in the open air when it closed behind me. I stepped on to the long front walk to the street, empty of people, where a few new cars shone in the late sun. Cathy's Nash was there, a weight in my heart when I saw it, a mental lump of dull nostalgia now that it was without its soul, but more fortunate than I because it would soon have her again and I, never, or so it seemed.

CHAPTER 27

One expected the talk to heighten now that Skip and Cathy were together again, but instead, it deflated into indifference now that their problem was resolved and everybody pretended it had never happened. Happy endings are so dull and uneventful! The only influence of the scandal was on Nancy; it helped her decide in favour of accepting a good post in the commercial design department of an advertising company in New York. The offer came unexpectedly and Nancy left immediately with the hopeful boast that at least New York was big enough in which she may find the perfect man.

She was gone within the week, and I was writing my exams back at Osgoode. As I was expecting a difficult exam the next day and had planned to re-read a chapter I hadn't understood well, the house waiter called me away from the dinner table to answer the telephone. Cathy was calling from Hamilton. She wouldn't tell me what was wrong, but she was in tears, and she wanted to see me. I had had enough of her wanderings back and forth between one man and another and of her involving me emotionally in her crazy little whims, but I agreed to her suggestion that she drive to Toronto that night to see me. Like most people, I had many weaknesses, the weakest of which was my capacity to sympathize. I rationalized that it was because she was crying that I was going to see her.

She arrived at the Frat House at nine, her face looking white and tear-stained under the porch light, where I was called to meet her as she had refused to come inside. We went to her car and sat there in the dark. She wasted little time explaining that I was the only person she could turn to for help, which she needed now more than ever before in her life. I thought her build-up typically feminine and ridiculously yet compellingly dramatic.

"Stop beating around the bush and tell me," I said.

I guess I sounded angrier than I was because she hesitated as if startled by my tone and spoke to me calmly in harsh contrast to the girlish pleading of a minute before.

"This afternoon the doctor told me I was pregnant."

"Fine," I said. "What's wrong with that? Skip'll want a child."

"But it won't be his. It's Peter's."

I was staggered by her news. Then the whole thing seemed ludicrous as if some huge joke were being played on me, as if I hadn't had enough of a nightmare with Melanie without finding myself in the grotesquely ironical position of advising Cathy, from a superior moral standpoint, to decide for once in her life against her interests.

"I just couldn't face Skip," she said, the horror of the ordeal spreading over her features as she imagined it.

"But if he loves you," I said, "he'd understand."

"Oh Tommie, you're a dreamer."

"Has something happened between you again?"

"No, no! We love each other now really deeply, deeply, deep. I love him so much I couldn't hurt him, and I would if I told him. Oh Tommie, don't you see, this is awful! I couldn't live with him ever again if he knew."

"But he's not like that," I said. "He'd love the kid no matter who was the father, wouldn't he?"

"He'd know who the father was, and you know how much he likes Peter. Oh Tommie, it would be awful!"

I could appreciate her terror. But despite my genuine sympathy for Cathy's predicament I could not help feeling secretly a warm sense of self congratulation at my own luck in winning Cathy now at last.

"Do you still like Pete?" I asked, my mind working mechanically ahead.

"I hate him! I hate him and I hate his child!"

"Are you sure? Hate is supposed to be the other face of love, so they say."

"Tommie, Tommie!" she groaned and let her head fall against my shoulder. "I love Skip so much that Peter just doesn't exist any more. I only hate that which I knew, and I don't hate it only but also that part of me that belonged to that past which doesn't have anything more to do with me now, don't you see?"

"Okay," I said. "Then you've either got to turn to the past which you hate, or to the future which you fear, to get out of this."

Since she didn't make any attempt to answer, I felt that she wanted me to take the lead in suggesting a course of action that would help her climb out of her present paralysis and boost her courage.

"You've made it almost impossible to go back to Skip," I said. "Have you talked to Pete?"

"No."

"Why don't you see him tonight?"

"Oh, Tommie, isn't there anything we can do?"

She wanted me to suggest the dreaded step, I thought.

"Nothing else that I know of," I said.

She looked at me, and I saw her wondering whether she should say what she wanted. She probably knew that I knew what she was thinking.

"Can't I get rid of it?" she said.

I couldn't look into her eyes any longer. She wanted the truth out of me, and I didn't want to help her. Of course she could get rid of It! But what about It? Does It always have to suffer because It happens to be in the way? Why can't someone else suffer for once?

"You don't want to do that," I said.

"But I want Skip!"

Cathy was a spoilt little girl now, wanting what she couldn't have. The sporty sex-cat that drove the Nash weeped like Raggedy Ann, and, for a moment, I wanted to help her but some kind of scruple, which made me uneasy, kept me from speaking. Intuitively, I felt it was wrong for me to advise. I had helped her enough in the past and now was the time to look on and let her make her own decisions; or watch fate make her decisions for her.

"Don't you think I should?" I heard her saying.

She wanted me to be her fate. I had the power of direction. She wanted me to play God with a power over life and death. But she was merely a girl of a woman lost in her distress, who sought guidance from a strip of a boy, who saw selfishly that if she entered a loveless marriage, eventually she would be ready for his love.

"You'll be sorry if you do. Life is more important than the rules of society, or the jealousy of one man, or the hurtful gossip of half the world."

"You're right," she said hopelessly. Then, wiping at her eyes, she tried to smile. "Will you go to the Millers' with me?"

"No," I said, and I pushed the car door open.

When I stood on the pavement looking in the door, I saw Cathy's frightened face, and I was glad because I knew she would mess everything up. I could see her babbling it all to Pete's mother and the old lady shaking a hair brush at her dutiful son and then at last it would be good-bye Skip, 'good-bye Mr. Chips.'

CHAPTER 28

I was right in what I had guessed. When the examinations were finished, and I was back in Hamilton about the middle of May, it was generally known that Cathy was divorcing Skip with the plan to marry the son of a wealthy Torontonian. The decision was popular with those who thought she had married out of her class and with those who were sure her marriage with Skip was ever doomed to failure. The Rymals were of the latter group. Now that their daughter was uniting the two rich and powerful houses, allying their wealth with that of a Toronto millionaire, they were quick to recognize how popular they had become amongst friends and neighbors, and so their attitude to Skip was not as sympathetic as previously. Assuredly, only the Millers knew that Cathy was with child, but the Rymals, who could not understand her sudden definite decision to marry Peter, fell in with the idea of her divorce and marriage and brandished banners which reflected the slogans of their society. Thus, Skip was shunted to the side from where he watched the whole charade like an unwanted tramp.

I heard that a great change had taken place in him. When Cathy had returned to him, he had never looked happier. But the news of her suit for divorce had hit him so sharply that he was severely stunned to a pitiable state of total inertia, which affected every aspect of his life. His new directorship floundered, and there was talk that he was becoming like the old Rymal, a burden to the company. There was, too, a reaction in the city against him. No longer supported by and at the top of society he felt the ladder pulled from under him and he fell hard to the bottom in a pitiably crushing heap.

At the end of the month, I heard the first real report on him. He had not been seeing anyone, nor leaving the Rymals' house much, but Tim Lake, whom I met walking downtown, said that he had seen him and was seeing him again that evening. He wanted me to come with him. Whether it was out of morbid curiosity or a true sense of sympathy that made me agree, I don't know, but I was looking forward to seeing Skip. Tim and I arranged to meet at a local drug store at eight o'clock and go to the Rymals' house from there. Tim ran off because the five minutes he had spent talking with me had made him late for an appointment with an insurance client. Like all of us, he said, he was not governed by his will, but by his obligations.

The time between then and the evening was a bore. I spent it being interviewed by a few legal firms who wanted cheap apprentices for the summer months when established lawyers took expensive holidays. In August business was slow and easily managed by a few intelligent university law students happy enough to earn paupers' wages. I knew, however, that I would have to work at the Legal Department of the Steel Company to make enough money to go back to Osgoode. I'd needed some understanding solicitor, perhaps a classmate's father, to say that I had worked hard with him and had proved myself invaluable as a searcher. I went home for dinner and, finally, when it was still light, I found myself waiting in front of the drug store window looking at the tooth paste advertisement in which a giant tube made me appear as if I was the little man who had just popped out of it.

Tim was five minutes late, which made me think that our earlier meeting had put him off schedule for the rest of the day. He was most unhappy about Skip.

"Poor Skip, the poor guy," he said. "I phoned him a while ago and told him you were coming. He's feeling miserable, but he said he wanted to see you 'cause he's leaving Hamilton so it's good that you're coming with me. I wanted him to go back into insurance; everybody wants him to, but he just wants to get away for a while."

Tim led me to his car and after a few sharp jerks the machine moved forward, he peering over the wheel as if he were looking through fog.

"Where does he want to go?" I asked.

"As far away as possible. Maybe Vancouver."

The idea of the West appealed to me just as it had to almost every other Easterner since Columbus had sparked the spirit of adventure in that direction, but I was like many people who never wished to go beyond the dream stage, which may help explain why so many novels of the West are popular. It is preferable to remain comfortable in one's home in the East than lead a life of hardship and sacrifice in the West. But I had seen photographs of Vancouver with its tall

ROMANCE

white buildings assembled under the snow white crests of the Rockies, a rich city of commerce, full of expensive autos, colorful tugboats, totem poles in parks, and where the god Mammon held hands with his big-brother south of the border. I admired Skip for his choice.

"But what about Rymal's beer?" I said.

"He resigned last week." Tim looked happy.

We said nothing more until we were at the house when the maid led us again to the sports room. Skip was standing at the window, his figure outlined in the twilight. He moved tiredly toward us and offered us chairs. It wasn't until the maid had drawn the curtains and switched on the lamps that I saw how thin Skip was, how long his face had become, and how his eyes were glazed with hurt and the attempt to protect himself from similar experiences.

"You see an old crock, Tom, don't you?" he said slowly. "No energy, no wit, no man, no nothing."

"Not yet," I said. "But after a while I might notice it."

"Yeah," he said. "Damn it, I'm sorry."

"You don't need to be sorry," Tim said sympathetically and inadvertently drawing attention to Skip's self pity. "You've got a right to feel as low as you want."

"How're your exams?" Skip broke away with an effort.

"Okay." That was all he wanted to know. "How's business?"

He shrugged his shoulders. "My bags are packed, and I'm leaving on a train early in the morning."

"Just tell us when you want us to go," Tim said. "We don't want to keep you up."

His concern was so obvious and his remarks so incongruous that even Skip managed to smile. "I won't see you again, Tim. I'm not coming back."

Tim gaped at him and then shut his mouth firmly, unanswering.

"This place is not for me," Skip said. "I should have had my head examined to stay here this long."

"Do the Rymals know you're going?" I asked.

"No. They're staying in Toronto now--away from their son-in-law, the untouchable."

"The gang'll be sorry," Tim said, frowning in disappointment over the thin rims of his glasses.

"No one'll be that," Skip grimaced. "I don't belong anymore, and I guess I never really did." He looked glumly around him at the animal heads on the walls, the trophies, the low modern lines of the furniture. "Let's get out of here. We can go and get a drink somewhere. This place is too full of ghosts--reminding me of too many things."

He disappeared up the stairway for a moment while we waited at the door. When he returned, he carried a suitcase.

"My other stuff'll be shipped," he said.

I could imagine the extent of his other stuff. One didn't live half a year with the Rymals without adding considerably to one's wardrobe. If one elected to uphold the personality of a millionaire, one had to be groomed and glitter all over like one. I bet all his pajamas were new.

"But your train isn't leaving till the morning," Tim protested.

"At four," Skip said. "A bloody hour, eh?"

When we were getting into Tim's car, Skip turned round to take a last look at the mansion and attempted a feeble joke: "Well, for me, I guess the honeymoon is over."

If I said I felt sorry for him, I'd be lying, but I wished I could feel sorry for him. He had adjusted himself well enough to his misfortune, and was now able to accept it reasonably. He was not leaving Hamilton, however, with the same ambitious confidence with which he had arrived. He was a thin, sad imitation of the one-time hockey idol. His big open smile was now a sarcastic twist. And when he sat in the car, he complained of pains in his bad leg.

Carefully, Tim drove us to a tavern in the East End. A few men in working clothes were discussing rudimentary politics at the counter, but we managed to get by them and order some bottles of beer. The tables were occupied by rummies or prostitutes except for one standing conspicuously draped with a red and white chequered linoleum cloth. We sat at it and ignored the eyes watching our comparatively clean and expensive clothes.

"I never thought I'd be back in one of these places," Skip said.

"We can leave soon," Tim said. "I know a cocktail bar that just opened up. A new thing in this city, you know."

"It won't last," Skip said. "Anything new just won't last."

We drank our beer as if we had an urgent thirst, but it was really because Skip was leading us, giving us the impetus as he savagely downed the contents of a bottle and held it out in front of him.

"See the label? This is Rymal's biggest competitor, and it tastes miles better than anything Rymal could ever turn out. Let's have another and toast to it!"

Tim fetched more bottles, and we drank quickly from them.

"I'm glad I've given up the beer racket," Skip said. "And they were glad I gave up too. Cathy's new husband ought to fit into my job pretty well. I guess she really hates me. She has taken away everything she had ever given me. I didn't think she was so rotten even when she was treating me so badly, 'cause I always thought deep down she loved me. I really thought that, you know. Geezus! how stupid can I be!"

Knowing what I did, I felt uncomfortable so I thought I should say something. "You can never tell a woman's mind, Skip."

"Boy! I know that now. Never again will I trust any woman enough to marry her. I pronounce my curse on all marriages right now." He swayed his hand over the neck of the bottle.

"Hey Skip, for a man who sold beer you get high quick," Tim joked.

A faint red glowed for seconds under Skip's cheeks. "Well, I was drinking a bit during the day," he excused himself.

We returned to swallowing until the bottles were empty. Because it was ten, the lights flickered and the clientele pushed themselves away from tables.

"If we go to your cocktail joint," Skip said, "we won't meet any snobs, will we?"

Tim hesitated as if doubtful about guaranteeing that no snobs will be there.

"If we do," I said, "we won't see them."

"Perfect!" Skip cried. "The best thing we can do! You know, Tom, you really belong to this city."

Poor Skip; he was confusingly identifying Hamilton with the snobbish society he came to know. But that society formed only a small segment of the city. There were several other regions that housed other classes of people. Hamilton was no different from other big cities, but its elite society was distinctively different in overall personality from other elite societies of other cities. Hamilton's was staid, provincial, whereas another city's might be sophisticated, broad-minded. So when he said that I suited Hamilton, it didn't bother me, because I didn't believe him. I never thought of myself as part of Hamilton's elite.

The several beers Tim had drunk seemed to have smoothed the kinks in his driving so that we breezed through the centre of town and stopped outside the Public Library with its high fluted columns blackened by years of industrial pollution. It stood alone, locked and barred for the night, while at the side of it, across a narrow street, was the cocktail bar called the "The Two O'clock Bell", painted in tasteless red under a huge false clock pointing out the hour of two o'clock. The cocktail bar overlooked a small area of slums which "powerful men" were going to clean up and replace with a parking area to "solve" the traffic problem. The "Two O'clock Bell" and its proximity to the slums symbolised the city's class divisions: rich over poor, the "cocktail-drinkers" over the beer guzzlers who snored six to a room in the ramshackle houses below.

"It says 'two' because it closes then," Tim said, enjoying his importance as our introducer to the bar.

Inside, we took a shiny, red-topped table surrounded by red-seated chairs and ordered strong drinks from a red-nosed man. If we looked to one side, we could see ourselves reflected in a wall mirror.

Tim bounced on the cushions of his chair. "It's comfortable though, isn't it?"

"Very," Skip said.

He bowed his head, and I knew he was thinking of the real wealth he had to give up for this cheap imitation. He knew now that he'd have to enter many such shoddy bars to charm and mix with the common brow to win his daily bread. How many gaudy liquor palaces he would have to go to, to carry on business for a company that belonged to someone impersonal, not his father-in-law's. No longer now would he associate in private comfort with those who owned their own businesses. He would miss the sense of belonging, of being surrounded by people with cultivated manners, sophisticated conversation, warm fellow-feelings, whose exquisite taste in

ROMANCE

food, clothes, furnishings made life so pleasant, easy, possible.

"Tom, did you see Cathy after she left me?" Skip questioned me.

He caught me hesitating as to whether to tell the truth or lie.

"Did she say why she was leaving me?" he persisted.

"Just incompatibility," I said.

"But that's nuts! For that week she was back with me we couldn't have been better suited. Even angels couldn't find more peace."

I shook my head in sympathy. "Women are unpredictable."

In the course of our drinking that night, Skip returned often to the subject of Cathy and the last time I saw her, but I always managed to avoid giving details and steered him into philosophical speculation of women in general. But then, when it was after three o'clock, and the club had not yet closed, when we were drugged with sleep and drink, I let slip the fact that Cathy disliked Peter Miller. Skip became wide awake at that admission of mine and eagerly resumed his questioning of me.

"Maybe she didn't know what she was saying," I said. "She married him so she must like him."

"I wonder if he made her marry him," Skip thought deeply.

Tim chuckled and swung his arms limply back on his chair back. "Detective Burke of homicide reporting, sir."

"If he did," I said, "would it make any difference to you?"

He gritted his teeth in intoxicated exaggeration. "I'd get her back."

"But what if she had done something awful and the fault was all hers," I said. "Would you want her then?"

"I'd want her no matter what she'd done."

For a moment I was afraid that I would lose control of myself and I would give way to my ego as someone who knew it all, and who in pursuit of praise and glory for having saved the romance of two lovers would blurt out the whole truth, but I subdued the temptation because I knew that when Skip heard the truth about the baby, not only would he take Cathy back, but she would come back, and that little baby would probably be the first of a number of children.

"Don't worry about her," Tim said. "There's thousands more in the sea."

"Not like her," Skip said. He put his head in his hands, and I was slightly embarrassed because a couple of waiters were looking at us.

"Your train'll be leaving soon," I said. "We'd better get you down to the station."

He straightened up at the sharp tone in my voice and looked hard at me before standing up. "My treat," he said and pulled money from his pocket.

Tim sped through the deserted streets so that we arrived twenty minutes before the train was due. The early morning chill had awakened us somewhat. Even Skip's teeth were chattering, Skip the hockey star who had spent a good part of his life on ice. We passed the time by tapping our toes on the platform, as Tim swung Skip's case with one arm to and fro in front of us. The darkness, interrupted here and there by station lights, drove us within ourselves so that the tapping of our toes was our only communication.

"If the damned thing doesn't come soon," Skip said, "I'll die here."

"Home Sweet Home," Tim laughed. He thought he was funny.

A knot of people gathered near us. Fedoras appeared in the lighted spots from the florescent lamps. We heard a whistle far in the distance. The three of us were like statues facing each other inwardly from the points of a triangle. We were waiting for time and the speed of the train to come and break us up. I had sudden remorse about Skip; he looked so alone. The engine wheezed by us, and passenger cars slowed their long brown bodies to a stop in front of us. Trainmen flashed beams to guide our group down the line of cars and up the steps, on which Skip paused and heartily shook hands with Tim, both of them smiling through the regret of parting, and then he turned to me with more reserve, as if it were official with us, as if I represented something, a thing, not a person, but then, in his eyes, I noticed a sad friendliness which went very deep into me, a regret, too, but more deeply felt than that with Tim, because he didn't bluff it over with smiles and hearty handshakes; instead, he left a part of himself with me, some part of a soul, which would float in a memory.

    Throwing his case ahead of him, Skip sprang onto the train. The lower half of the door swung shut behind him, and he stood in the dull yellow light of the bulb silhouetting his head and shoulders, turning his brown hair to copper.
    "Hey Skip," I said. I began to walk as the train moved forward. "Hey Skip! Cathy loves you. I know." And when he only looked at me, I told him again, but the train was moving faster, and he slowly shook his head and passed a hand in front of him as if to knock the idea away as being silly. But he could have believed me; he could have got off the train, and he could have come back, but I guess, once he was moving, he thought he was well on his way.
    I ran for a little-ways, thinking he might jump off, but I saw him turn his head as the train left me behind, so that the light shone on his sad limp face which wore a trace of a smile, more indulgent than happy, and I didn't recognize him as the same person pictured on those blue bubble gum cards that I used to pin up on the walls of my room when I was a kid.

-30-

ROMANCE

GIVE A GOOD BOOK TO A FRIEND; CLIP AND SEND TO DAVUS PUBLISHING, P O BOX 1101, BUFFALO, N.Y. 14213-7101 UNITED STATES or to 150 NORFOLK ST. S., SIMCOE, ON. N3Y2W2 CANADA OR ASK YOUR BOOKSTORE. Or order with your credit card by calling Christie and Christie distribution at **1-800-263-1991**. [Libraries call Coutts 800-263-1686]

SEND ME............... COPIES OF HAMILTON ROMANCE for $19.95 Cdn., $14.95 Am. a copy.
..........COPIES OF CHOCOLATE FOR THE POOR;; a story of rape in 1805 FOR $11.95 U.S.($13.95 CAN) PER COPY.(Mass. Berkshires in 1805; a father accused of raping his daughter) "Held me spellbound," Angela Ariss, Children's Rights Advocate
.... COPIES OF THE JENNY; A NEW YORK LIBRARY DETECTIVE NOVEL AT $7.95 (U.S..&Can) PER COPY Library detective solves case of biggest stamp theft in U.S. history. "Held me rivetted" *Rotary on Stamps;* "a fascinating tale," *Stoney Creek News.* "fun reading," *Global Stamp News.* "The solution is as surprising as it is ingenious." *The Simcoe Reformer.* It gets Gold for the "whodunnit" plot and the exciting, don't-put-me-down read that it is.-- *Canadian Stamp News.* The writing is fast paced, and for this reviewer the novel offered a pleasant diversion on a hot summer afternoon.--*The Canadian Philatelist.*
.... COPIES OF THAT OTHER GOD, A NOVEL AT $18.95 (U.S. and Can) PER COPY. American mystic brings people through telepathic communion into the universal subconscious to a realization of the God of humanity. "Compelling, really interesting, exciting...a cry for peace at a time of anarchy," *Brantford Expositor;* "Absorbing.... Gripping style, detailed observation, poetic images. Vital, entertaining, apocalyptic," Peter Rankin, NYC. "Compelling story [of] the saving values deep within the human spirit," *Human Quest.*
.... COPIES OF THROUGH PAPHLAGONIA WITH A DONKEY; A JOURNEY THROUGH THE TURKISH ISFENDYARS AT $9.95 PER COPY. $11.95 Can. "Charmingly written," *Explorers Journal;* "Now that I have concluded my fourth re-reading, I have become... a thorough-going dweller in Paphlagonia and an ardent partisan of Bobby, the donkey" *Local 1930 Newsletter;* "...insightful for students of cross-cultural communication," *International Journal of International Relations.*

PLEASE INCLUDE $3 FOR POSTAGE AND HANDLING FOR ORDERS FROM 1-3; $4 FOR 4-7; $6 FOR 8-10. FOR LARGER ORDERS CALL DAVUS 519 426 2077.

NAME:
ADDRESS:

ENCLOSED PLEASE FIND A CHEQUE TO DAVUS PUBLISHING FOR $......................

HAMILTON

BOOKS BY DAVID BEASLEY IN PRINT ELSEWHERE

The Canadian Don Quixote; The Life and Works of Major John Richardson, Canada's First Novelist (Erin, Ont: Porcupine's Quill) $6.95 (C) "Definitive "; "Not only a good read but the fulfillment of 'an aching void'." *Brick;* "very useful... mass of new information," *Toronto Globe & Mail.* "a roaring good adventure yarn about a highly eccentric dreamer," *Library Journal.* "brings to life the early history of this country," *Kingston Whig Standard;* "well-researched book gives the reader an insight never before documented," *Niagara Advance.*

How To Use A Research Library (New York City; Oxford Univ. Press) $9.95(U.S.). "Beasley writes clearly. Useful information on the many services of research libraries. Communicates well the excitement of doing research," *Library Journal.* "ideal for first course in 'fact-finding' at either undergraduate or graduate levels," *Florida A&M University.* "Plenty of excellent insights," *Loyola University of Chicago*

The Suppression of the Automobile; Skulduggery at the Crossroads (Westport, CT, Greenwood Press) Hard cover only, $45 (U.S.) "Railroad interests did all they could to prevent the development of the automobile in the 1830s" *Journal of Economic Literature* "Excellent...superbly spun story...thorough research,... Only automobilists whose interests begin after Wold War II will not find this an engrossing book." *SAH Journal..* New enlarged edition: Who Invented the Automobile?; Skulduggery at the Crossroads (Montreal. P.Q.: Black Rose Books) Hard cover $48.99 Cdn., soft cover $19.99 Cdn.

EDITOR
MAJOR JOHN RICHARDSON: SHORT STORIES (PENTICTON, B.C.; THEYTUS BOOKS) "They deal largely with the American Indian. Major Richardson was recognized as the best writer of Indian tales-"-*CANADIAN CONSULATE GENERAL, NEW YORK CITY* $5.95(U.S.), $6.95 (CAN)

DAVUS SUM, NON OEDIPUS